Dust to Dust

Also available by Audrey Keown

The Ivy Nichols Mysteries

Murder at Hotel 1911

Dust
to
Dust

An Ivy Nichols Mystery

∾

AUDREY KEOWN

CROOKED
LANE

NEW YORK

Copyright © 2021 by Audrey Keown

Published in the United States by Crooked Lane Books, an imprint of The Quick Brown Fox & Company LLC.

Crooked Lane Books and its logo are trademarks of The Quick Brown Fox & Company LLC.

Library of Congress Catalog-in-Publication data available upon request.

ISBN (hardcover): 978-1-64385-734-3
ISBN (ebook): 978-1-64385-735-0

Cover illustration by Alan Ayers

Printed in the United States.

www.crookedlanebooks.com

Crooked Lane Books
34 West 27th St., 10th Floor
New York, NY 10001

First Edition: August 2021

10 9 8 7 6 5 4 3 2 1

For Michelle,
whose fresh courage lifts us all.
Sic itur ad astra.

I am not willing you should go
Into the earth, where Helen went;
She is awake by now, I know.
Where Cleopatra's anklets rust
You will not lie with my consent;
And Sappho is a roving dust;
Cressid could love again; Dido,
Rotted in state, is restless still;
You leave me much against my will.

—Edna St. Vincent Millay,
"To S. M. If He Should Lie A-Dying"

I

What Happened About the Statues

‽

My first reaction to the water gushing from below the men's room door was the impulse to phone Mr. Fig and marvel with him over the reflection of our Narcissus statue in the puddle, a rare perfect moment of myth brought to life. But I was a plumber's daughter to my core. I knew to shut off the water, and how, without calling our already overworked general manager in the dead of night.

For a minute, I worried the current cold snap had broken a pipe and caused the leak, a situation I couldn't begin to deal with on my own. But the hotel's plumbing, although more than a hundred years old in places, ran down from here through the heated basement. It wasn't likely to freeze in any kind of temperatures we got in Tennessee.

I went for the mop bucket in the closet at the top of the old servant staircase, but as I wheeled it, squeaking, through the hall, the gold-filigreed front doors split open, and two couples burst through, shaking snow from their hatless heads. Guests arriving for check-in, if I knew my business, and I liked to think I did.

1

Mr. Fig would not approve of them seeing housekeeping equipment during their first impression of the otherwise glamorous entry hall.

Of course, he wouldn't appreciate me letting the main floor flood either.

While the guests busied themselves in the doorway, I shoved the bucket out of sight, dashed daintily across the hall, and sloshed through the puddle into the men's room, realizing only then that I should've announced myself.

Thankfully, the stalls were empty. I spotted the leak spurting from the supply line under one of the vintage sinks and closed the offending valve nice and tight.

"Look at this, would you?" The voice of one of the freshly arrived women echoed in the hall.

I hoped she was remarking on a classical painting or an early-twentieth-century piece of furniture rather than the deluge.

"Watch out. Floor's slippy," said a man with a stronger version of the woman's slightly mumbly northern accent.

I swung myself out the door, lifted my heavy skirt, and waded back through the puddle.

The four guests plodded across the room like a desert caravan, slowed by their shoulder bags and rolling suitcases.

One of the men, massive and stiff in his bearing, paused in front of an oil painting to look around and reminded me of a graying moose as the leafless branches in the painted tree behind him seemed to extend from either side of his head. He maintained an unaffected expression, but the wide eyes and mouths of the other three told me they were having exactly the transporting experience that Mr. Fig and Clarista King, our exuberant and often eccentric boss, had curated for them.

Pausing by one of the two naiad statues at the foot of the staircase, I folded my hands neatly at the tight waist of my dress, took a deep breath, and delivered my most devastating smile. "Welcome to Hotel 1911."

I gestured toward the bathroom. "I'm afraid we have experienced a leak. Please avoid the wet floor."

And to think, regular hotels had signs to do this work.

One of the women, a pretty brunette of about fifty with a demure smile, let her eyes trail across my Titanic-era dress as if I were another period fixture. "It's like we've stepped back in time, Autumn."

"Let's not overromanticize things," said the woman beside her, evidently called Autumn, who was near her age and had short red hair. She glanced at me. "This girl reminds me of the guide who gave us the Mount Calvary Cemetery tour in costume. Remember?"

Cemetery tour? That was unusual.

I returned to my station behind the antique reception desk and opened the booking book on the marble desktop.

The freak snowstorm that had powdered our guests on their way in had coincided this year with a semiregular March freeze that longtime Southerners called redbud winter. The intersection of the two meant some of the white fluff might remain with us a day or so.

I was overjoyed.

Like many in these parts, I nursed a starving hope that this year might finally bring snow worthy of making men and angels. I blamed Hollywood for this fantasy of charming white winters. Christmas movies were nearly always set somewhere up north.

The moose-ish man opened a bag of pretzels from his pocket, sat down in the nearest armchair, and began to slowly munch his noisy snack.

"A real charmer, isn't it, hon?" The other man in the foursome clamped his arm around the waist of the brunette woman, who had started to wander away. He was blondish and sixty-something with a slight paunch but good posture, the physique of someone who had a casual relationship with the gym. "Not too different from how I remember it."

"Just like you said." She nodded politely.

He reached up and untucked her hair from behind her ear, then fastened one more button on her blouse.

She frowned, twisted out of his embrace, and joined the red-head at the wall mural beyond the wide staircase, as if to inspect its classical garden scene more closely.

Dissatisfaction spread over the blondish man's face, but as he turned to meet me at the desk and eyed my poofy suffragette hair, a smile replaced it. "You're part of the scenery too, aren't you?"

Here for your entertainment, I thought. The most aggravating drawback of this or any customer service job had to be constantly biting one's tongue.

His eyes didn't stray below my face, though, so maybe he hadn't meant anything objectifying by the comment. Then again, the men who best hid their ogling were often the most dangerous, in my experience.

"Yes, sir." I smiled back at him. "All of the staff uniforms sport a contemporary design, the latest 1911 fashion."

Buttoned up from my waist to my throat, I wore the same style gown as the housekeeper who had worked for my great-great-grandparents when they'd built this house near the turn of the twentieth century.

The guest stuck out a hand and chuckled. "Dr. Clyde Borough."

He certainly wasn't *treating* me like a prop. Most guests didn't bother shaking my hand.

I was charmed. "Ivy Nichols. It is a pleasure to make your acquaintance, Dr. Borough."

I usually maintained this pseudo-period language through check-in with a guest and dropped it sometime after, despite Clarista's expectation of consistency. "Did I hear you say you've been a guest of the house before, sir?"

"Great question. I was, but that was well before you got here. Before this mansion was a hotel, it was actually a private residence."

Did he think *he* needed to explain that to *me*? I disguised my frown with a mock cough and focused on the intriguing part of what he'd said. In the nine months or so that I'd been working at Hotel 1911, no guest had mentioned visiting my family here. "You were a guest of the Morrows, sir?"

"That's right. Back in my college days." He lifted a finger toward the desk. "Our group booking is under my name."

"Yes, sir." I flipped open the book where we had such things recorded by hand. Our period theme meant any anachronistic office equipment was hidden behind a curtain in a tiny room behind me.

It was just as well he'd changed the subject. Having never known the Morrows, I still struggled with impostor syndrome and wasn't ready to be telling outsiders I was a descendant of the original owners.

"I see we have you and Ms. Gallagher in the Achilles suite, sir—a fine choice, our grandest room," I said.

One of Clarista's odd regulations was that each guest's name appear on the booking. She thought it made for a more personalized check-in experience when we greeted them by name, which I aimed for half the time. Doyle (the day clerk and my nemesis) almost never did.

"Achilles? I'm honored. Although I probably have more than one fatal flaw." He lifted one eyebrow.

5

"Well, let us hope we don't find that out while you're here."
I handed him paperwork to sign, pushing away thoughts of
another guest of the Achilles whose singular weakness had been
the end of her. I glanced at a note scribbled next to Dr. Borough's
booking. Shoot. "Sir, you were probably informed when you
made your reservation, but I should remind you that because
our staircase from the conservatory to the second floor is under
construction, one of your balconies in the suite will be off-limits
during your stay."

"That won't be a problem for us. We'll hardly be in the
room, what with the conference during the day and visits with
my daughter. She's going to school here—at Covenant?"

"Oh yeah, I've heard of it." *Covenant College* was the answer
to the question, *Is that a castle up there?* frequently heard when
driving past Lookout Mountain on the way out of the city.

He lifted his chest. "My alma mater, actually."

"How nice. And what conference are you in town for?"

"Great question. It's the annual meetup of the Association for
Gravestone Studies at your little convention center off MLK.
Our whole group is here for it, actually, the four of us and the five
who arrived earlier today. We're all members of the Gravestone
Friends of Greater Pittsburgh. I'm the club president."

What the Dickens? I had checked in the five he'd mentioned—a pair of women in their eighties, a father and son,
and a quiet man on his own. I'd been too busy to ask what had
brought them to town, but I wouldn't have thought of them
sharing this same weird interest. You just couldn't peg people
on sight.

I feigned a smile. "How fascinating."

"I know it seems a little odd at first." He smoothed the lapels
of his sport coat. "I guess I've become used to the macabre,

spending so much time with the nineteenth-century poets. The Victorians were obsessed with death."

"Oh, so you're a teacher?" I filed his paperwork away to transfer to the office computer later.

"Yes, professor actually. Anyway, there's a lot to know about gravestones—from the symbols engraved on them to the material they're made of and how it disintegrates over centuries. In fact, we're jazzed about exploring the historic grave markers you have here. They're remarkable."

Jazzed.

"Mm-hmm. There are some cool cemeteries in the area," I said. "Some of them date back to before the Civil War, like the one where the early missionaries to the Cherokees are buried."

"Yes, I believe that's on one of the tours the conference is leading," he said. "But I was referring to the graves here on the hotel property."

"Oh." My fingers froze, pen in hand, and my eyes flicked toward the garden doors and back to his face. There were no graves *here.*

Sure, we had classical statues, elaborate formal gardens, and even secret passages, but no graves.

I hated making people unhappy, so I wasn't about to tell him they'd booked the hotel on false pretenses. As general manager, or "butler" as far as guests were concerned, Mr. Fig would want to handle the misunderstanding himself, but he'd gone home hours ago, and I wouldn't disturb him for something that could wait till morning.

As I handed Clyde the skeleton keys for the Achilles Room, Renee Gallagher followed Autumn out of the theater. (According to their booking, Autumn's last name was Truman, and the imposing man with the pretzels was her husband Tom.)

At my offer to help with the group's luggage, the two men protested and began throwing bags over their shoulders.

Renee glanced around the room again with a gleam of amusement behind her benign expression, reaching up to touch each ear in turn, as if checking that her pearl studs were still in place.

"What is it?" Autumn asked her, without joining in her fun.

"It's a little overdone, isn't it?" Renee said under her breath, more like she was unsure of her own opinion than trying to keep me from overhearing.

"What, the decor?" Autumn said.

Renee's smile opened up and her face lifted. "I mean, all these reproduction Greek sculptures and the faux marble and fake gold frames and—" She broke into a musical laugh, bending forward and catching a hand on her collarbone.

I bristled inwardly—and probably outwardly, if anyone was paying attention. Her comment would have offended Mr. Fig too, on behalf of the Morrows and this place that represented their legacy. But he would have found an assertive yet respectful way to set her straight. I needed to learn exactly how he did that.

"You must be delirious from traveling," Autumn said to Renee, her face drawing downward in disapproval. She grabbed the brunette's arm to direct her toward the elevator. "All this stuff is real and historical, by the way. I read about it on their website."

Well, that wasn't as good as what Mr. Fig would have said, but I was thankful for it.

"I'm tired too," Tom said flatly.

"What's going on with you?" Autumn, the apparent manager of everyone in the group, squinted at him. "You know, you've been tired ever since you gave up drinking—not that I'm not glad you did."

Their conversation trailed off as the four of them got on the elevator.

I, meanwhile, turned to the soggy disaster at hand.

I began by mopping up the bathroom floor, propping open the door with the yellow bucket and working my way out to the hall. Wrapping up, I admired the gleam of my handiwork on the pale marble, shiny enough to reflect the gold chandelier over my head. I turned around to get the bucket out of the doorway, only to see that a new puddle had formed on the bathroom floor.

I knelt and checked the valve. It was still nice and tight, but the leak continued dripping down from the supply line onto the floor. Darn.

Mr. Fig would insist on being notified of such a thing, even during his off hours.

*   *   *

Our esteemed butler arrived pressed and combed to his usual standard, but instead of the period three-piece suit I was used to seeing him in, he wore a nut-colored cardigan over a linen button-down. Most men I knew would have considered the outfit up to par for Thanksgiving dinner. For Mr. Fig, it was evidently just something to throw on in the middle of the night.

Although I worried that inconveniences like this made him think twice about retiring, he didn't seem bothered to be called here after ten o'clock. Only a cast of silver aged his red hair, but he was in his midseventies now, so it had to be a sense of purpose, and maybe pleasure too, that kept him on the hotel's payroll.

Still, if packing it in after all these years was best for him, I could support that. But if we didn't work together, would I ever see him?

Mr. Fig knelt and peered under the sink to check the handle of the valve himself. "You're well suited for taking care of the hotel while I'm away, Miss Nichols. I'm glad you're on the night shift."

I wanted him to follow up with, *Although it means I don't see as much of you*, but outright displays of affection weren't his style. I'd met him the day I started this job, and it hadn't taken me long to latch on to his peculiar blend of warmth and rigidness.

"Thanks," I said. "I know the pipes couldn't have frozen, but it's weird that I shut off the valve and there's still a drip."

"I agree, yet it may be as simple as worn parts. These supply lines aren't original to the house, but they aren't new either." Mr. Fig stood, removed a handkerchief from his pocket, and dusted his knees and hands with it. He wasn't afraid to get dirty if he had to. He just didn't like staying that way.

Not that the hotel floors were ever less than clean. None of us would stand for such a thing.

He folded his handkerchief and tucked it back in his pocket. "I'll call a plumber in the morning to inspect the pipes. For now, I'll turn off the water supply to the main-floor bathrooms, and you can place the 'out of order' sign at the door."

After a quick trip to the boiler room, he met me back at the desk. "Did everything else go all right tonight?"

"Yep." Except for the gravestone group. "Actually, there was a small issue."

"Yes? How can I help?"

"You know the group that was booked to arrive, the grave-studying club?"

"Ah, right. Unusual hobby, don't you think? If only it were Halloween."

I smiled. "So, they seem to think they're going to tour graves here."

He brushed a stray thread from the surface of the desk. "Here," I said. *"At the hotel."*

He looked at me expectantly. "Did they want to preview the tour information? I'll bring it back with me in the morning."

"You're giving them a tour? You mean there *are* graves here on the property?"

He scrunched his eyebrows slightly and lifted one side of his mouth. "I thought you might have figured that out by now, Miss Nichols. Of course, Ms. King has gone to great lengths to keep them secret."

I thought of Pan, of the satyrs, of Aeneas, whose story Mr. Fig had told me after I had found the secret passage last year. "The garden statues are memorials?"

"Many of them."

A cold drip seemed to trickle down my spine, and I shivered. "I guess Clarista thinks a cemetery out back might put guests off."

"Precisely." He folded his hands. "Mr. Zhang keeps the plants trimmed neatly, but by design, they are allowed to grow tall enough to cover the inscriptions."

Mr. Zhang, our secretive gardener, was technically bound to the same restrictive period standards as the rest of us, but out on the grounds, he had more freedom from Clarista's and Mr. Fig's examining eyes than us indoor staff.

"I guess I haven't looked at the statues closely enough," I said.

"Well. I'm awake. You're awake."

A laugh burst out of me. He was never this casual. "What? Now? And leave the desk unattended?"

What had come over him?

"Just this once." He narrowed his eyes conspiratorially.

11

I sighed with satisfaction. The times he bent the rules for me were few and far between, but I'd never seen him do it for anyone else, definitely not for day-shift Doyle.

Mr. Fig knew he could trust me to keep this between us. If I explored my shadow self, which by Carl Jung's definition was the *un*explored side of the psyche, I was sure I'd find a buried urge to gloat about the special treatment. However, I'd never give in to that instinct and let the others think Mr. Fig was susceptible to a character flaw like favoritism. (My dad had expected me to be bored with Jung by now, but I was still heartily obsessed.)

My jacket was in the staff dressing room downstairs, but we kept a few coats in the hall closet for this sort of occasion, most of them forgotten relics of former guests.

I slipped my arms through a vintage fur cape. Something so lux would never have been worn by a servant in this house, and I enjoyed the incongruence.

Mr. Fig had a manner of turning and walking away that encouraged me to follow him, and he did so now, although he was slightly less debonair wearing his cardigan than his butler's uniform.

As I passed my great-great-grandfather Murdoch's painting, I threw him a quick salute before catching up to Mr. Fig at the end of the portrait gallery.

He opened the beveled glass door when he reached it and paused to let me go before him.

A gust of frigid air blew my skirt against my legs.

It was thirty degrees out there, which wouldn't have felt so cold except that yesterday's low had been sixty. Tennessee weather was fickle like that, but it conditioned us inhabitants into vigorous people.

We stepped out and rounded the corner of the terrace, my dress sweeping a wide trail in the snow. Most of the statues were in the back garden.

"Be sure to take the rail," Mr. Fig said. "The stairs are coated with ice. I'll salt them before I leave."

"The temperature's going back up tomorrow, right?"

"Yes, but there'll be little sun to warm the northern exposure. I don't want anyone falling."

When we reached the foot of the long staircase, the frosted garden wrapped around us on three sides. The greenish-copper lampposts shined little moons on the silver ground.

At the sight, I almost forgot the cold. It'd been years since Chattanooga had seen a blanket of white like this one.

Mr. Fig offered me his arm, and we strolled down the path together. At one corner, he stopped and faced the nearest snow-topped statue—or memorial?

Long Grecian braids framed her attentive face. She had eagle wings, and a tail fanned behind her. In her arms she cradled something small and perhaps human.

"What is she?" I looked at Mr. Fig.

"A harpy."

"I thought harpies were ugly monsters."

"Indeed, sometimes thieves of children even, but the earliest mention of the creatures is more complimentary than that. They were often agents of justice."

If it was a memorial, there would be an epitaph on the base, which was shielded by shiny green gardenia leaves. I put a foot into the snowy bed and pushed a branch back to read the inscription. *Lucretia Lillian Morrow. 1896–1920. Kings might be espoused to more fame / But king nor peer to such a peerless dame.*

"Shakespeare," Mr. Fig said. "From his poem about the most famous Lucretia."

"Oh. But Lucretia Morrow was who? I mean, in relation to me."

"Your great-grandfather Blandus's sister."

That meant she was the daughter of Murdoch and Lillian, who had built the house. Her middle name was her mother's first.

Mr. Fig shifted a leaf off the path with the toe of his shoe. "Your family often called her 'Good Lucretia.' She worked as a nurse overseas in the First World War, I believe, and died shortly after, quite young, as you can see."

An image of war-era nurses in their distinctive white, folded caps popped into my head. My mental picture was black-and-white, removed by several degrees from Lucretia's experience. An ache tightened my throat, and I walked away.

Mr. Fig followed me to the next-nearest statue, centered in a trefoil-shaped, fluff-topped hedge.

"A replica of the famous statue of *Marcellus as Hermes Logios*, a first-century Roman work," Mr. Fig said.

Maybe it was the snow obscuring the figure's features, but the man looked like George to me, with his long Roman nose and lean shape. Even the sculpture's marble was like George's pale skin.

But Marcellus wasn't wearing a stitch, and as close as my best friend and I had been for the last sixteen years, I'd never seen him in the buff.

A memory surfaced of the time I had accidentally walked in on George changing into his soccer uniform at fourteen. He'd had his boxer shorts on, so it wasn't *that* big of a deal. If anything, the encounter had taught us just how much awkwardness we were willing to get over in order to hold on to our friendship. Anyway, the fleshy sight of him then hadn't ignited any feelings in me. He'd been all height and no muscle. Not like now.

My face felt hot and cold at the same time.

"The original Marcellus sculpture was owned by Pope Sixtus the Fifth and France's Louis the Fourteenth before ending up in the Louvre," Mr. Fig said.

"Wow," was my highly educated response.

Around the plinth were rosebushes that had broken free of their winter dormancy just weeks before the frost. When I pushed aside their branches, the Latin inscription was barely visible.

"This one is dedicated to Blandus," Mr. Fig said. "Marcellus, like your great-grandfather, was a powerful and effective leader."

I saw now at the base of the statue a rectangular marble slab that clearly marked his grave.

"Miss Nichols." Mr. Fig inhaled. "I want to prepare you, if I may. Your family has been, in your mind, whatever you wanted them to be . . . for a long time."

Behind him, the hemlocks' white sleeves reached for the darkness at the end of the bluff.

"They've been a frustrating mystery mostly," I said.

"There's a touch of the romantic in mysteries. While they last, they're open-ended and, therefore, full of hope."

I'd never heard him talk this way. Almost—what was it?—wistful.

"However, filling in the very real details about your family's lives and character . . ." He looked pointedly at me. "Sometimes it can be difficult to take a revered loved one off the pedestal one has built for them."

Our current positions next to a statue on a pedestal, whose purpose was to immortalize my ancestor, underlined his words with irony.

I didn't want to argue with him. I was sure he was right. Digging into the past was always a risky endeavor.

But reality was so much better than fantasy in the end. The truth was something firm to build your life on. I wasn't an orphan, and yet, for years now, I'd felt like a leaf lost in the wind. I needed to root myself to the people who had come before me.

"Are you talking about their mental health?" I said. "I know about my great-great-grandmother Lillian's psychosis. And I know she must have passed it down."

"Those aren't character flaws, as much as the family tried to hide them," he said.

The same strand of mental illness caused my panic attacks— at least I'd always thought so. My old psychiatrist and the therapist I'd started seeing last month had suggested that parts of my past were also to blame.

Mr. Fig knew all about my panic disorder, and he gave me leeway when I needed it, but he never made me feel pathetic.

"I don't blame the Morrows for trying to hide their issues," I said. "They lived in a time that was less understanding." *Even less*, I should have said.

I glanced up at the house. Its golden limestone walls, lit softly by the terrace lamps, faded into shadow toward the roofline. On the third floor, a light flicked off in the Romulus or the Remus room. I wasn't sure which.

"I should get back to the desk," I said.

"I believe I am up to the task." He smiled softly. "Take your time."

I watched him walk back to the house, all my affection for him squeezing my throat.

Before last October, I hadn't been able to see why he favored me. The small allowances he made for me were like floaters in my eye that disappeared when I tried to focus on them. When I found out that he had worked in this house decades ago and knew I was a descendant of the family to whom he was still so loyal, I understood the reason for his soft spot.

For him, I was already one of them.

I was still trying to figure out what it meant to fill those Morrow shoes, but I was pretty sure I wasn't doing it yet.

The need to feel closer to my family ruled me, but I was careful not to use Mr. Fig for information or overwhelm him with my constant questions.

We had years, maybe decades, to be friends.

Of all the people who must have worked for my ancestors, only he had found a way to come back. And now he was the backbone of this place. It couldn't run without him.

II

Burning Love

～

I waited until I got to work the next afternoon to talk to George about the graves.

He'd be more responsive in person than over text. Three-quarters of his communication was in the angle of his shoulders, the dance of his coal-black eyebrows, and a variety of nonverbal sounds that, over the course of our friendship, I'd learned to interpret. Fluency in this language really paid off when he was at his moodiest—when he felt guilty or misunderstood.

I came into the hotel through the basement-level service entrance and the whitewashed hall, changed into my constrictive black dress, and pinned my brown hair into the requisite poofy bun on top of my head.

As I scaled the narrow servants' staircase, the front desk bell rang out.

It was 3:55, still five minutes till my shift technically started, so I let Doyle get it. (Any nearer to the end of *his* shift and he would refuse.) I needed the time to see George.

But before I could swing through the kitchen door, where I was sure to find him stirring sauces and pickling vegetables, the bell pealed again.

I popped into the hall and found no Doyle at the desk, only an especially grumpy, cardiganed guest tapping his fingers on the crook of his cane. He'd stayed with us before, and the glad tidings of his repeat visit hit me like a shovelful of coal.

When he saw me, the folds of his paraffin face tightened, and one hand lurched forward on the desk like an anxious crab.

"Mr. Wollstone," I said with all the pleasantry I could muster and stepped behind the desk. "How nice to see you. How may I help you?"

"If I'd've known you were harboring a colony of rats in this old place, I'd never have returned." With his white, flyaway hair, he was something like a snowy owl who'd been abruptly awakened during the day.

I sighed patiently. "I apologize, Mr. Wollstone, but whoever told you we kept rats here was mistaken."

A mouse now and again, maybe.

"Nobody *told* me. I heard 'em myself scratching in the walls last night. They woke me right after I'd fallen asleep." He grumbled and twitched his mouth.

Like a reflex, I glanced at the wall opposite me, almost thirty feet away on the other side of the entry hall.

Something was out of place—a strange, letter-sized paper tacked up in the empty space between the classical paintings. "I am sorry, sir. How dreadful. I will inform the butler, and we will refund a portion of your stay."

"Well. That's more like it." He nodded, thunked his cane in place, and frowned with satisfaction.

I didn't say *what* portion.

As he cantankered back to his room, I crossed the hall and examined the strange paper a little closer. It was a crayon drawing, a simple one with only three or four colors.

I tugged the paper, and it came off the wall with a few pieces of Scotch tape stuck to its back. Only a kid would do this kind of thing, and there was only one staying here at the moment. Was his name Parker? He was the son of one of those gravestone goobers.

But where had he even gotten tape? It wasn't the kind of thing most people traveled with, and we didn't keep it anywhere a guest could find it. Tape would be anachronistic, after all.

I was sure Mr. Fig would not approve of this kind of "art," so I carried the drawing back to the desk and stuck it in the lost-and-found, where it would probably stay until it yellowed like the expired kale in Dad's and my vegetable drawer (over which I still suffered buyer's remorse).

I turned toward the kitchen again but heard voices and footsteps on the second-floor gallery. "No, he tried to kill him though."

It was Clyde Borough, president of the gravestone club. What was he saying?

The other voice was a woman's, his girlfriend Renee Gallagher's, perhaps. I missed the first of her reply but made out, "—thought that he died."

My ears pricked. Were they discussing an attempted murder?

"Poseidon rescued him," Clyde said.

Poseidon? That was fishy.

Maybe I shouldn't have been listening in, but there were so few ways to pass the long hours at the desk.

"Oh, so Aeneas challenged Achilles to a duel that he would have lost?" Renee said.

"Yes, well, Aeneas is a tremendous symbol of self-sacrifice."

I quickly lost interest. They were talking about three-thousand-year-old fiction, not a real life at stake. Staying in the Achilles suite must have sparked their conversation.

Every room in the place was named after some Greek or Roman figure or region, and of course there were the Greek replicas, old texts, Roman numerals and such scattered about, but I hadn't known how personal my great-great-grandfather's enthusiasm for the classics was until I had discovered his secret basement passage with Mr. Fig.

Holding hands, Clyde and Renee rounded the second-floor landing at the top of the staircase. Renee wore a matching sweater set with pearls, but she wasn't at home in them. It seemed more like she was dressing for a role as a midcentury TV mom.

I wondered if someone else had bought the outfit for her.

Clyde's banana-colored polo nearly matched his hair.

Renee stopped at the top of the stairs and leaned on the carved balustrade.

Clyde swiveled around to look at her. "What?"

The brunette closed her small eyes and pinched the skin between her eyebrows.

Forcing an exhale and dropping her hand, Clyde said, "Don't tell me it's one of your headaches."

"It's not like I can *control* them," she groaned.

"Wait here." He climbed up two steps. "I've got something in the room that will take care of it."

"But what is it?" Renee lowered her hand, and her eyes whined at Clyde.

"Some kind of magic pills. Ms. Velvet gave them to me for the next time this happened," he said, still climbing the stairs.

Velvet Reed was one of the two octogenarians in the gravestone cohort who had checked in a few hours before Clyde and Renee the day before.

"Wait," Renee called.

Pausing, he slapped a palm on the banister and huffed. "What now?"

"Well, I don't know that I want to take something if I don't know what it is," she pleaded.

An ugly, mean smile slid across his face. "I see what this is. You're just trying to get out of the tour tonight."

Renee glared at him and turned to go back up the stairs. "Fine. Give me the drugs. And don't bother reading about dosage or side effects. I'm sure I'll survive."

As she marched past him, his eyes met mine, and he sent me a pleasant but strained *Everything is good here* glance.

Now that he'd gotten his way, I imagined it would be.

When the lovely couple was gone, I stepped through the curtain behind the desk, through the little office, and into George's kitchen. The sharp sweetness of herbs hit me first, followed by a wave of salty air that reminded me of the Gulf Coast where Dad and I vacationed sometimes.

"So what's for dinner?"

It was Bea's voice from across the room.

In her period maid uniform with its white pinafore, Bea's petite figure appeared even smaller next to George in his long chef's coat. Both had their backs to where I stood.

He unloaded a crate from the dumbwaiter, and she leaned against the dishwasher a foot away.

"Filet and crab perloo," he answered, as if trying to impress her. This wasn't new. He was an excellent chef. He knew it, and he enjoyed being admired routinely by newspaper columnists and social media influencers.

I for sure shouldn't eavesdrop on *this* conversation.

"Ooh." Bea turned to look up at him. Her lips pouted obviously, and her blond curls blew back softly as she fanned herself with a hand. She leaned closer. "What's the steak *wearing?*"

My stomach turned, and I backed toward the doorway, crouching a little behind a steaming pot on the stove. Bea liked to play up the sexy-maid routine, and it was sometimes funny, but I didn't like her using it on George.

He cleared his throat. "Um, just a beurre blanc. It's an emulsified butter sauce."

"Mmm. And it's French, *oui?*" Bea smiled.

"Oui, mademoiselle."

Okay, the French was the last straw. This was really getting on my nerves.

But then, maybe it was harmless flirting. Maybe I was being overprotective of him.

I'd sacrificed a lot for George last year, and I'd never been sorry about it for a second, but I wondered if those sacrifices had changed something in me, in the way I felt about him. I was aware enough to see that I was becoming possessive.

A hot wave of shame welled up from my gut.

And intensified in my arm. My arm burned. Pain seared my skin. I jumped back from the stove.

My sleeve was on fire.

I yelled something unintelligible, and my brain fired off *Stop, drop, and roll.*

I was vaguely aware of raised voices and of George and Bea skidding toward me.

I buckled and rolled and kept rolling.

George dropped to the floor at my side and used his coat to beat at my arm.

The fire was out, but the pain raged on.

I lifted my arm in front of my face. My sleeve smoldered.

"I'll call an ambulance," Bea said.

"No, I'll take her. I'll be faster." George handed Bea his keys. "Pull my car around."

She disappeared.

My heart chambers fired fast and hard just like they would if this were a panic attack. But it wasn't. Only adrenaline from the pain.

"Come on." George put one of his arms behind my back and the other under the bulk of my dress and lifted me.

"I can walk!" I shouted, although my face was inches from his.

"You're not heavy, if that's what you were worried about."

I groaned, partly from the intense sting of the burn but mostly from the irritation that he could see right through me.

He backed through the swinging door and carried me out through the entry hall.

"What happened?" Mr. Fig shouted, hurrying toward us.

"Ask Bea," George answered without stopping.

I remembered Mr. Fig carrying me last year, although I'd been unconscious at the time.

I thought briefly of my mother.

*　*　*

You haven't been to the emergency room until you've done it in early-twentieth-century dress. The stares I got from middle-aged women in yoga pants and men in screen-printed T-shirts made it clear that they thought I belonged in the psychiatric unit rather than this one.

But the hours George and I spent together at the hospital amounted to the longest single block of time I'd had with him since my college classes had started back in January. It was definitely worth the funny looks, if not the physical pain.

While we waited, he asked how I'd gotten close enough to the stove to catch on fire. I lied and said I'd been tasting what was on the stove. Not only would the truth be humiliating to me, but I was afraid he might also think I was trying to control him.

My arm was treated and bandaged, and for once I was grateful for these sturdy cotton sleeves, which, along with George's quick reaction time, according to the doctor, had kept a barely-second-degree burn from becoming a third.

As George drove me back to Dad's and my apartment, my head was heavy against the seat back, and I blinked hard to keep from dozing. It was only nine o'clock. I didn't know if it was the hospital drugs or coming down from the adrenaline, but the pain wasn't enough to keep me awake anymore.

I let the side of my face rest against the window glass and closed my eyes for a moment. Besides the burn, there was another new sensation taking up my attention, a charge along the side of my body, like an echo in my skin of when George had carried me. I didn't know what it meant, if anything.

"Fig called while you were talking to the nurse." George turned his pale face toward me in the darkness before looking back at the road. "He was concerned. I told him you were all right."

"Thanks. I guess he covered for me at the desk?"

"Guess so."

Mr. Fig was supposed to have given that tour to the grave-stone geeks. Though I wouldn't put it past him to have figured out by now how to be in two places at once. "So. You and Bea?"

"Uh, we've been hanging out a little," he said.

"Nice," I said, ignoring the niggling dread in my chest.

"It's just—you've been busier with school and stuff."

"No, yeah, that makes sense."

He tapped my leg. "Hey, did that ER doc remind you of anyone?"

"Your old neighbor!"

"Mr. Duff. Yeah, the same beady eyes," he said.

"And the way he kept saying, 'Now, folks!' "

George laughed. "Now, folks, you can't just cut through my yard. Now, folks, this is a serious burn here."

I laughed too, but it came out slow and wheezy.

"It's been six years since they buried him," George said.

Death and burial had haunted my last twenty-four hours like the rhythmic call of a katydid on a June night. "I didn't get a chance to tell you about the graves Mr. Fig showed me. That was why I came in the kitchen."

"What graves?" he said.

"At the hotel. The garden statues." The snow-powdered harpy towered in my memory.

"Wow. Weird. They just seem like . . . art."

"Yeah, but if you look closely, there are inscriptions. After my shift last night, I walked around in the snow for a while reading them."

He raised one corner of his mouth. "You know, when you said you wanted to be closer to your family, I thought you meant metaphorically."

"Ha-ha. You know, I looked pretty hard for my grandparents' graves, but I couldn't find them."

"I thought your grandparents were still living when they sold the house."

"That's what Mr. Fig said, but he doesn't know what happened to them after that. I asked him this afternoon about their graves, and he said he doesn't know where they're buried, and it's always been sad to him that they weren't buried on the hotel grounds because the city, who they sold the property to, probably would've allowed it."

"Maybe he overlooked them?" George asked. "Like they're at the edge of the property where the trees have filled in?"

"You and I both know he doesn't miss much, but it's possible, I guess."

"And you still don't feel like you can ask your dad about it?"

"I mean, Dad doesn't even mention his own parents. And when we talked last year about my mom leaving, all the things I didn't remember well, it was so hard for him."

"And for you."

"But if any of my grandparents were still living, surely I'd know them. Surely my mom's parents would have been in my life when she left. They would've helped look for their daughter, right?"

"I guess so. Things happen in families, though. People cut off contact for the dumbest reasons," he said.

"I don't wanna be like that."

"Of course not. You won't be."

My uniform felt even more uncomfortable than usual. I started pulling the pins out of my hair and sticking them one by one into his cupholder. "It's like, I don't just want to know *about* my family. I wanna know them."

George sighed.

"But . . . they're dead, and I can't, and I'm obsessed anyway. Does it seem weird to you?"

"Not really," he said. "Besides my parents and my sister, all my family is still in Romania. Overseas isn't as inaccessible as dead, but still—I'd like to know them better."

"*Înțeleg.*" *I understand.* One of the Romanian phrases I'd picked up around his house growing up.

"Now, a bunch of people obsessed with graves of people they don't even know?" He raised one eyebrow. "That's a different story."

"Yeah, it's creepy, right?"

He turned into the parking lot just outside our building. The snow had mostly melted here, but a few slushy piles hung out around the pansies that had grown leggy over the warm winter.

As George pulled into a space, I saw Dad leaning casually against a car I didn't recognize, a green Hyundai of some sort. From this distance, the most obvious things about him were his short silver beard and his torso, which always reminded me of a bag of chips. And then there was the fact that he was talking to a curvy blond woman I also didn't recognize.

As George shut off the Jeep, the blond reached up and brushed something off Dad's shirt. Irritation hiked up my shoulders. "Who the heck is that?"

George grunted in a way that meant he didn't know either and understood I wasn't really asking him. He opened his car door. "I'll walk you up."

They were across the lot from us, but there was no way we could get upstairs without being seen.

"Quick. Give me your coat," I said to George.

He hesitated. "You *still* haven't told him about working at the hotel?"

"I *will.*"

He frowned and passed his long jacket to me. "I think he can handle it, Vee."

I pulled my skirt up and tucked the hem in my tights so they were the only thing visible below the coat. Dad would think I was wearing leggings. "Yeah . . . maybe. But it's my choice to spend so much time digging around in my mom's family history, and I don't want my choices making him sad."

"He probably thinks of your mother anyway, though. Whether or not you bring her up."

I sucked my lips in. He was right.

As we made our way down the sidewalk closer to Dad's car, we stepped into a circle of light, and Dad looked up.

He jerked a bit like someone had goosed him, his eyes widening then narrowing, and he eventually waved.

George nodded at him, but I kept moving. If Dad didn't want to tell me about his relationship, that was fine. I knew how to give him space.

Inside, George put on the teakettle while I changed clothes in my room and stuffed my uniform dress under my bed, just in case Dad were to peek in here.

I brought a pillow back to the couch with me and propped up my bandaged arm.

"Strange that you burned the same arm you broke last year," George said, slipping his hands gracefully into his pockets and leaning against the kitchen counter.

"Yeah, I guess it has the bad juju . . . like your old Ford that kept getting hit even while it was parked."

"You should probably just amputate and get it over with."

I giggled, but it turned into a yawn.

The kettle whistled. George poured the water in to steep the tea and set the mug on the coffee table in front of me. "All right, I'm gonna leave so you can rest."

"You don't have to go," I said. "Stay while I drink my tea."

"If I do, I'll be too sleepy to drive."

But he looked at me a moment before turning to the door, and I knew that he wanted to.

"Need anything else?" he said.

I shook my head. "See you tomorrow."

"Far away from open flames."

As George went out, Dad came in.

I threw a blanket over my gauze-wrapped forearm.

"Oh, hi, Paul," George said.

"George. My man!" Dad reached out a hand.

The two of them executed their secret shake. Raised by a man, I liked to think I understood their gender pretty well as a whole, but the handshake thing still mystified me. Back in high school, when George was on the basketball team, I had asked him at what point in a relationship two men decided it was time to design their own handshake and how they went about working it out, but his answer had mainly included a lot of shrugs.

"Take it easy," Dad said and closed the door behind George.

I turned on the TV.

Dad laid his jacket over the back of the recliner, sat down, and steepled his hands in front of his mouth. "Hey, punkin'."

"Hey." I glanced at him and back at the TV.

"Listen. That was Kimberly. We've only been out a few times. I was going to tell you about her if it got serious . . ."

"Uh-huh. I understand." I made short eye contact, keeping my face calm, but tension still laced up my shoulders.

I didn't want to let him get away with hiding something from me, even for a little while. But I realized how hypocritical that was, and I took a slow breath. "Looked like you were having a good time."

He twisted his mouth and hiked up one cheek into a crooked smile. "Yeah."

"Good."

Running both hands down the tops of his thighs and standing up, he said, "Hey, you want a cup of tea?"

Maybe he was nervous, talking to me about a woman. I gestured toward my mug on the table. "I'm all set, but thanks."

"Oh, right." He lifted his eyebrows. "Is that the ginger?"

I picked it up and smelled it. "Uh, no, the sleepy one."

He refilled the kettle in our little kitchen, only a dozen feet away from the couch where I sat, and I thought about how strange it must be for him to try to date while he had a grown daughter at home and nowhere that was private.

The cost of school meant I couldn't afford my own place right now. I knew that Dad wouldn't trade my going back to finish my degree for more privacy (even though my major was psychology, and let's face it, could be more practical). But I wished there was a way, financially, to give him space and me the independence I should have at twenty-eight.

A reporter blipped onto the local news show.

I hadn't been watching, but my eyes snapped to the screen.

The reporter stood, microphone in hand, in the glare of the news camera. In front of the hotel.

My hotel.

The kettle squealed in the kitchen, and my internal alarm blared too. What was happening? What was a big enough story for the news? Another accident? A fire?

I craned my head toward the TV, clenching the remote and trying to make out what the reporter was saying.

". . . unidentified person has died at Hotel 1911," she said. "More on this and other stories at ten."

A death? My whole body stiffened. I couldn't wait till ten. I needed more on that story right now.

Dad brought his tea into the living room. "You all right?"

I stood up and let the blanket fall. "I've gotta go. I'm sorry. Can I have the car?"

"You just got home." He sat his mug on the side table, and his eyes landed on my bandage. "Ivy, what the—"

Irritation and worry stormed his face.

"I'm fine. I'll explain later." I started putting on my shoes.

"What the heck happened?"

"I really need to go." I reached for the car keys on the kitchen counter.

But he swiped them first. "First an explanation."

"I got too close to George's stove, and my sleeve caught on fire."

"You got burned? What were you doing?" He stared at my arm in horror. "How bad is it?"

"Second deg—"

"*Second* degree—"

"*Barely* second." I put a hand on his arm to comfort him.

He frowned and reached for my arm gently. "So that's why you're home early. Did he take you to the hospital?"

"Yes. And I'm really fine." I grabbed the keys he was still holding. "Let's talk more about it tomorrow. Please?"

"You bet we will." He narrowed his eyes. "Were you and George . . . busy starting a different kind of fire in the kitch—"

"*Dad.* No."

He let the keys go. "See you in the morning."

"Thank you," I called as I swiped my jacket and rushed out the door.

III

The Dangerous Edge of Things

I swung the Volvo through the hotel's front gate, but the drive was already crowded with police cars. News vans squatted willy-nilly all over the lawn, their dark windows reflecting blue flashing lights.

My stomach cramped. Someone was dead, and others could be hurt.

A flock of camera-laden, microphone-proffering TV crews huddled in front of the house.

They wouldn't be here for a death by natural causes, would they? News of something more sinister must have been leaked to them. How could this be happening again?

I threw the car into park and ran toward the huddle across the slick grass. Clarista was talking to reporters at the hub of the crowd, composed as ever. Her relaxed black hair was swept up in a neat chignon, and her heels matched her champagne pantsuit.

I wedged myself between two camera people to listen in.

Clarista gestured with one manicured hand in a winding circle. ". . . and then there's the question of family and so on. Of course, we should be sure that no one else . . . But even if that's the case, it's just a thing we have to deal with." She shook her head sadly and emphatically as if she was finished speaking.

Several reporters swapped looks of incomprehension. One took a straightforward approach. "Can you tell us how the victim died?"

Victim. Someone hadn't simply died but had been murdered.

Clarista bobbed her head. "Well, first we've got to cover our . . . you know, and then we can talk about getting into that, and even then we don't want to mislead anyone, naturally."

The reporters were openly annoyed now. One mouthed a solitary *What?* to his camera person.

Past experience had taught me this was all we were going to get from our eccentric hotelier. Clarista's brand of noncommunication was my every day, so seeing it fresh through others' eyes was validating. And would be hilarious if not for the worry that gnawed at me.

I had to know who died. Was the victim a guest? Or an employee? George had been with me the whole night, but where was Mr. Fig?

Assuming he was unharmed, he could fill me in on what had happened. In sentences that actually ended.

Based on the aftermath of the last death here, the drawing room would be the best place to look for him—and everyone else, for that matter.

I darted up the outside steps and through the double doors. An eerie quiet permeated the hall. Police tape guarded the foot of the staircase. All was still except behind the front desk, where an officer rummaged through papers.

I had nothing to hide, but I felt intruded on anyway.

The officer behind the desk didn't notice me cross the hall, but at the closed door of the drawing room, another stood sentinel.

Bingo. Either the drawing room was the scene of a crime or guests and staff were behind that door.

Think fast, Ivy. "Hi, Officer—" I glanced at her name tag. "Officer . . . Slatten. Excuse me. I'm back."

"Back? Who're you?"

"I just stepped out. Little girls' room. Thanks. I can go back in and sit down now."

She scanned me head to toe. "No, you wasn't in here. Who are you?"

"Oh, nobody." I waved my hand. "Staff."

"Wait here a second."

Uh-oh.

She ducked her head and talked into her radio. Another officer strode over, taking her attention.

I took the chance to disappear, winding my way through the morning room and the conservatory to the back terrace. A day's worth of sun had wiped away every trace of snow from the stone floor, so I sprinted without fear of slipping.

I could see the action of the drawing room lit up on the other side of the French doors, as clear as any TV screen. No one was visibly injured.

Mr. Fig stood calmly near the wall by the piano, his hands folded neatly behind his back, ready for service at a moment's notice.

I wiped my sweaty palms on my pants and exhaled, relieved to see him in one piece. The whole scene felt a little less dire now.

I tried to figure out who was missing.

Eight members of the Gravestone Friends of Greater Pittsburgh were scattered around the room, plus Mr. Wollstone, looking more like a dozing owl than a waking one at the moment.

I realized that everyone inside the drawing room could probably see me, too, in the light of the brass lanterns on the terrace, and I stepped back from the glass. I picked up a pebble from a nearby pot and tossed it toward the French doors.

It hit with a satisfying tink, and Mr. Fig, alert as ever, turned to investigate the sound. He crossed the room and muttered something to the officer guarding the door. She frowned, admonished him with words I didn't understand, and allowed him to pass.

I reminded myself to breathe and peered through the glass again to glean what I could from body language and lip reading.

Huddled together on the settee in front of the fireplace were Velvet Reed and Deena . . . Deena who? It was one of the presidents . . . Reagan? Nixon? I didn't know which of the ladies was which. Both octogenarians and members of the gravestone society, they drew the most attention because of the fabulous period clothing they wore—one a sapphire-blue gown with a silver beaded overlay, the other adorable high-heeled boots that buttoned up one side.

"Sideways telephone in Lincoln's popsicle," said one.

"Exit until mum sequence," replied the other.

I was not a great lip reader.

A chilly breeze ruffled the ornamental cabbage in the planter outside the nearest window, and the cold helped keep me alert.

On a second settee in the drawing room, the oversized Tom Truman was eating beef jerky from one hand and had the other arm curled around the thin shoulders of his wife Autumn, the stern redhead. If not distraught, she at least seemed tense. Although her slightly vacant expression could be a sign of shock more than anything else.

It was the first time I'd seen the Trumans since they'd checked in with Clyde and Renee. I guessed they'd all been busy with the conference.

Furnell Rogers, also from the—

A footfall on the terrace behind me spun my head around.

"Miss Nichols." Mr. Fig's angular silhouette stood outlined by fuzzy backlight. His forehead wrinkled as he glanced at my arm. "I was sorry to hear of your accident."

"Thanks. George told me you'd called."

"I wish you had stayed home and rested tonight."

"You know I had to come. Tell me who died. And when? And where?" I spread my upturned fingers as if I could catch the answers in my hands.

Mr. Fig took a step back.

I folded my hands.

"I'll take those one at a time, and in a sensible order, if you don't mind." He reprimanded me with a glance.

If he was able to be so calm, no one we loved here could be in danger. I relaxed my shoulders a bit and tried to lean against the balustrade ever so nonchalantly. "Of course. Whenever you're ready."

"Dr. Borough—"

"Clyde, right?" The lit professor.

"Yes," he said. "Dr. Borough returned from the club's tour of the estate to find Ms. Gallagher—"

"Renee?"

"Yes—to find Ms. Gallagher dead. How, we don't yet know, but from the angle of her head, her death didn't seem at all natural."

"*The angle of her head*?" I asked.

"I glimpsed her body before the police arrived."

"In the Achilles?"

"That's right," he said.

"When did she die?"

"During the tour, it seems."

"What's this?" A shadow loomed behind Mr. Fig with a familiar, gravelly voice. "You said refreshments, Fig, and I believed you. I believed you."

"I apologize, Detective." Mr. Fig turned, and the light fell on a neat, brown beard and a pair of bagged eyes I knew all too well.

"Inside," Detective Bennett barked.

He herded us back into the drawing room with everyone else. Several faces peered up at me with questioning looks that turned slowly to understanding as they realized I was that girl they knew from the desk, but out of uniform.

"Interviews are done," Bennett announced. "You can all return to your rooms—but don't leave town."

"We're here through Monday for the conference anyway, so . . ." muttered a guest with a dark widow's peak. Leonard Chaves, maybe? Homer Room. His whole body seemed drawn in protectively, and he didn't look at anyone dead on.

Autumn Truman swiveled to look at him, her deep-set eyes glowing with disdain.

Dr. Chaves pulled his phone from his jacket pocket and focused on it, apparently unaware of the carelessness of his comment.

As soon as Bennett disappeared, Officer Slatten, who'd been guarding the door, stepped forward. "Uh, actually, just to clarify, we don't have any legal means to hold any of you. But leaving town may draw suspicion if you later become a suspect."

This was all too familiar. I turned to Mr. Fig. "What else can you—"

"You—uh—Ivy." Detective Bennett had popped back in the room like a cockroach that wouldn't die. "You're not done yet."

I lifted my eyebrows at him, disrespectfully I hoped. "Me?"

"I have some questions for you."

* * *

The detective forced everyone else out of the drawing room, rested one hip on the arm of the settee by the window, and pulled a pen and a little spiral-bound notebook from his pocket.

"I don't know how I can help you." I leaned on the wall by the bookshelves. "I was gone all night."

"People don't always know what they know. Now then"—he flipped over a page in his notebook—"what did you think of her?"

"Ms. Gallagher?"

He grunted something like a yes.

"I mean, I barely interacted with her—actually, I didn't at all."

"I understand you checked the couple into the hotel last night. You didn't have any thoughts about them?"

"I have thoughts about everyone."

"And . . . ?" He tapped his pen on his notepad.

I shrugged. "I guess if I were you, I'd be looking at her partner, Clyde, uh, Dr. Borough."

"Eh? Why's that?"

"I heard them arguing this afternoon." So I *could* tell him something he didn't know. I felt pretty smug. "It seemed like Clyde bullied her. Like he made the decisions, and she complied but then whined about it."

"Uh-huh." He scribbled. "And . . . what of the other couple, Mr. And Mrs. . . ." He flipped a few pages back and forth. "Truman?"

"I've only seen them once, really. He was quiet and tired . . . and snacky. She was serious and guarded. She seemed to be pretty close to Renee."

"How would you describe the interactions between Ms. Gallagher and Mrs. Truman?"

"Well, they seemed friendly, like I said. After they checked in, Renee, Ms. Gallagher, kind of fell over laughing—it was late—and Ms. Truman told her she was getting slaphappy. Not the kind of thing most people would say to an acquaintance, right?"

Detective Bennett twitched his moustache. "What was she laughing about?"

There he went in the wrong direction again. "Oh, it wasn't like it was important—she thought the hotel decor was over-the-top or fake or both."

He made a few marks, pocketed his notebook again with a flourish, and stood. "You've been more helpful than you know."

What could he mean by that? "Okay. Great."

I felt an uneasy rush of acid in my stomach. A fear that, like last year, Bennett would get things tragically wrong.

* * *

After the detective released me from the drawing room, I lingered outside the door.

There was no sign of Mr. Fig.

I wondered if George had heard about the murder.

An officer with a manila folder passed me on his way into the drawing room. "Coroner says the ligature was something soft. She's not sure what yet, really."

Strangulation, then. What a terrible way to die. I glanced back through the door.

Bennett snatched the folder from the officer. "Shut it, you idiot. That's confidential."

I slid out of his line of sight just before he reached the door and slammed it.

A soft ligature? Hmm. My curiosity was piqued, but I told myself not to get involved as I stepped into the conservatory to call George.

A familiar sweetness filled the air, something I'd smelled before . . . but not in here.

I scanned the cavernous space for some new blooms that would give off that fragrance and spotted them just beyond the bronze fountain in the center of the room.

Permanently frozen middance, five naiads took turns spraying water into tiers of seashells, and behind them, a thigh-high drift of white Easter lilies picked up the moonlight.

I'd never seen these lilies before, but I'd also never seen the conservatory through a spring.

Left to their own devices, Easter lilies were naturally late-summer bloomers, but they were forced by commercial gardeners to do their thing early every year in order to fulfill their name's promise.

Had Mr. Zhang manipulated these plants to be ready for Easter Sunday in a couple of weeks, or was it some memory of their past lives that had pushed them to flower ahead of schedule?

I had a feeling of being reunited with an old friend. I knew that this particular species had been important to the Morrows because my mother had told me so, one rainy day.

Maybe it wasn't just the flower but the presence of the gravestone society that brought the memory to mind.

I must have been about seven. The three of us—Mom, Dad, and I—stood in a cemetery for the funeral of some relative. An

Uncle Herbert, I wanted to say, a relative of my dad's, not on the Morrow side of the family. It wasn't that long before my mom left us, in my memory at least.

The afternoon was bright, humid, and hot, like every Tennessee funeral I could remember, somehow, as if the grim reaper had conspired to get us all dressed up in our black layers of mourning just to make us sweat.

I stood in my shiny black Mary Janes holding my mother's hand under a tent at the graveside. Dad in his dark suit jacket, sweat running down his temples, helped the other men carry Uncle Herbert's casket, which was blanketed with roses and mums.

My mother bent low to whisper in my ear. "If he were a Morrow, there would be Easter lilies. Your grandmother Mary's casket was covered with them. Yellow ones."

"I don't remember," I said.

"You were just a baby." She wiggled my hand and smiled.

Did she smile at the thought of me as a baby or at the memory of her mother? Or something else?

I didn't know.

A few years later, there were Easter lilies on the casket of a coworker of Dad's. "Look," I told him, pointing, "like the Morrows, right?"

He frowned at me and stared ahead, and I understood from the shift in his face, the tightness around his eyes, that I'd said something wrong. As if he wasn't already sad enough. He clearly didn't want to be reminded of anything to do with my mother.

I hadn't brought up the Morrows again to him after that. Not even when I'd taken this job. Keeping it secret from him hadn't gotten any easier over the last nine months. But neither had the thought of coming clean. I just couldn't convince myself to bring up my mother's family again, to do or say anything that would cause that tension to come back into his face.

After checking to make sure I was alone in the conservatory—or as sure as a person could be in these dim, leafy environs—I sat down on a bench under the towering date palm. Over my head, three clusters of ripening fruit dangled from its branches like unlit copper chandeliers.

I looked at my phone for the first time since I'd arrived at the hotel. George had texted to check on my arm and see if I'd found out about Dad's new friend.

I called instead of texting back and worked the answers to his questions into my saga of all that had happened in the last hour.

He groaned. "This is . . . strange."

"That's the understatement of the year."

"Another murder at our hotel? And how dare Bennett show up there? That piece of—"

"Come on. He makes a lot of noise, but he's harmless," I said.

"It didn't seem that way last year when I was the one in his sights."

"You're right. Not my place to say, is it?" After a guest died at a dinner last year, George had been targeted first by Bennett and then his superior, Captain De Luna. Bennett had bothered him more because the detective refused to listen to reason.

It was quiet on George's end of the line. Maybe he was going to bed. I pictured him that way, in flannel pants with bare feet.

"Anyway, I couldn't find out much from Bennett," I said. "I gave him an excuse for coming back to the hotel tonight and got out of there pretty quickly."

"What did you want to find out from him?"

"I don't know—who killed the woman and why. Her boyfriend is a real smooth talker, but things seem . . . strained between them. Of course, the intimate partner is always the most obvious suspect."

"This is just your natural curiosity, right?" he said. "You're not thinking of getting involved."

"What? No. I'm way too busy with school and everything else. And no one I love is threatened like last time." I must have told him I loved him a hundred times in the years we'd been friends, but this time, when I said it, even in a roundabout way, my arms prickled. We said good-bye and ended the call.

There was a rustle of leaves behind me, and I turned expecting to see one of the songbirds that lived in here.

But it was Tom Truman, alone, his face half covered by tree limbs and towering above me. He stuck both hands in his pants pockets and ducked his head in apology.

"Sorry n'at." He followed the walkway past me and headed out toward the morning room. His grumble sounded more like a question than a statement.

What? Where had he been hiding when I'd checked the room? He'd have heard everything I said to George.

But it didn't matter. I wasn't going to get caught up in whatever was going on here.

I'd gone to great lengths to solve a murder last year, but the tracking of a killer had exhausted me and revived old hurts, throwing gasoline on my panic disorder. I wouldn't do it for just anyone.

Whatever had happened to Renee, it was between the killer and the justice department.

IV

Girl, Interrupted

~

I skipped my first class Friday, figuring that if my professor needed an excuse, my emergency room bill would be enough to gain her sympathy. I got out of Cognitive Science at three and went on to the hotel, even though it meant arriving forty-five minutes before my shift.

I couldn't have said why, but I felt like the hotel was the place to be at the moment—a pleasant surprise, since Fridays were usually the night I dreaded working the most. While other people were on dates or girls' nights out, I was stuck here. At least I had George's company.

It was warmer outside today, so I walked through the garden one more time, checking the inscriptions of more statues but not seeing my grandparents' names on any of them. I was distracted by the formal beds of optimistic crocuses and daffodils that behaved as if there hadn't just been a killing freeze here . . . and a killing.

A sneaking hope had followed me since Mr. Fig brought me out here—a wish, really, that Hortensius and Mary Morrow might not be found in any grave anywhere. I decided to look for my grandparents' obituaries as soon as I got the chance. Knowing one way or another would be better than this.

My usual dressing room operations took longer with my arm smarting from the burn, and since I had ruined my uniform dress, I'd been forced to replace it with one that was too big for me and unpleasantly bulky around my shoulders.

I met Bea as I entered the hall. Leaning her elbows on the desk, she squinted her sky-blue eyes at a paper in her hand and turned it toward me. "Any idea whose masterpiece this is?"

It was a simplistic drawing, like the one I'd found the day before, but the subject matter was different and so were the colors.

I shook my head. "I hoped it wouldn't come to this, but I'll talk to the guest in the Byzantine Room. I think it's his son, Parker. I put the last one in the lost-and-found, but no one's come to claim it that I know of."

"I guess it's just a week for weird stuff." Bea tugged on the crisp white collar of her maid uniform. "I found a wig in the trash can of the men's room."

"What, like a toupee?"

"No, like . . . long, wavy hair," she said.

That really was strange. I wondered for a second if it had anything to do with the murder last night. Maybe the killer had worn it as a disguise? But that seemed farfetched.

A much funnier idea elbowed into mind. "Think it was Wollstone's?"

" 'S'possible." She wrinkled her nose and grinned.

I tightened my lips. I was still ruffled about how she'd flirted with George, and I didn't want to make nice. I didn't want to laugh.

But I couldn't help it. The mental picture of the old grouch's scowling face framed by flowing locks was just too much.

A silent laugh shook me, and Bea joined in with her own mischievous chuckle.

I burned through the last of my breath and supported myself on the crooked marble arm of Hestia, who guarded the entry hall, spear in hand.

She was not amused.

Bea straightened up and looked at me thoughtfully. "Hey, this might seem . . . no, I'll just . . ."

"What's up?"

"You're good friends with George . . ." She looked at me sideways.

Fuzz. Please no. Nuh-uh.

"I wondered if he had said anything about me."

Be kind. Be honest. Definitely don't lie. "Yeah, sure. He said, uh, that you've started hanging out some, which is cool."

"George is cool. You know, he didn't—I didn't think he was that attractive until I got to know him."

Attractive? My arms and legs stiffened like someone had dipped me in concrete. I liked Bea, but dammit, this was not a conversation I wanted to have with her. Then again, she *had* asked me last year if anything was happening between George and me, and I'd basically given her the go-ahead. And we were friends.

Her eyes focused on the entrance behind me. "Oh, who's that?"

I glanced back, and my blood froze.

"A plumber," I answered.

Middle-aged and silver-headed, the man wore coveralls and carried a toolbox at his side. He stopped in the entryway by the

bust of David and surveyed the room, his mouth set with deter-
mination and his eyes pained.

Not just any plumber.

My dad.

"Gotta go," I whispered to Bea and ducked into the office.

It took me a second to understand why he was here.

I'd known Mr. Fig had called a plumber about the leak, but
there must have been a hundred of them in the city. How in the
name of Zeus was my dad the one who had taken the call? And
why would he have taken it, when this hotel was a place he tried
so hard to avoid?

I couldn't go out and greet him. That would be the worst
way for him to find out I was working here. It was always better
to confess a lie in person than to be caught in one. Dad and I
hadn't even finished dealing with the girlfriend-in-the-parking-
lot situation, and we sure didn't need this conflict piled on top.

It was probably past the shift changeover now, but I didn't
think Doyle was gone yet. I could still smell him, like old pop-
corn and Pepto-Bismol. I popped my head into the kitchen.
"Hey. Is Doyle in here?"

"Hey. He was a second ago," George said from the walk-in
freezer.

I checked the hall outside the kitchen. Doyle's stout back
was disappearing down the stairs.

"Doyle!" I called. "There's someone at the desk. Can you—"

"Nope. My shift ends at four, Ivy." He didn't even turn
around.

"Please, will you? Two minutes. I'm *begging* you." I couldn't
see him anymore, just the dim staircase down to the basement
level. "I'll get here early tomorrow. I'll take your shift next weekend." Anything beat facing my dad at the moment.

"No can do." His voice echoed from the lower hall. "Got a big show at the library."

"Please," I yelled with my last measure of hope.

No reply.

"Yeah, have fun at toddler hour then!" I bellowed and skulked back to the kitchen. Sometimes I wished he'd go from hobby magician to David Blaine overnight so he could finally leave us in peace.

The bell rang again. Dad wasn't going to go away no matter how much I wished for it. "*George.*"

He stuck his head out of the walk-in cooler. "Yeah?"

"Hello?" Dad called politely.

George's eyes widened. "Is that your dad's voice?"

I grimaced and nodded.

"No answer?" Clarista's smooth voice said from the lobby.

Nooooo. I couldn't just ignore him anymore, and I couldn't send George out in his chef's coat. She'd kill me.

"Ivy?" Clarista called.

Fear and shame stabbed me like a hot poker to the gut.

"Ivy!" More insistent this time.

It was over. Even if I didn't come out, he would be onto me now. Curse my adorable, uncommon name!

I pushed through the part in the curtain and lifted my eyes to the firing squad. Clarista and my dad both stood there frowning at me, albeit for different reasons.

Dad's eyes squinted as if caught in a permanent wince. He scanned my hair, my collar, my sleeves, like he was putting it all together—the trouble George had been in last year, my lies about working at a bar, about sharing the hotel's parking lot. He scrubbed the back of his neck with one hand the way he did when he was most upset.

Shame reared up inside me, and I turned subtly away from Dad's gaze, feeling worse than I had that night in middle school when he'd caught me lying about joining the basketball team to cover for having a boyfriend.

"Ivy, the leak . . . you know, don't you?" Clarista flapped her hand like an injured wing.

"In the men's room." I pointed lamely and checked Dad's face.

But he picked up his toolbox wordlessly and disappeared into the men's room.

Some once-healthy limb of my pride shriveled and fell off. I had lied to my own father, my only family, and I couldn't hide from the fact a second longer.

"It took you much too long to answer that bell," Clarista started.

I prepared myself for a good talking-to.

But Clarista didn't have time to finish lecturing me. The front doors banged open again, and a trench-coated Detective Bennett took two steps inside and planted his feet. One arm guarded his side while the other brought a fat cigar to his mouth.

A smoking cigar.

Mr. Fig was going to flip out.

Two uniformed officers stepped in behind Bennett. The handcuffs on one's utility belt flashed in the sun glaring in from the window.

"Detective." Clarista glided over to greet him. Her fingers fidgeted nervously at the pocket of her wool skirt. "How can I help you?" (Read: *How can I get you out of my hotel before you're seen by a guest?*)

Bennett lowered his cigar and exhaled a cloud of smog that obscured his face. "Here to see Ralph Fig."

All I could think was, *Ralph?*

"I can help you with anything you need," Clarista said.

The detective exhaled a thunderhead. "Where's Fig?"

Clarista shifted her feet. "He's in the basement. He's . . ."

Her eyes darted from side to side, like she might do a runner.

"Doing the wine inventory." My voice cracked as I finished Clarista's sentence. I didn't want to connect the dots here.

Bennett nodded at his officers. Clarista, wide-eyed, led them into the elevator, and he shoved in behind them.

I didn't want to jump to the wrong conclusion. Maybe Bennett needed more information about the hotel on the night of the murder. Maybe he knew Mr. Fig could answer his questions best. But a sharp finger of dread picked its way under my skin.

I took the stairs down to meet them, leaving the desk unattended again, but I couldn't worry about that at the moment.

I followed Bennett's cigar exhaust and caught up to the group as they filed into the wine cellar.

Mr. Fig, who had been kneeling by an open shipping crate, stood slowly, dusting off his pants. He faced Bennett and locked eyes with the man as if he'd already prepared himself for this moment.

"Ralph Fig, you are under arrest for the murder of Renee Gallagher. You have the right to remain silent." Bennett drummed the Miranda speech like he was on *Law and Order*.

But I didn't hear the rest of it. I couldn't hear or think or feel anything besides the shouting in my brain. *Not Mr. Fig. Not Mr. Fig. Not Mr. Fig!*

One officer pulled his handcuffs from his belt.

A groan escaped my lips, and a wave of nausea flipped my insides.

Clarista gasped and covered her mouth. Her face, normally bronzed like the underside of magnolia leaves, lost its warmth.

"You don't have to do that," Mr. Fig said calmly. No one had more respect for law, or order, than he did.

" 'Fraid we must." Bennett said.

Mr. Fig turned around and put his hands behind his back. I'd never seen anyone so vulnerable and brave at once.

The officer with the cuffs snapped the steel against Mr. Fig's wrists where his skin was thinned with age.

I couldn't feel my own body, just a weightless chill where my skin used to be.

The police walked Mr. Fig back out the way they had come. I rushed up the stairs, racking my brain for something I could do.

"George!" I yelled as I raced past the kitchen door.

Clarista caught me by the arm at the top of the stairs, her face crumpled with fear and disbelief. "It's better if you . . ."

I pulled away from her, gathered my thick skirts in my hands, and ran through the entry hall toward the door.

By the time I got out to the front steps, an officer was already shoving Mr. Fig into the back of Bennett's unmarked car. Mr. Fig's white bow tie was crooked, and one lapel was flipped up.

He was an old man, for pity's sake, and an innocent one.

I needed to stop this, but I felt as frozen and powerless as if I were handcuffed too.

"No," I yelled feebly.

Mr. Fig paused, raised his eyes, and locked them on mine.

I ran down the steps. "No."

In my mind I rushed Bennett and knocked him to the ground.

In reality, I stopped just short of contact, my hands taut and hovering in the space between us. "What's wrong with you? Are you just screwing with us? We cooperated. We've told you everything we know!"

He hadn't flinched or shifted from where he stood. "Get control of yourself, or I'll take you to the station with him."

I did as he said and lowered my hands.

But I raised my voice. "That wouldn't surprise me. Evidently you're used to arresting people without just cause."

He ducked his head so he could sneer at me. "I'm warning you. Shut your mouth, and keep out of this. If not for your sake, then for his."

I gritted my teeth. My breath came in short huffs. I needed to do something.

Bennett tossed his cigar onto the drive and ground it out with a foot, leaving an ashy smear on the brick. He glanced at Mr. Fig, already his prisoner in the back seat, then at me, as he got behind the wheel and slammed the door.

Mr. Fig blinked hard. He was trying so hard to fend off his emotions—whether for our benefit or his pride's, I didn't know.

I stared into his face.

He looked right back at me for several seconds, his hardened mouth holding the rest of his face in check. In his eyes, there was something like concession, and as he lowered his head, I wondered if it was shame.

Bennett started up the car and pulled away.

I couldn't pull my attention from the sight of Mr. Fig's bowed head.

George put an arm around my shoulder.

I jumped a hair. I hadn't realized he was outside, much less next to me.

His face, above mine, displayed the rage and confusion I felt.

Together we watched the black car slice down the drive, taking away someone we couldn't do without.

V

Hints and Shadows

∾

It wasn't until after they'd taken Mr. Fig away that I noticed everyone else standing with us under the porte cochere. Bea, Mr. Zhang, and even a few guests had come out to watch the ordeal. Clarista clenched a tissue in her hand and cried silently.

George hugged me, but all I could feel was the angry flow of lava in my veins and embarrassment for Mr. Fig, for having been made a spectacle. I pulled away, and we stood there staring at the empty drive until the others went inside.

George seemed to be concentrating on something far away and painful. "I wanna lock Bennett up for a crime *he* didn't commit. See how he likes it."

His indignance comforted me.

I dropped down to sit on the step, and George took off his chef's coat and lowered himself down beside me. I stared at the brick pavement, but his long leg filled up the periphery of my vision.

It was like we hoped that if we sat there a little longer, we could find a way to undo what had just happened. After a few silent minutes, we forced ourselves to go back into the house.

There was no sign of my dad in the hall or the men's room. He must have repaired the leaky line and slipped out while all my attention was on Mr. Fig. All this time, I'd thought he was avoiding this place, avoiding talking about it, avoiding thinking about it. So why had he taken that call? He had enough seniority to turn it down, give it to someone else.

I was a walking fireball of frustration, so this wouldn't have been the best time to talk to him anyway.

When I reached the desk, I heard Clarista at the computer behind the black curtain, but I was sure she wouldn't really be working yet. She wouldn't have the presence of mind.

George opened the door to the basement, and there was a flash of green baize behind him. The felt fabric—like my dress, like Mr. Fig's suit, like the period language we often employed around here—had always been purely ornamental, but in the face of the disaster we'd just witnessed, it seemed a silly relic.

Green baize was another symbol of division between upstairs and down, a way to muffle the noise of the long-ago staff, to remove their concerns from the world of the family. But just like the servant rooms in the basement had disappeared to make way for a modern garage, the hard division between employer and employee had faded in this house. Although Clarista owned the place, she and Mr. Fig held each other in high regard, and she would be worried for him.

I returned to my post, completely unbothered for once by her rule against sitting down in a guest's presence. The gravestone people were away at their convention anyway. I paced in the five-foot space, stewing over Mr. Fig.

I pictured his face. What was the look he'd passed me at the end? It was impossible for me to believe it was guilt.

But you've known him less than a year, said a small voice of doubt. *You know nothing of his past.*

It didn't matter. He wasn't capable of murder, especially not strangulation. It was a cruel and inefficient way to kill.

But it was a clean method, said the small voice. *Strangulation spills no blood. Mr. Fig likes things clean.*

Like my mother's life, Mr. Fig's story was unknown to me. While I avoided thinking about what she'd experienced after leaving me, when it came to Mr. Fig, I simply painted in the blank bits with a wash of optimism.

A picture of him—his hands clenched around Renee's neck, her fingers prying at his—encroached on my consciousness.

I forced out a breath and wiped my hand across my face. No. Not Mr. Fig.

What would a psychologist say about these intruding dark thoughts? Was there some part of me that wanted Mr. Fig to be guilty?

Well, I would banish that part of me, if it existed at all.

As far as I knew, Mr. Fig had only met Renee after she checked into the hotel. Even if he had the capacity to kill someone, how in Hades would he have come up with a motive in a single day?

I needed to talk to him. As impossible as it seemed, Bennett must have had some evidence in order to arrest him.

George came up from the basement and stood by the desk.

"Where were you?" My words came out accusingly, but I didn't mean them that way.

He still had a dinner to finish preparing, I realized. How could we all be expected to go back to work like it was a normal day?

"Just walked Bea out to the parking lot." He was patient, not defensive.

"Oh. Sorry." I couldn't escape the raw feeling when I thought about them walking out together.

"You gonna be okay?"

"Yeah. It's just . . . this is so crazy. They can't possibly hold him, right?"

He cocked his head. "Well, they have enough to make the arrest, so—"

"But what could they have when he didn't do anything?"

"You know more than I do about what's happened. But I wonder if it's about opportunity. Sounds like everyone else was on the grave tour when Renee was murdered."

"Then it's my fault," I said. "He should've been giving that tour. He would've been, if I hadn't been so clumsy in the kitchen" (i.e., if I'd minded my own business).

"Look, you can't know that." He touched my shoulder. "There may be some other reason they suspect him. We'll just have to wait."

"I'm going there as soon as I get off."

"What, at two in the morning?" he asked.

"Well, then I'll go now. I'll ask Clarista for the night off. I'll fake a stomach bug if I have to."

He leaned on the desk and brought both hands together in a fist. "They'll be booking him, Vee, and it's a long process. Just wait till morning. He's not going anywhere."

"I wish you didn't have a reason to know so much about the process." I had hated the thought of George in jail so much last year that I hadn't let myself even picture it. Now, an image of Mr. Fig, in his bespoke suit, his handkerchief wiping the seat in a dirty cell, shoved its way into my head.

George looked at me squarely. "Ivy, you said before that you wouldn't get involved—"

"But that was before Mr. Fig was—George, I have to." Sure, my schedule was already full with classes and work, and sure, it was risky, especially with Bennett's warning. But the dramatic detective had run off the rails on this one. "Bennett's far enough gone to arrest Mr. Fig, so he won't let a little thing like truth stand in his way."

I had done this before, and I could do it again. I would find what Bennett was overlooking.

"I get it," George said. "And part of me's glad you're doing it. Just—" He pinched the corner of the bandage on my arm. "Be careful, okay?"

"Don't worry," I said. "I know where Clarista keeps the gun."

I was half joking. After the danger last year's investigation had put me in, she had installed a small safe below the desk to contain some kind of pistol, but I didn't know how to use it. I hoped I wouldn't have to.

* * *

It wasn't simply that Mr. Fig was the steel backbone that kept this place from sinking into bankruptcy—or worse, in his eyes at least, becoming a three-star hotel. He'd also been my personal support more than a few times. When I craved connection to the past, he was there with a story to tell, and when I clung too tightly to my own history, he had solutions for that too.

After all the years I'd thought about my mother and wondered where she was and how she was doing, I hadn't been brave enough to actually try to find her, and I hadn't understood my hesitancy until last fall.

Mr. Fig had shined a light on my motivations the first time we were together in the secret passage, the one that began underneath the conservatory.

I'd tipped the iron heron's wing and taken the stairs as quickly as I dared to, ending up in the dark hall where I'd been injured the week before.

We reached the first doorway, and Mr. Fig flipped on the light.

A long, gray coffin filled the center of the room. *No, a tanning bed?* I thought.

But ancient. A gauge and fan stuck out from one side and three X-shaped handles from another.

My eyes were still adjusting to the brightness. I blinked at the thing and then at Mr. Fig. "What *is* it?"

"*Sic itur ad astra*," he said. That cryptic phrase he'd used before. It meant "thus we go to the stars."

But I didn't understand how that applied here.

"It's a full-body fever machine," he said.

"Well, I . . . what's that?"

"A person would lay inside, and the bed, heated by steam, would slowly raise their body temperature. The treatment was thought to cure psychosis."

"Whoa. And it's here because . . ."

"Mr. Murdoch had this entire hall planned out from the time the blueprints were designed in order to take good care of your great-great-grandmother. You probably know, but at the turn of the last century, treatments for mental illness were few, and families often sent their ill to asylums." He grimaced.

"Where the conditions were horrible," I finished for him.

I thought of Lillian's heart-shaped face. Instead of picturing her in the fine dresses that the paintings upstairs captured, I saw her in a straitjacket. I shivered. "I'm thankful that she and her husband had the resources to keep her out of there."

"And others after her, I believe, although I have little evidence."

"I wish they'd found a way to stop it from spreading to the next generation," I said.

"Before your mother came along?" he asked.

I bit my lip and nodded. I took a deep breath and questioned out loud what I'd never had the guts to ask my dad. "You don't have any idea . . . where my mother is now, do you?"

Mr. Fig took a step back and stared at the floor for a long moment.

"What is it? If you're trying to decide whether or not to tell me, the answer is yes, you know. I deserve to know, don't I?"

He nodded, and for a moment, I thought I was going to get the answers I was looking for.

"You do deserve much better than you have received, dear. I wish I could make your mother's leaving make sense to you, and I wish I could tell you where she is now, whether she thinks about you, whether she regrets her mistakes." His shoulders dropped. "However, I cannot."

My eyes burned in the corners, and tears flooded in. For a moment, while the possibility of knowing had hung in the balance, I hadn't been sure. Some part of me *did* want all of those answers, and yet, as Mr. Fig was speaking, I realized that what I really wanted wasn't to understand the present but to undo the past. I wanted to make her different—no, not just different. I wanted her to be better, to be whole. And not only for my sake, but for Dad's and for her own.

"As impossible as it may seem," he went on, "I believe that a different answer, one that you did not expect, will come to you before long."

I narrowed my eyes at him. "You aren't going to tell me what you mean by that, are you?"

His troubled smile was so full of affection that I let it go. If he was right, and he always was, I would find out eventually.

The darkness I'd felt about my mother's leaving had lightened a shade that day as we explored the rest of the passage and I got to know my family a tiny bit better.

A part of me would always want to bring her back, to make her answer for her crimes. Another, more idealistic side of me hoped she would come back on her own someday, full of grace and apologies, having done her own work and ending up healthier.

But these days I found it easier to set aside those expectations, unrealistic as they were after all this time. And for that, I had Mr. Fig to thank. I would do whatever I could to repay him.

* * *

After all the staff went home Friday evening, I made the rounds to lock up. Mr. Fig would always do the bulk of this at the end of his shift, and I would just handle the front doors and servant entrance when I left at two. Tonight, of course, was different. There were at least ten exterior doors. It took a lifetime after a day that had already felt endless.

I ended in the drawing room where the lights were dimmed by an automatic timer that Clarista had finally agreed to install earlier this year (against her desire to keep everything as historically authentic as possible).

A distant giggle bounced toward me from the direction of the back terrace, and I slid over to the glass doors for a look.

A white pixie cut belonging to either Velvet Reed or Deena Nixon (not Reagan—I'd looked it up) bobbed just above the level of the swimming pool water. The other member of the pair lay on a chaise nearby, her hair in a voluptuous French roll and her tall figure draped in a green silk caftan printed with enormous, art nouveau–style poppies.

No part of the hotel had a posted closing time, and the pool was heated, so it wasn't surprising to find guests taking advantage of that. Then again, it was after ten o'clock, and I wondered if the sounds would carry to the upstairs windows.

This pool wasn't the kind with a diving board, and there was no slide. The whole thing was only maybe fifteen by thirty feet and not deep enough for diving. Still, it was romantic, with the stone Gorgon heads spewing water from the height of the balustrade and the old fern planters at the corners.

I decided to give the ladies a few more minutes before asking them to tuck in for the night and turned back toward the hall.

One of their voices reflected off the water. "Well, Renee did give him the cold shoulder on the way to the conference yesterday morning."

It sounded like they were talking about other members of the gravestone group, and as far as I was concerned, all of them were suspects. I spent less than a second deciding that eavesdropping was not so unethical if it had anything to do with getting Mr. Fig out of jail. I cracked open the door enough to hear the women well and see their faces while keeping myself out of the light.

"Only because you brought up that thing about her business," said the one with short hair—Deena, I thought. "No, I simply can't believe it was Clyde." She spoke with a subtler version of that same accent I'd heard from Tom, a Pittsburgh accent evidently.

I caught a whiff of chlorine mingling with the scent of the hyacinths that bloomed at the edge of the terrace.

"Why not?" asked the one in the caftan—Velvet?

Yeah, why not?

"For starters, he was giving the tour the whole time. All eyes were on him."

That was a good point. But besides Mr. Fig at the desk, only Clyde would've had a key to the Achilles suite. Of course, there might be several people in the group who Renee would have simply opened the door for.

"What I can't figure out is how anybody could've got upstairs without the butler seeing them," Deena continued.

That was right. With the conservatory staircase out of commission, the only way to the Achilles suite on the second floor was via the main staircase, planted in the middle of the entry hall, or the elevator, just a few yards from the front desk.

"Oh now, surely he strayed away from the desk for a minute," said Velvet.

It didn't sound like Mr. Fig to leave the desk unattended. But if he'd seen anyone go upstairs during the grave tour, he would've told the police. Was this the sticking point for Bennett?

I stepped out onto the terrace and pounced on their conversation. "Wait a second. What if Clyde—"

I stopped myself midsentence.

The one in the water was naked.

She was swimming *naked*. I hadn't seen it from inside, but I did now, yards of bare white skin, wrinkled first by time and more so by the pool water.

"Oh, hello, Ivy," both women said, almost simultaneously. Their faces recovered from the surprise of my interruption and shined up at me, awaiting the end of my sentence.

I took a breath. "Um, what if Clyde killed her when you all returned from the tour?"

"Impossible," said the naked one. "We were standing just across the way when he flung the door open."

"He screamed and flew out again with his hands up by his face." The one with the French roll pantomimed to illustrate her tale.

"Velvet's such a good storyteller," said the naked one, who was therefore definitely Deena, in an aside to me.

"Just like that painting," said Velvet. "By Munchausen."

Did she mean Munch? I opened my mouth to correct her and closed it again. Arguing with white-haired people was strictly against the Southern code of conduct by which I had been raised, not to mention that it was no way to treat a guest.

"But maybe it was before he led the tour," said Velvet.

"How long was the tour, anyway?" I asked.

"Oh, an hour I guess," said Deena. "There's so many interesting statues in the garden."

She said *hour* like *ahr*, reminding me of a college friend I'd had who hailed from just north of Alabama. But the two accents were altogether distinct.

I took a pool towel from a cabinet camouflaged into the stonework and slipped back into historic verbiage to separate myself from the situation. "Ms. Nixon, I regret disturbing your bathing time, but I must ask you to dress yourself. Period-appropriate clothing is not required here, simply clothing."

"I knew this was an old-fashioned place. I didn't expect such old-fashioned values," said Deena as she swam my way.

I craned my head away so that I couldn't see her body leaving the water and stretched the towel like a screen to protect her privacy. And perhaps my psyche. I liked to think I was okay with the idea of growing older, but I wasn't immune to scares.

"Gosh, we'd better not tell her about the weed," stage-whispered Velvet.

"You mean CBD," I said. Surely they didn't have marijuana.

Deena shrugged her bare shoulders, smiled, and donned a robe that had been draped on the balustrade. Velvet got up slowly, revealing ankles that hadn't aged as quickly as the rest of her, and joined her friend.

I held the drawing room door open for them and locked it behind us. "Good night, ladies."

They resumed the conversation I'd interrupted as they meandered toward the elevator.

"But my lands, what reason could anyone but Clyde have to kill the woman?" said Velvet. "Renee never hurt a fly."

"Well, she was a little annoying with those headaches n'at," said Deena.

"Not that that's a reason to harm anybody."

"No, it's not."

"Hey, doesn't her company run security for your nephew's building?" Velvet held the elevator door back so Deena could scoot in.

"Oh, yes. They do a darn good job too. Autumn's company, actually. Renee works for her—worked."

Velvet swiped a hand in the air. "Anyway, she's not the kind of person anyone would want to murder who wasn't jealous or something like that."

"No, it's just like the old movies, I think," Deena said. "The butler did it."

What was this *n'at* word several of them were using? Some kind of Pennsylvania lingo?

I liked these ladies. They asked a lot of good questions.

But they didn't know that Mr. Fig was incapable of murder. He was a consummate rule follower, and I'd be shocked if he'd ever had so much as an overdue library book. Felony was out of the question.

I just had to prove it.

Even if he had a gravestone-solid alibi, Clyde was Renee's partner and therefore an obvious suspect—maybe too obvious, George would say. But statistics were on my side. Not only was he the only other person with a key to the Achilles, but something like half of female murder victims were killed by intimate partners these days.

If Clyde was guilty, then one of the following was true— either he'd killed Renee right before the tour, or he'd found some unlikely moment while everyone was in the garden and he could leave the group. But how had he slipped past the desk unnoticed?

VI

Ivy Looks Into a Wardrobe

～

Since I couldn't talk to Mr. Fig until tomorrow, I switched gears for now.

I needed to see the crime scene if I was going to investigate this murder properly. It was really unfortunate that I hadn't been able to take a look last night, and I was unlikely to hear any more leaked info from police.

I wished I had the relationship with Detective Bennett that I had with his boss, Captain De Luna, who I felt owed me one since I'd given her the goods to clear George's name last year. But homicide was Bennett's department, not hers, so I wasn't likely to see her this time around.

I couldn't at this point examine the body—not that it would tell me much, since I had no kind of expertise with corpses. (I made a mental note to start watching more *CSI* in my off hours.) I did have expertise with Google, though, and would've especially liked to have seen the victim's neck.

My only hope was that police had left some evidence behind that didn't need to be taken in or couldn't be. Stains on the carpet, that kind of thing.

It was worth a look.

I popped another pain pill for my arm and propped the *brb* sign (whose text was Clarista's novella-length explanation for the attendant's absence) on the desk, hoping no one would actually need me in the middle of the night (they never did). It was after twelve, which gave me two-ish hours to the end of my shift, if I should need them.

I climbed to the second floor and locked the door of the Achilles suite behind me, leaving the lights off as I stepped through the alcove and into the heart of the suite. If anyone was outside in the garden, I didn't want them noticing a lit window where one shouldn't be. No one needed to know I was here, including the killer. I'd learned last year how dangerous it was to let a murderer know you were onto them.

My phone was handy as a flashlight and in case I needed to photograph anything. Keeping it with me on shift used to be against Clarista's rules, but the events of last fall had changed that.

The room was large and daunting, considering I had no idea where the body had been found. There was no dramatic chalk outline on the floor. I hadn't seen the police do one last year either, so I started to suspect they weren't as common as the movies would have you believe.

Judging by the smudged mirror at the dressing table and the personal items here and there, it was clear that neither Bea nor anyone else had cleaned the room yet. Maybe there hadn't been time between the police releasing the crime scene and the end of Bea's shift today. That was lucky.

I wondered, too, what Clyde was using as clothing at his new hotel, since his suitcase was still by the bed.

I knew enough *Sherlock* to understand that if Renee had died on the floor, she'd have left the carpet fibers mashed down somewhere on this plush Persian. I got on all fours and held my flashlight beam parallel to the carpet, working my way across the room. I congratulated myself on finding a footprint but saw nothing like the outline of a body.

Could Renee have been strangled in the bed? That would seem to point toward Clyde, or another lover, if she had one. Tom came to mind. He was attractive (if you liked that fill-up-the-doorway look) and close to her age, and since they'd arrived here together, they seemed to be friends.

But before I reached the bed, I could see that it was undisturbed, as if I had turned it down only a minute before. The covers were flat and smooth. Even the mints sat primly on the pillows.

In fact, there was little out of place on this side of the room. The roses on both nightstands were as they should be, and the velvet bed-curtains hung neatly to the floor.

A sofa and two chairs gathered in front of the fireplace. I walked over, and the soles of my Chuck Taylors ground in soot on the hearth. Either Bea had done a poor job cleaning the room after the last guests (a filmmaker and a location scout who liked the look of the area) checked out, or a fire had been lit the day Renee died.

I sat down on the settee and imagined Renee here beside me, her coffee-brown hair shining in the firelight. Perhaps she'd be reading. No, she'd had a headache. Maybe she had curled up on the settee and thrown an arm over her eyes.

There would be a knock. She'd sit up, perturbed, open the door, and smile with recognition.

Would she fight back? No one around here had visible scratches from what I'd seen, and the room didn't show signs of a conflict.

Maybe Renee had turned her back on the visitor and from behind they'd wrapped something—a scarf, as I imagined it—around her throat. She would've yanked at the fabric, but if it was long, maybe she couldn't have reached her attacker's hands or face.

Of course, a lot of different scenarios were possible.

I lifted my arm to knead the tension from my neck, and some kind of filament caught the light against the burgundy velvet of the settee. A strand of hair, pale and about two feet long.

I searched over the brocade and found several more, some much longer than the first. Could it mean anything? Bea's hair was blond, but chin length and curly, while these strands were straight.

None of the guests had hair both long enough and blond enough to match these. Definitely not Renee, with her shoulder-length mahogany tresses.

I slipped the loose strands into a pocket of my dress and stood to check the armchairs for clues.

A metallic click sounded from the door. The lock.

Caesar's leaves! Who had a key to the room? Clyde had returned his to the desk when he checked out. And who but the killer would sneak in at this hour?

I had to hide.

The armoire seemed to me an ideal spot, but fear had rooted me in place.

I took a breath, peeled my feet from the floor, and absconded to the cupboard's dark depths, leaving the door cracked behind me, since, as everyone knows, it's foolish to shut yourself in a wardrobe.

In my haste, I knocked the empty hangers, and they scratched against the back of the furniture. I caught my breath and reached up a hand to still them.

The floorboards squeaked near the door.

Had the intruder heard me?

I hoped I might glimpse them through the sliver of the armoire opening.

Alas, they also kept the lights off, which both confirmed that their intentions were nefarious and meant I could see only hints and shadows in the moonlight.

I couldn't think for the life of me why anyone, even Renee's killer, would need to be here, but that old adage popped into my head about murderers always returning to the scene of the crime.

Footsteps sounded on the wood floor.

I could barely hear over the whooshing of blood in my ears. I held my breath and kept my eyes on the blue darkness beyond the crack.

A streak of light zipped around the slice of room I could see.

I leaned into the gap.

The armoire door flew open. Brightness blinded me.

I let slip a frightened warble and covered my face with my hands.

It was too late. I'd been seen.

My hands shook as I lowered them and opened my eyes warily into the darkness that had returned. There was a white overlay on my vision.

The intruder's footsteps retreated, and the door closed behind them.

Whoever it was didn't want to be seen here.

But had now seen me.

My poor heart blipped and blinked and launched into a quiet tattoo against my rib cage. Doom clawed at me.

I felt the familiar chill in my legs. My hands froze into numbness.

Deep breaths would have been calming if my chest weren't a block of cement. I was paralyzed in the dark.

I employed the grounding technique from my therapist, squeezing my eyes shut and concentrating on the feel of my feet on the wardrobe floor, the sharp scent of cedar, and somewhere in the distance, the haunting call of a bird.

*   *   *

It was two thirty AM.

The panic that had come for me in the armoire had sucked away all my energy. On the way to up to Dad's and my apartment, I paused to catch a breath outside our neighbor Ms. Franklin's door. She'd put out a spring wreath, a circle of green grass with carbuncles of chicks and bunnies.

I was tired of climbing these stairs every time I came home, but I still had to save money for my own place, which was slow going while working only part-time and keeping up with school.

I hoped Dad would be asleep, honestly. At some point we'd have to talk about the hotel and the lies I'd told him, but I had more urgent matters to handle now, so I had to set everything aside and get some sleep myself.

Before the murder at the hotel last October that had sent me reeling into snake pits of anxiety, I'd thought I'd outwitted my disorder by using positive thinking.

Now I understood that the beast only responded to a multipronged attack. I'd been taking better care of myself lately—sleeping enough, exercising, journaling, going to counseling, even eating better. It seemed like I should have reserves to offset this crisis.

I thought back to the moments before the panic had set in, in the darkness of the armoire. I hadn't seen the intruder, but what about my other senses? Had I smelled or heard anything helpful?

Mudderpucker. I couldn't stop these ruminating thoughts.

I dug through my bag for my keys, but as soon as I laid my hand on them, the door swung open.

I looked up at Dad's blue eyes, visible in the sallow light from the apartment stairs. Behind their usual kindness was an aching question—why had I lied to him?

"Hi," he said flatly. One hand throttled the doorframe. The opposite arm stood tense at his side.

Was it a good sign or a bad one that he'd met me at the door? At least he hadn't thrown a suitcase at me and told me to go find someone else to take me in. Not that I would expect such. He didn't lord it over me that he paid most of the rent here or bought most of the groceries. He never treated me like a charity case, and only now and then like I was still a child.

I took a breath as if it were my last before a forty-fathom plunge to the ocean floor and exhaled it all out again before stepping over the threshold.

I was afraid that the day's events and my reactions to them had robbed me of the patience to have a good talk now, but this was the way life happened. For months at a time, it was all smooth sailing, and then in the course of a few hours, the skies would darken, the crew mutiny, and the sharks begin to circle.

Dad turned his back to me as he stepped into the little linoleum kitchen.

I tensed at the hint of rejection implicit in his body language. "I guess you want to talk about the hotel."

It was the first time I'd said those last two words to him, and I gave them the full weight of all they contained. The mansion was the childhood home of the wife who had left him and the font of her mental illness, which had been the ultimate cause of her leaving. Those were the reasons both for my working there and for my keeping it secret from him, but now my lies had added insult to injury.

"We have to talk about it." He turned toward me again with a steaming mug in each hand. A peace offering of tea, perhaps?

I hoped he knew that the hotel brought me pain too, that I hadn't taken the job lightly, that every time I glimpsed those golden walls, I had to steer my thoughts quite purposefully away from my mother.

"I've been working there for nine months," I blurted, and took a mug from him. It had been nine months exactly on the night the gravestoners checked in.

He flinched slightly.

I almost didn't see it. A person who knew him less wouldn't have.

We both sat down, me on the couch, him in the adopted but well-loved corduroy recliner facing me. I felt the same cold sweat under my arms that I had during my interview with Clarista for the hotel job.

"Nine months. Congratulations."

I frowned. "Sarcasm. Great."

"No, I mean that," he said, reaching a hand out, even though he was too far away to touch me. "I know the anxiety makes it hard to stick too long to anything."

"Yeah." I tucked a piece of hair behind my ear, a gesture that wasn't even my own. I thought of a friend from school who did it constantly. "It helps that George is there."

I spoke slowly, as if every word was a pin in his flesh, as if slowing them down would give him time to process. But I couldn't have predicted what he said next.

He straightened up. "I wondered when you were going to tell me."

I blinked twice.

"Yes, I knew. Your old dad managed to piece it together." He tapped the side of his forehead.

My mouth crinkled with sadness. "I'm sorry."

"Ivy, I have tried to cultivate a relationship between us where we can both be honest and vulnerable. I know I don't talk about the hard stuff very often, but it doesn't mean that I don't want you to."

"No, you're right. I know. You've been great at that."

"Do you? Do you really know?" He shook his head. " 'Cause it feels like you're holding back, like you think I can't handle it."

Oh, he was right. That's exactly how I'd behaved. As if it was my job to protect him from the hard feelings, as if I could. I looked at my left Converse where a worn place was starting near my big toe. "I guess, yeah. I have assumed that any talk of the hotel, of the house, would just be so painful for you."

"Of course. I have a lot of negative associations with it. But like I said, I can take it."

"Okay."

"I know why you lied." He waited until I made eye contact. "But don't do it again."

I nodded. "I won't. I'm sorry."

He wasn't finished. "Whatever happens to you, anything that's part of your life, matters to me. I wanna hear about it."

When you feel bad about your behavior, turning the tables on your accuser is a natural reaction, so of course the desire to bring his new girlfriend into the conversation surfaced, but I checked myself.

His mind must have gone there too, though. "And in the same vein, I have held things back from you. The fact that you're the child and I'm the parent works in my favor, but still, you are an adult now, and I have to learn to trust you too."

"So I get to hear all about your *girlfriend*?" I cuddled my mug and settled back into the couch. My curiosity was genuine. I felt more open to the situation now than I had a few nights ago. Was it the life-and-death nature of the past two days' events that put everything in perspective? Or maybe the way Dad was loving me well by opening this conversation, by being so vulnerable, by forgiving me already? I hadn't even said sorry yet, I realized.

"She's not my girlfriend."

"Yet?"

He jiggled his head. "Yet."

We spent a few minutes talking about Kimberly, but I started to yawn.

"All right. That's enough for now. We're both tired," he said.

"I'm glad we talked."

"So'm I. Now we just have to follow the talk with action." He stood up. "Hey, one more thing. That leak at the hotel?"

"Yeah?"

"It wasn't just worn parts. It looked like the supply line was probably cut."

"Cut? Like intentionally?"

He raised his eyebrows and nodded.

"Wow. Okay. Thanks."

"Hey, stand up, will you?"

I set down my tea and did as requested.

He put both arms around me and hugged me tightly. "I will always have room for you."

After a moment, he released me.

I turned toward the hallway. "Okay, so I promise to share everything with you. If I get a paper cut, I'll tell you. If I have tuna instead of egg salad for lunch, you're gonna hear about it."

"Watch it."

I laughed. "But in general we'll be less protective of each other and more communicative, right?"

"Sounds like a plan."

VII
First Fig

⁓

I followed the guard down a narrow, peeling gray hallway as a fluorescent light flickered overhead. Rust stains dripped down the wall under a vent. I was not in Kansas anymore.

Outside, a ceiling of clouds hung over the city so it was barely light out, but from inside the county jail, you wouldn't know there *was* a sun.

I'd woken up as early as I could to see Mr. Fig before my appointment with my therapist. I couldn't cancel it now because the late notice meant she'd charge me anyway. And maybe I had things I needed to say to someone.

The guard stopped in front of a holding cell full of men lying on benches or on the floor or else pacing, leaning, sitting. There were a couple dozen of them in this cell that was maybe twenty-five feet long.

I could describe the smell as that of a kennel for incontinent dogs, one that was never cleaned. But that wouldn't quite do it justice.

Most of the men glanced up when we appeared. One yelled something profane at the guard. Several stared outright at me.

I felt the oppression of the place like something crawling on my skin.

One man, in a nice but wrinkled suit, stood from a bench near the sole toilet and threaded his way toward us. Platinum stubble dusted his jaw, but his ginger hair had been patted down neatly.

I flinched and my throat spasmed as if someone had punched it. My dear Mr. Fig.

A thin man in the corner whistled at me and oozed a few foul words.

"Some decorum, please, Mr. Jones." Mr. Fig frowned.

"Sorry," the thin man muttered and sat up a little straighter against the concrete block wall.

So Mr. Fig earned respect wherever he went. I'd have expected no less, even here. He stopped on the other side of the bars from me and ran his hands down the front of his jacket.

The lines on his face were creases he couldn't smooth. Normally they inspired admiration in me, but now they stood out like scars. For the first time, he looked haggard.

"Miss Nichols? What is it?" he said.

"Mr. Fig." I couldn't just jump into my questions. I couldn't even form a sentence. "Mr. Fig."

He looked down, as if taking in the condition of his appearance through my eyes.

I followed his line of sight and realized he was in his sock feet.

When his eyes lifted, there was shame in them like there had been in the back of Bennett's car, only clearer now.

I shouldn't have come. It would have been better to let him be lonely here than to shame him by my presence.

"I'm sorry." My throat burned. "I'm just really sorry that you're here and that I'm here, and I . . . I wanted to talk to you."

"It's all right," he said gently.

Great. He was the one in jail, and I was the one being comforted. I wanted to rip my hair out.

"Can we talk?" I said instead.

"Of course. How is the hotel?"

"Oh, fine." I glossed over things so as not to alarm him. I didn't mention Deena's skinny-dipping, but I did tell him about the strange drawings Bea and I had found—in case he could explain them. He couldn't.

"So . . . have they set bail?" I asked.

"Monday." He frowned.

"*Monday?*"

"The first available arraignment and bail hearing when one is arrested on a Friday afternoon."

"Oh. I'm sorry." That timing felt purposeful on Bennett's part. All I wanted was to pull Mr. Fig out of here, legal or not. "But why? I mean, do you know *why* they arrested you?"

His square shoulders rose and fell. "I told Detective Bennett that while everyone was out taking the tour—except Mr. Wollstone, who was in the theater, and Deena, who came inside to use the restroom—I was at the desk alone. I didn't see anyone use the stairs or elevator."

"You were at the desk *the entire time?*"

"The entire time."

"Well . . ." *Well what, Ivy?* "Well, couldn't Clyde—or anyone, really—have killed her and then joined the tour?"

"Apparently not."

"How do you know?" I said.

"I took her a bottle of wine while the others were out. And she was perfectly alive."

No. That looked really bad. "You told the police that?"

"Oh yes," he said. "Several times."

How long had they questioned him?

"Ms. Reed and Ms. Nixon don't think he had time when he came back from the tour and found her," I said.

"I'm inclined to agree."

"Maybe . . ."

"Miss Nichols." He smiled at me.

He seemed to emphasize my last name in a way that had become familiar to me.

"It's terribly kind of you to show such interest," he said.

"Of course I'm interested."

"However, I must ask you to stop. You have your studies to focus on, your shifts at the hotel, and I know there must be other responsibilities on your shoulders."

"I can do this." The skin around my mouth tightened involuntarily.

He leaned forward and lowered his voice. "You are entirely capable. You've proven that by now, but I cannot have you jeopardizing your health for mine."

If only it were just his health and not his freedom and reputation. "Just tell me this. Is there any other way upstairs? Anything the police are overlooking?"

"There was a servant staircase going all the way to the third floor originally, but it was closed during the conversion to the hotel."

I sighed. "And the balconies, the outside one and the conservatory side?"

"The door to the conservatory balcony is sealed and locked while the spiral staircase is being rebuilt, as you well know, and the outside balcony entrance would require a ladder tall enough to be dangerous and quite noticeable to one of the staff, or else some kind of machinery like a cherry picker, which I feel sure we would have heard and seen also."

"Is it possible someone could have scaled the wall?" Chattanooga was a rock climbers' mecca.

He shook his head and drew down the corners of his mouth. "Please. Don't pursue this. The truth will out."

The truth would be great. The facts troubled me. "Let me get this straight—you were the only one with access to the room during the tour, the last one to see the victim alive, and since you're staff, your DNA will be all over the room. Yeah, the police are bound to get it right this time."

*   *   *

"So I know we've addressed some of the ways you've responded to your mother's leaving, Ivy." My therapist, Gina, sat catty-corner from me without a notepad.

After I told my dad last year that I'd stopped seeing my psychiatrist, he'd recommended that I try a counselor next, and Gina had come highly recommended by a college friend of mine. Sometimes I felt like sending that friend a thank-you note. Other times I considered a chain letter.

Gina was competent and professional, but I wasn't sure that I liked her. As taskmaster of the self-exploration I had to do, she was relentless.

She glanced down at her lap and back at me, as if she could see the thoughts behind my eyes. "But I suspect that there are memories from before the day your mother left that are also continuing to cause you distress."

I shifted in my seat. "It's possible, I guess."

Her office was all white and greige, pale pillows and soft angles. But the work we were doing in here was dark, dirty, and uncomfortable.

There was a danger in letting things lie.

The childhood trauma I'd experienced hadn't died but hibernated. When I finally revisited its dark lair (dodging briars and cutting back overgrown branches), I'd found a ravenous, waking monster surrounded by the bones of my positive thinking.

I didn't blame myself. Seven-year-old me had made all the sense she could of what happened, but the unprocessed hurts that I had left in the forgotten woods grew sly and dangerous and watched for me now to lose my footing.

"You can think about those memories, see if anything comes up, and I'll ask you again next time." Her tone brightened slightly. "Have you ever heard of attachment disorder, Ivy?"

In front of the window, a blast from the vent agitated a snapped frond on her potted fern.

It was hard in the moment to care about things that had happened to me a million years ago when I had a murder to investigate. I knew that putting on my own oxygen mask before helping Mr. Fig was best practice, but sorting out what was going on with me wasn't a one-day fix.

"Um, yeah. It happens to kids who are, like, neglected by a caregiver, right?" I said.

"Yes, that's a common way for the disorder to set in, and like we've talked about, we were all kids once. People with attachment disorder learned to stop trusting other people early in life."

"I think I know what you're saying. My mom left, and it was hard, and now I can't form proper attachments to people."

"You're an insightful person, Ivy. I know I'm not really telling you anything you don't know. As a child, you attached yourself quite firmly to your dad, before the trauma that caused you to isolate yourself. But since then, you seem to have very few close relationships."

Ugh. I hated when she said things like this, but that probably meant she was doing a good job.

Since time was money, I had to choose carefully what subjects to bring up in therapy, and sometimes that left holes for Gina. I was attached to more people than George and my dad. I had some friends from school and other jobs who I still met up with now and then. And Mr. Fig. I would count him as a friend, even though he was my manager.

"What effects do you think this lack of connection has on you?" Gina asked.

The clock behind her said we had fifteen minutes left in the session.

"I don't know." I clenched my toes inside my Chucks and unclenched them again.

"That's okay. You can think about it, and we can circle back. In the meantime, I want you to be aware of how you may be pulling back from people out of the belief that any relationship you form is suspect."

Suspect. After this, I had to figure out an excuse for visiting Clyde. He was still the most likely suspect in my mind. "Okay, sure."

Now that the police had released the Achilles Room, maybe I could get some of Clyde's things and bring them to him.

I decided to run out the clock on a topic that seemed more immediately helpful to me. "I had another panic attack out of nowhere last night."

"Oh, I'm sorry, Ivy." She tilted her head. "Were you able to try the grounding techniques we talked about?"

"Yeah. It was dark, but I focused on sounds and sensations."

"And did that help?"

"Maybe," I said. "I think I pulled out of it faster this time."

"That's great. Any progress is something to celebrate. And that doesn't mean it's a steady climb from here, but you are growing."

"Thanks. But I—I don't understand how I'm able to do things sometimes that are really significant and hard, and then other times, I turn to slush at the first sign of conflict."

"I can see how that's troubling." She nodded. "You mentioned that your dad is seeing someone new?"

"Right."

"And you feel like you're getting less time with George lately."

I nodded back at her. Dang it, she was good. I'd mentioned that last month, but I hadn't even told her about Bea flirting with him.

"So, it's likely, given what you've been through, that a part of you feels deeply threatened by those things."

"Oh."

"Your brain is responding to those threats the best way it knows how, but we're going to work together to train it to respond better. Speaking of which—I want to loan you this book on epigenetics." She stood up and went to her bookshelf.

"Epige-who?"

"Epigenetics." She pulled the book she wanted and offered it to me. "It's the study of how factors other than DNA can change your gene activity, including the way your body responds to certain stimuli."

"Okay. Thanks." I took it from her, knowing I wouldn't have time to look at it for a while.

Even the hour I'd spent at this appointment felt like more than I could spare. I'd picked up an extra shift tonight, since Mr. Fig's absence left us stretched thin at the hotel. If I'd known more about the suspects in Renee's murder coming in today,

I might have been able to redeem the time questioning Gina about traits and motives. There could be a psychological element to this case, but I didn't know enough about Clyde or anyone else yet to confirm that.

As I hefted myself onto my hand-me-down Schwinn outside the counseling office, Gina's questions, rather than my own, rang in my head. I stomped my pedal in frustration.

* * *

I rode a rickety wagon down a track through a dark tunnel of rock. I pulled a lever in front of me, and the brake engaged.

My small leather trunk was surprisingly difficult to lift from the cart and set on the rough stone floor. Before me was an enormous green metal door with a dozen latches and locks, each one distinct and powerful. One by one, they clicked and slid and turned open, as if by telekinesis.

I put a palm against the cold metal and pushed the door open with a loud squeak.

Stacks of boxes, canisters, and chests filled the vault, and a space beckoned under a nearby shelf, just large enough for the trunk I carried. I dragged it into the room, feeling the grit of the floor under its edge, and slid the trunk back against the wall. I turned my back on it, closed the door and all its locks, and walked away.

I opened my eyes. My shoulders felt lighter already. My eyes, more alert.

It was a compartmentalizing trick Gina had taught me, and I was suspicious of it, but it worked today. Mostly. My worries about George, Dad, and especially my mother would be somewhat deactivated, stowed away until I was ready to look at them again.

Now to tackle the doors that stood in front of me in reality. I couldn't stand the thought of Mr. Fig in that gross cell even one more night, and Captain De Luna of the Chattanooga Police Department owed me a favor. Without my intervention in the murder at the hotel last year, a killer would still be on the loose.

At the downtown station, I told the small man behind the desk that I was headed to the captain's office.

"Aw, nah, she's still on vacation, Little Bit."

"Vacation, huh? When will she be back?"

"End of next week, I think? Anyway, doll, it's Saturday. Even if she wasn't gone, she wouldn't probably be here. You should've emailed first."

"Right. Thanks," I said. "Doll." Sure, email would've saved me a trip, but I was impatient, and I knew I'd get more results from De Luna in person.

Gravity felt double as I trudged back toward the entrance.

But I wouldn't be so easily defeated. I'd come all the way here. It was worth talking to Bennett. I'd bet he was working this weekend, seeing as he had a case to solve. He might be overdramatic and wrong about nearly everything, but he wasn't cruel, not from what I'd seen. There had to be something human behind his grim detective front. Maybe I could make him care about Mr. Fig's predicament.

I wandered the halls until I found his office and knocked on the open door. Bennett's moustache twitched, and he greeted me with a frown. I caught him noticing the bandage on my arm. I didn't mind the sympathy if it got me somewhere.

"May I come in?"

He didn't answer, so I took that as permission.

Bennett's office was nothing like Captain De Luna's. Where hers had a window, his had a corkboard. Where she displayed framed photos, he had a row of books with titles like *The Process of Investigation* and *The Forensic Casebook*, props that made him seem like a more serious detective than her, although I knew the opposite to be true.

I stood across from him, splayed my hands on his desk, and conveyed with as little sentimentality as possible the indecent conditions in which I had found Mr. Fig that morning.

He clicked his mouse and stared at the desktop screen in front of him, from which he'd barely raised his eyes since I'd come in. (Solitaire, I guessed.) "Due process must take its course."

"Please."

"I already told you to stay out of this." Bennett looked pointedly at my hands.

My fingers were spread on his desktop calendar. I withdrew them but didn't apologize.

"You know what's really criminal? Locking up innocent people before they've even been tried." I'd bet there was a name that would get his attention, if I knew it. Some commissioner with power over him, or better yet, a local organization for citizens' rights that cared about the conditions of the jail and the fact that people were held there without bail and without arraignment.

"Take it up with your county government. That's nothing to do with me." Bennett strode to the door and gripped it, looking at me meaningfully.

I didn't move. Still facing his desk, I glanced down at his calendar. "I can find out things for you, you know. The people who actually knew Renee—unlike Mr. Fig—are coming and going from the hotel all the time."

Among Bennett's calendar appointments for the day was *Truman, 2:00*. Was that Autumn or Tom?

The detective stepped toward me and swept his long arm in my direction. "Ralph Fig will await arraignment just like any other defendant."

"Listen, I understand that at face value, he was the only one in the right place at the right time." I had no choice but to back toward the door. "But it's illogical. What motive could he even have?"

"You can thank yourself for that."

"What?" How could I have had anything to do with it?

"If there's one thing I understand about Ralph Fig, it's that he's loyal as a retriever to that big yellow house."

I stared at him. He was right about that, but what did Mr. Fig's loyalty have to do with Renee? "So?"

"So—" He got out his little notebook and flipped a few pages. "You told me yourself that Ms. Gallagher, quote, 'laughed at the furnishings.' "

Whaaaaat? I shook my head. "You think this was some kind of honor killing? Or you think Mr. Fig's *feelings* were hurt?"

"Not quite. You see, I did a little digging. It turns out our Ms. Gallagher was a"—he checked his notes—"an 'Instagram influencer.' She's got more than ten thousand followers, and she's reviewed a few hotels already this year."

I never would have pegged Renee for an influencer, but an online platform could be the one place she felt free to speak her mind. "You're saying Mr. Fig murdered this woman to stop her from ruining the hotel's reputation?"

"Bingo." He rested both fists at his waist. "Especially considering your hotel's lost some business since those murders last year."

"But Mr. Fig wouldn't commit violence over some small offense like that. And wouldn't another murder hurt the hotel's reputation just as much?" I couldn't keep my voice under control. "You're . . . you're unhinged!"

His thick moustache twitched once. "If you're not careful, Ivy Nichols, you're gonna find yourself on the wrong side of the law."

On the last word of his sentence, he slung the door my way. I jumped back so it wouldn't hit me in the face.

Jeez. If he wanted to be menacing, he needed to stop using so many clichés. Still, there was real authority behind his theatrics.

When I got back outside, I couldn't seem to move on. I paced back and forth in front of the station. My shoulders knotted up again, and my hands were two dead trout on the ends of my arms. It was bad enough that Bennett wouldn't help *me* but worse that he wouldn't accept help or input from anyone else.

I shoved a hand in my pocket and remembered the hairs from the Achilles suite that I'd put in there this morning. Was it worth going back to give them to Bennett, or would he dismiss them anyway?

I was overwhelmed by how much the police already knew about Renee's murder. And how little chance I had of getting that info.

I'd meant what I'd told Bennett about playing witness to the guests of the hotel, and I knew that was important, but did I need to figure out the murder weapon too, or was it enough to know that Renee had been strangled?

Deep down, I was afraid I didn't have it in me to solve another crime.

I remembered Mr. Fig's relief last year when he realized I'd cleared the hotel of scandal. Even though he didn't want me doing the same for him now, he *had* said he believed I could.

I admired so much about him, but what qualities of mine could he think would help me solve this? My stubbornness? My willingness to break the rules?

Bennett was just as stubborn but legally bound to follow procedure, to slog through paperwork like wet sand.

I just needed to start talking to people. There was treasure buried in the memories of those gravestone association guests, and I would dig down and find it.

VIII

See Seven States

❧

I zipped around a bend on the eastern side of Lookout Mountain in Dad's Volvo. I certainly wasn't going to conquer the steep highway on my Schwinn, and this was faster.

On my right was a wall of shale dusted with snow. The higher I climbed, the lower the temperature dropped and the more snow hung around on the landscape.

To my left, the forest along the bluff was budding out in early green, crimson, and purple, getting dressed for the full, leafy goodness of spring. As I neared the top of the mountain, the trees dropped away, the view opened up, and the signature precipice of Rock City jutted out into the clear blue sky over the valley.

Just ahead, streaming out from underneath the arched bridge past Lover's Leap, the High Falls weren't any less breathtaking for having been artificially created in the 1930s.

If I dared peel my gaze from the road and look down from the mountain, it was one of the best views around. I could see all of Chattanooga at once and more.

As advertised on barn roofs near and far, Rock City touted a view of seven states. When I was a kid, I'd expected to see borders showing me the familiar shapes of all of them, as if the landscape were a life-sized map.

"See seven states" had its origins in journal writings from both Union and Confederate soldiers during the Battle of Lookout Mountain claiming that landmarks from all seven could be spotted from the overlook. But that was before modern air pollution.

When I reached the town on top of the mountain, I pulled into the pea-gravel parking lot of the Chanticleer Inn, which, like most of the buildings around here, was overwhelmingly adorable and built out of stone. Little storybook cottages sprang up around a central office that looked straight out of Hansel and Gretel.

This neighborhood, Fairyland, had been developed in the 1920s by local entrepreneur Garnet Carter and his wife, Frieda, whose fascination with European fairy tales had resulted in all of these streets being named "Peter Pan Road," "Mother Goose Trail," and the like. Their original concept for the community included a golf course, which was downsized to become Tom Thumb Golf, the country's first mini golf.

I loved mini golf.

Back at the hotel, I'd overheard Tom and Autumn saying Clyde had taken sanctuary up here, and having just lost Renee, he was more likely to be in his room than at the convention center today, I thought.

As Renee's significant other, he seemed an obvious suspect, so why wouldn't the police see him that way? I didn't know what I didn't know about him or their relationship, but I was going to find out.

On the front patio of the reception building, an old couple shared a magazine. They nodded at me as I went inside.

"Clyde Borough?" I said to the small girl behind the desk.

She was school age, but it was a Saturday. I had a cousin growing up who'd had to pitch in like this at her family's restaurant on weekends. It was an understatement to say her indenture made me thankful my dad didn't own the plumbing business he worked for.

"Borough." She checked a screen, clicked a mouse once or twice, and answered, "Cottage number six."

Either she didn't know better than to give out a guest's room number, or my confidence and the box I carried (professionally, as if for a delivery) told a convincing story.

Every surface was lined with mountain stone here, including the snowy path she directed me to take and cottage six, which stood at the end of a landscaped walk past the pool.

Before coming here, I'd detoured to the hotel. All of Clyde's and Renee's possessions the police hadn't taken with them were being stored in the office.

With his overnight bag over one shoulder and a box of his other things balanced against the opposite hip, I knocked at his door.

After a minute, it swung inward. Good luck at last.

It wasn't Clyde but a blond girl (woman?) maybe twenty years old. Long straight hair. Hoodie. Flip-flops.

"Hi, I'm sorry—" I leaned back to check the room number. "I'm looking for Mr. Clyde Borough. I have some things for him from the last hotel he was staying at."

She walked away, leaving the door ajar, and yelled into the room, "Dad."

Clyde popped up a second later. "Oh, Ivy. How are you? Come in."

He asked about my arm, and I explained briefly as I followed him into the open-concept living area dotted with wicker furniture and flowery curtains. Everything in here was precious as a baby bluebird.

Clyde's chipper attitude was tuned to match the room's pitch. Was he pushing his feelings down for some reason, or was he really not grieving for Renee?

He turned to me as we reached the middle of the room, and his face went blank.

I realized he was staring at the overnight bag. I held it out to him. "Thought you might need this."

"Oh, ah, thank you." He took it from me, but his face blanched as if I'd handed him a bucketful of spiders.

"I'm sorry. You didn't want it?"

"Um, it belonged to . . . my girlfriend . . ."

"Oh. Sorry. I just—sorry." It was plain and black, and I would've thought her bag would be a flowery print or maybe pastel, something to match her pearls and sweater sets. I offered him the box. "Maybe these are yours?"

He set the bag on a chair and the box on the breakfast table, then opened the flaps and glanced inside. "Yeah, thanks so much. I've been without clothes and things . . . as if it wasn't hard enough, losing her."

"I'm sorry," I said lamely for the third time, but I still couldn't be sure there was genuine grief in his statement.

He gestured for me to sit down and did the same himself. "Please."

"How are you holding up, Dr. Borough?" I took a chair.

"Call me Clyde." It wasn't a request.

"Okay," I said.

He shrugged. "What can I say? I'm glad Selena's here with me."

"Your daughter?"

"Oh, yes, you haven't met. Selena?"

She returned from what was probably the bedroom, her hips taking turns sinking as if the earth pulled harder at her than it did other people. Her frown was left over from opening the door for me.

"Selena goes to school here on the mountain," Clyde said.

"Your alma mater, right?" I asked Clyde as I greeted Selena with a little wave.

"That's right. She's an excellent student."

Hands in the pockets of her jogging pants, Selena scoffed, then retreated to a stool at the kitchen bar, where she perched, crossing her arms. Her eyes were alert and on her father.

"She's a little annoyed with me right now," Clyde said, his body relaxed in his chair like he was used to her attitude.

"A *little* annoyed?" Selena said.

"I don't have to stay." I bluffed as if to stand up.

"No, it's kind of you to stop by and to bring the things." He glanced at Renee's bag. "See, Selena and I were just arguing about her—"

"Renee was a terrible person," Selena said to me. "I'm not happy she died, but I'm not going to pretend I liked her just because she's dead."

Clyde clenched his jaw but smiled softly. "She's defensive. Because of her mother."

"Yeah, maybe I do take Mom's side sometimes, but at least Mom doesn't break promises to me."

"We'll talk about this later," he said, then turned to me.

"And anyway," Selena continued, "whoever's side I take, it doesn't change the fact that your girlfriend was awful."

Clyde leaned forward in his chair, gripping both arms. "It was your mother who chose to leave. Now drop it."

"Because she was tired of you controlling her."

"I'm not—" Clyde caught himself yelling, looked at me, and lowered his voice as he started again. "I'm not controlling."

Selena adopted an expression of feigned interest. "Oh, you're not? So you didn't ask Dr. Larsson to spy on me, then?"

He swallowed hard and mustered his patience with a deep breath, as if he were being asked to mediate a conflict between two hostile nations. "It's only natural that an old friend of mine, who also happens to be a professor of yours, would be interested in your success as a student."

She opened her mouth to speak, but he talked over her. "That's *all* it is."

She rolled her eyes, shot up from her stool, and stomped across the kitchen, as much as one could stomp in flip-flops, anyway.

"You see this?" He looked at me. "I move up to this hotel to be near her, and this is how she thanks me! Now. While I'm grieving."

I frowned sympathetically but didn't want to say anything so supportive as to alienate Selena. I might need to talk to her later.

He turned his head back to yell into the kitchen. "If anything, you should talk to your mother about how she's treated *me*."

Selena leaned against the wall and squared herself to him. "I've told you. She's not the one vandalizing your house."

Hello. What was that? Vandalism?

"Who else would have a vendetta against me?" He spread his hands. "In fact, I wonder if your mother had anything to do with—"

"That's too far." Selena shoved a finger at him. Her face held more anger than I'd thought possible a few moments before.

He'd been about to say *with Renee's death*, hadn't he? And why was he looking for someone who had something against *him*? Why make it all about himself? That seemed a touch narcissistic.

The two of them stared at each other silently but not without communication. It was almost like they'd forgotten I was here.

"So someone's tearing up your house?" I said to Clyde. "Back in Pittsburgh?"

"Yes," he answered, still staring at his daughter.

"Is that where your ex-wife lives, Clyde?" Although he'd asked me to use his first name, the word felt cottony in my mouth.

"Yes," he said.

"No," Selena said at the same time.

He threw up his hands and slipped me a wry smile. "I'm sorry, Ivy. We're evidently not in a position to entertain here."

Oh, I was plenty entertained. "Of course not. I should be getting back anyway."

He walked me to the door.

There was one more thing he could tell me. "Could I talk to you sometime about your visit to the hotel before—"

"I've never been to the hotel before." He opened the door.

"I mean, when it was a house—"

"No, I was never there." He smiled politely.

"But you said at check-in—"

"That the *city* was just how I remembered it, when I lived here on the mountain, as a student."

"Oh." I didn't buy that for a second.

Behind him, in the window on the other side of the room, there was a flash of movement, as if someone had been watching us through the glass.

"Thanks again." He shut the door behind me.

I zipped around the back of the cottage as fast as I could, but no one was in sight. I spent another minute circling the little house and still didn't see anyone. Maybe it had only been my imagination.

But under the window where I thought I'd seen someone peeking in, a Cheez-It bag littered the flowerbed. Two footprints, big enough to swallow my own, were just visible in the thick pine-bark mulch.

I positioned myself back at the cottage window where the snoop would've stood.

Yeah, it was an excellent vantage point. I was mostly hidden by the curtain and could see straight into the suite's living room.

Clyde, alone now, paced the floor and looked at his phone.

"Jill says the transfer still hasn't come through," he said as if to someone in the next room, plenty loud enough for me to hear him through the windowpane.

Whoever had been standing here would have been privy to Clyde's and my entire conversation. But what were they looking to find out? And why at this moment? Had I been followed here from the hotel?

"I swear it's on the way," said a woman coming out of the bedroom, not Selena but Autumn Truman, the stern redhead from the grave group.

When had she gotten here? And why had she come?

A wisp of cigarette smoke hit my nostrils, and there was a short *hmph* behind me.

I swung around.

Selena, a few yards away on the path, was smoking a cigarette and smirking at me.

I slipped a hand awkwardly in one pocket. "Oh, hi, again."

"Don't let me interrupt your eavesdropping." She looked at me pointedly, then continued along the path to the far side of the cottage.

I considered going after her and trying to explain, but inside the cottage, things were heating up.

Clyde crossed the room to stand just a few inches from Autumn.

His body language was intense, threatening. He grabbed her pale, thin arm, and even from the window, I could see her skin go white around his fingers from the pressure. He pulled her close, close enough to kiss her, and said something in a low, menacing tone. I didn't have to understand the words to know they were a threat.

Autumn jerked away from him, grabbed a purse from the coffee table, and marched out the door. Clyde's temper flare alarmed me, but I didn't know Autumn well enough to tell if she was more frightened or riled by it. She played her cards so close to her chest.

I didn't have long before I needed to head to work. It was a twenty-five-minute drive downtown from here. But without Mr. Fig at the hotel, the only person to be concerned about my lateness was Doyle, and the idea of pissing him off turned the corners of my mouth up against my will.

Anyway, I wouldn't be annoying Doyle in vain. I couldn't miss this chance to talk to another member of the grave gaggle in relative privacy. Now that I'd been seen in the Achilles Room, I had to be more careful not to let Renee's killer know I was hunting them.

Had Autumn entered the cottage the second I left, or had she been in another room of the cottage the whole time and able, along with whoever was at the window, to listen in on our conversation? Maybe that gave me a hook that would open her up to talking.

In a few seconds she rounded the corner of the cottage and continued down the stone path toward the parking lot, head up and eyes alert.

I took off in the same direction. Autumn was more removed from Renee than Clyde, so I felt better about pumping her for information.

It turned out I didn't need any sort of lead. She was a direct person.

She spotted me just before getting to her car and jetted toward me, swinging the hand that gripped her keys to propel her. "So the hotel told you to give Renee's things to Clyde?"

I shrugged. "The police have released all of the belongings that they didn't take to the station."

Up close, Autumn's eyes were cold and lichen colored.

I thought of gray-eyed Athena. Like the goddess, Autumn came across as proud, tactical, and single-minded.

"Is he listed as her beneficiary somewhere?" she asked. "Yinz contacted her lawyer?"

Yinz? "Um. I guess Ms. King, the hotel's owner, must have."

Autumn was interviewing *me*. I needed to turn this around. "Do you know Clyde in some way other than the grave society?"

"Why're you asking me that?" She took a step backward.

"I'm wondering . . ." I said. "Do you think the police are on the right track, arresting the hotel manager for her murder?"

"I don't know. I can't imagine what motive the manager would have. Renee didn't mention knowing him. She didn't mention him at all." She tightened her lips. "Although I guess some people are sociopaths and don't need a motive."

Explaining away hot-blooded murders with sociopathy was comforting to people. But so far, this murder didn't point to that kind of killer. Sociopaths had trouble forming connections with people (even more than I evidently did), and they usually committed crimes that were spontaneous and disorganized, leaving fingerprints and DNA at the scene.

If this was that kind of murder, the police wouldn't have arrested Mr. Fig.

I changed gears. "Have you met the ex-wife?"

"Linda?" She glanced behind me at the cottage. "Yes. She worked for me a while."

"You're in the security business, right? What did Linda do for you?"

"That's right. Linda was my office manager." Autumn turned ever so slightly toward her car and clenched her keys in her hand.

"And Renee was . . ."

She sighed. "I gave her Linda's job."

Wow. So at the time of her death, Renee had not only Linda's ex-husband but her former job too. At the risk of pushing her away, I pressed on. "So . . . she quit?"

"I had to let her go."

I opened my mouth to ask why.

"But let's not get into that," Autumn said, slicing one hand through the air.

"What about Clyde? Does he have it in him to hurt someone?"

"I don't know." She shook her head, and her cheeks hardened. "I can tell you that I never liked Renee being with him. Selena and I agreed on that, if nothing else."

I wasn't the only one feeling possessive about my friends. "What is it about Clyde that you don't like?"

"He steamrolls people, and Renee made herself easy to run over. I joined this little club of theirs mostly to keep an eye on her, but it wasn't enough . . . obviously." She folded her arms, tightened her mouth even more, and shifted her weight. "And Clyde can be weirdly obsessive. Do you know what he gave her for Christmas? This bizarre Victorian mourning locket, jet black with a curl of some dead woman's hair inside. Makes me think something's wrong with him sometimes."

"Yeah, that's a really strange present," I said, nodding. As much as I loved my dad, I couldn't imagine walking around with his hair in my jewelry. "And what about Selena? Is she into that sort of thing too?

"Ha. She doesn't like *anything* her dad likes. But Selena is . . . *volatile* is a good word, I guess."

"You think *she* could have . . ."

"Committed murder? I wouldn't have thought so, but then, how could anyone?" Her neck reddened. "When I think about how she reacted when he proposed, I do wonder."

"Clyde? He proposed to Renee?"

Autumn nodded.

"What did Selena do?" I asked.

"Wrecked her car to spite him. And then she bought that motorcycle." She nudged her head in the direction of a scarlet Yamaha in the nearest parking bay.

"Wow, all because her father got engaged?"

"No. Because he *proposed*." She smirked. "Renee turned him down. Selena doesn't know it, but Renee and her father weren't even sleeping together for months before this trip."

"She told you that? You must have been close."

"Yeah. She was my little sister."

IX

Found Objects

∽

I got to work right at four and was only ten minutes late to the entry hall by the time I changed. My mouth watered instantly. The whole place smelled of the garlic focaccia George was baking.

Doyle, who was talking on the phone, slammed down the receiver, and his mud-brown eyes glared at me.

"Was that a potential guest you were talking to?" I said.

He grunted at me like an angry pig, turned on his heel, and left without giving me a chance to apologize for being late.

Not that I was going to.

Now that I was sure Mr. Fig hadn't left the desk during the gravestone tour and that someone must have found some alternate route to the Achilles suite, I had new goals to add to my usual work duties. Top priority was figuring out where the servant staircase ended and if it could have been reopened.

Unfortunately, I wouldn't have the time to find a mystery staircase or anything else until most everyone was asleep. If I was quick, I could squeeze in a little exploration after turndown service while the guests were at dinner. But I had a feeling I'd need longer than that short window would allow.

Part of me wished I had some kind of sedative at hand that I could add to all their drinks at dinner (and that doing so was within the universe of ethical behavior). I envisioned them all conked out, leaning on the dining table—Leonard Chaves's drooling face smushed into Autumn's severe shoulder, Tom's giant hand slipping into the cream sauce on Velvet's plate. No, I wouldn't really do that, not to them or anyone else, but I let myself smile at the image.

The desk ledge was a mess by Mr. Fig's standard, so I set about aligning everything perpendicular or parallel to everything else. I straightened Clarista's freshly printed copy of the 1911 edition of the *Chattanooga News*, but it read the wrong date—yesterday's. Replacing it must have been one of the many tasks Mr. Fig did daily without anyone noticing.

I picked it up to throw it in the recycling bin, but the name *Morrow* in a headline below the fold caught my eye: *Alderman Morrow Backs Negro Firemen Against Railroad Brotherhood*.

I flinched internally every time I read the word *Negro*, and I was white, so I marveled at Clarista's ability to keep these papers around in their original forms, the nuanced way she could evidently appreciate some parts of history while knowing there was a lot of bad with it. But I wouldn't expect any less from a woman who, against the odds, had taken this mansion from rags to riches.

I scanned the article. The headline referred to my great-great-grandfather Murdoch. Management of the Queen and Crescent railroad had assigned three Black firemen to a part of the line connecting Chattanooga and Oakdale, Tennessee that had been staffed only by whites before. The white firemen and engineers in the union had begun their protest strike on March 9, one week and 110 years ago today. Along the train route, rural supporters of the strike were attacking trains and pulling crew members off cars to beat them. Murdoch Morrow had spoken in defense of the Queen and Crescent's hiring decision at a council meeting.

The article also said his son Paulus had been in attendance. I hadn't heard the name Paulus before, much less known there was one in the family. I guessed it was just a Latin version of my dad's plain old *Paul*.

I set "yesterday's" paper aside to take home and went to the library, where I was pretty sure I'd find "today's".

*   *   *

Even at four in the afternoon, the library was dim. It had something to do with the book-lined walls and ubiquitous walnut paneling. And let's face it, gunmetal gray as an accent color didn't brighten things up any.

Two familiar voices, thin with age, echoed in the cavernous room. Dwarfed by the high-backed armchairs in front of the fireplace, Velvet and Deena both looked up as I came in. They weren't in period clothing today, just simple buttoned blouses and slacks more appropriate for their convention, but I hoped they would dress up for dinner again.

"Good afternoon, ladies," I said.

They greeted me in turn and continued their conversation.

"Where did Autumn say he was staying?" Deena asked.

Standing in the same room with them, I didn't feel like I was intruding as much as I had when they were at the pool.

"Lookout Mountain," said Velvet.

"Is that the one you can see from over there by the aquarium?"

"No, that's Signal Mountain. Lookout is the one with Rock City and Ruby Falls, on the south end of town."

"You're so smart," Deena said. "You just know everything about this place."

"I just know how to use the internet." Velvet shrugged. "Sort of."

They dropped into conspiratorial whispers, and I focused on my mission.

Beside the glass case of rare first editions was an ancient file cabinet, where I found the newspaper reprints. I had just laid my hand on the March drawer when Deena raised her voice again.

"Why not ask her? She's not biased."

I retrieved the paper I needed and turned their way. I could smell a thick perfume like lilacs as I got close.

Velvet sized me up, but Deena's eyes were on her friend rather than me.

"Ask me what?" I said.

"We've been thinking about people who could have strangled Renee to death," Velvet explained matter-of-factly.

Jeez. "So you don't think it was Mr. Fig after all. I'm listening."

Velvet went on in that expressive voice of hers. "Apparently Deena thinks Dr. Chaves is a natural-born killer, but I told her she only says that because he's Latino."

Jeez. Jeez. Wow. These two had a gift for saying out loud what most people wouldn't.

"But Velvet's wrong," said the accused. "I'm not racist. I don't like Leonard because he speaks too little and too quietly. Plus, his acne scars make him look like Robert Davi. I never did trust that man."

I didn't get the name reference, but I wasn't sidetracked by it. In part, I could agree with Deena. Leonard Chaves had appeared quite shifty in the drawing room after Renee's death, closing himself off with his tightly folded arms and not making eye contact with anyone. Of course, I didn't know how he behaved at the conference, but when he was here, he ate every meal outside or at odd times of the day—in order to be alone, I imagined.

But none of that made him a killer. "So you think I look like a person who wouldn't judge someone based on how they look?"

They shrugged in tandem.

"You're a Millennial," said Velvet.

I guess that explained everything. "Well, acne scars and quiet speech don't seem like good reasons to suspect someone of murder. Is there some other basis for your suspicion, Ms. Nixon? What motive would Leonard have?"

Deena pulled her purse, an enormous blue thing decorated with a painted peacock, onto her lap and began to dig through it. "It's just a feeling."

"She gets these feelings," Velvet said. "Sometimes she's right, but not this time."

"How long have they known each other, Renee and Leonard?" I asked.

"Who knows?" Velvet said mysteriously, as if I'd asked her the meaning of life.

"They met through Clyde. He and Leonard work together." Like an ancient embalmer, Deena began removing the internal bits of her purse—crumpled tissues, cough drops, keys—and lining them up on a side table. "And that widow's peak! Have you seen it, Miss Nichols?"

I nodded. Combined with Leonard's nearly black hair, it had a rather vampiric effect on his appearance. But George's father had a slight widow's peak too, and on him it was endearing. "They're both professors, Leonard and Clyde?"

"That's right, at Carnegie Mellon," said Deena.

"Yes, they both teach literature," Velvet said.

"Like you did," Deena said to her friend.

Velvet coughed. "Oh, well, I was just a high school teacher. Not like them. They're important men making big contributions in the world of the arts. Anyway, Dr. Chaves is quiet but kind. I think he was heartbroken by Renee's death, in fact. I saw him in the conservatory very upset." She began to rock in her chair, and used the momentum to push herself up to standing. "Excuse me. Must powder my nose."

Velvet's accent was less Pittsburghese than Deena's, and I wondered if Velvet had purposely lost hers when she became a teacher.

With Velvet gone and Deena silent, my thoughts drifted back to Renee. Had she known Leonard well enough to open the door to him that night? Even if she had, there was still the issue of how he would've gotten from the tour outside to Renee's room on the second floor without Mr. Fig seeing him.

I should have asked Mr. Fig if he'd heard anyone moving around upstairs that night. If the entry hall had been quiet and the first floor mostly still, it would have been easy to hear the Achilles door open and close, since the first floor was open to the second and third. But surely Mr. Fig would've mentioned that to the police.

Deena looked as if she might nod off.

"What did you do for a living, Ms. Nixon?"

She blinked. "I'm sorry, dear, it's the cannabis making me sleepy."

An unwilling smile overtook my face. I didn't know whether or not to take her seriously. The lilac perfume hadn't lightened when Velvet left the room, so it was Deena's. I wondered if she used it to cover the scent of weed or if, as I'd suspected before, she had meant to say CBD oil instead.

"I was a mortician." Deena's eyes flicked up, noticing something behind me.

Parker Rogers had just entered the library. He was about ten or eleven and must have been drug along on this trip by his dad, Furnell, either as bonding time or in lieu of finding a sitter.

Short black twists covered his head, and he reminded me of a young Trevor Noah. He plodded, head jutting forward, to the biography and history section.

"Good to see a young person using the library," Deena said to me, and then louder, "Hello there, Packer."

Packer? *Packer*, then.

The boy turned when he reached the shelves, reached out a finger absent-mindedly, and traced along the ledge at shoulder height.

I walked over. "Hi, Packer. You're welcome to borrow a book. Can I help you find anything?"

He angled his head but didn't look at me. "Parker."

"Oh, *Parker*. Sorry."

His finger stopped its linear path and made a right turn, sliding up the spines of three books. Stopping at the last, he pulled it from the shelf, tucked it under his elbow, and walked slowly toward where Deena sat putting all her purse accoutrements away.

Following Parker, I got close enough to see that the woman's key fob bore a Porsche crest. That fancy orange Cayenne in the garage belonged to her.

Velvet returned from the restroom, and Parker followed her feet with his eyes.

Deena tutted and shook her head, looking at her purse.

"Did you lose something?" I said.

"Just misplaced my blood pressure meds again."

"Oh, I think they're by the sink in the room, dear."

The Romulus and Remus Rooms shared an adjoining bath.

Without looking at her, the boy said to Velvet, "Where will they bury you?"

I clenched my stomach. What a strange question. And rude to say to . . . well, anyone.

But neither Velvet nor Deena reacted as if it was.

Instead, Deena narrowed her eyes at her friend puckishly. "I think he's tired of waiting on you to make plans, V."

I hoped I would still have people around to call me Vee in fifty years.

"I still don't know, young man." Velvet turned a beaded bracelet on her wrist and smiled. "God willing, I have plenty of time."

Parker cocked his head and held it that way as he made for the door.

I turned to the women. "What was that about?"

"Oh, he's an unusual boy," said Velvet. "Very direct. Very observant."

"Hmm," I mused. Parker seemed well behaved and too mature to assume he could hang his drawings wherever he liked, but if he hadn't done them, who else could have?

"Yes, inquisitive," said Deena. "Reminds me of my granddaughter at that age."

I had to get back to the desk, but I thought of another question before I left them. "Ladies, do you happen to remember who suggested that Clyde and Renee take the Achilles suite? Was it Leonard?"

"The what sweet?" Deena said.

Velvet patted her friend's hand. "She means the big bedroom they stayed in."

"Oh. I don't remember," Deena said.

"Neither do I." Velvet shrugged.

"Well, thank you anyway, ladies." I nodded good-bye.

"See you later, Ivy," they said in unison.

I stopped at the door and turned back. "Hey, isn't the conference going on now?"

Velvet giggled. "We're playing hooky."

"She really only comes along on these things to be with me," Deena said.

That was how it was with long-running friendships (if they *were* friends and not something more to each other). I often went along with George to some kind of kitchen demo show, and he came with me to shop for plants. I always ended up buying more herbs when he was with me. I found myself smiling as I placed the recovered newspaper carefully on the front desk's ledge.

As I went around to the other side, something new stood out to me, an apple-green hardcover book with no jacket. *Robert Browning* was embossed on the front inside a decorative ellipse-thing that reminded me of the stone carvings on the outside of the hotel. *Cartouche*, that was the word.

Did the book belong to another desk clerk? It couldn't be Doyle's. Maybe Sarah's, though. I lifted the cover but couldn't find a name written inside. If it were part of the hotel library collection, there would be a stamp on the first page, and there wasn't. There was no bar code for any other library either, so I dropped it in the lost-and-found bin—on top of the drawings Bea and I had found on the walls.

I could hear Parker Rogers humming to himself in the morning room, so I grabbed the pictures and found him curled over a book on the window seat on the far side of the room.

"Hi, Parker." I stopped a few feet from him. "I don't mean to interrupt your reading . . ."

He didn't look up.

"I wondered if these are yours." I held the drawings up so he could see.

He glanced up quickly. "No," he said flatly, and resumed his humming.

Maybe he was ashamed to admit to them. "They're lovely, but I'm afraid if they stay on the hotel walls that you'll forget to pack them when you go back home."

No answer.

"I'll just leave them here for you." I placed them on a table near him. "Okay, see you later."

A stack of paperwork waited for me in the office, along with a paper on signal detection theory that was due in my Sensation and Perception class on Monday. One of the perks of this night shift was having long stretches to study and write papers, and I'd planned to use tonight to catch up, but the work I was doing for Mr. Fig was too important.

I sat down behind the desk and let my mind shift.

Deena seemed a little flighty but seasoned. I didn't want to discount her intuition just yet, so I added Leonard Chaves to my mental list of people to be interviewed, which also included Selena, Tom because he was Renee's brother-in-law, and Clyde's ex-wife, if I could get to her.

I hoped there was nothing intensely scientific about this case. It was against my personal code to ask help of a rival, not that Bea was one necessarily. George had room in his life for both of us. It just annoyed me that she might be toying with him. He was slow when it came to bonding with people, and I didn't know if her interest in him had more in common with Super Glue or those removable 3M strips.

It was Bea's day off, but I should get my head straight for when we were both back here together. I had a fleeting idea that, equipped with a microscope, she might be able to tell me something about those hairs I'd found in the Achilles. I'd wait to see if I could puzzle out their source on my own first.

I heard the swinging door to the kitchen swoosh open, and George slipped through the black curtain behind me.

"Hello, stranger." I smiled.

"Getting anywhere, Detective?"

"Well, the field of suspects is pretty swampy." I drummed my fingers against the desk. "And I still haven't figured out how anyone got to Renee's room that night."

"It's confusing. This crime was clearly planned in advance. But strangling is a crime of passion." His eyes were locked on mine.

Had he said *passion* emphatically? No, that didn't make any sense. But why did he keep staring at me?

I turned away from his gaze to stack up the comment cards. "Right. It would have to be premeditated if the killer knew how to get to the victim without being seen."

"But how would the killer know they were going to have an opportunity to find her in her room alone?"

I shrugged. "It sounds like she had headaches like that a lot and maybe used them to skip out on the group's events sometimes."

"Mm, yes, so the killer had to have known her habits. And must have hated her at least a little." He leaned his elbows on the desk a few inches from me and rolled a pencil between his fingers. "Or been jealous of her, or some other dark motive."

George smelled like basil and butter today. It occurred to me that there weren't a lot of people to whom I could stand close enough to smell without it being weird.

"That still makes Clyde the most obvious choice, especially given that there was trouble between them," I said.

"Looks like you're making progress."

"I hope so." I watched his fingers as he doodled on someone's check-in paperwork.

"How are you sleeping?" He nudged me in the arm, well above my bandage.

"Okay, so far." Several times a night, I'd roll over onto my sore arm, making my skin scream as if the burn were fresh. I loved that he asked, but there was no sense in worrying him any further.

"Good," he said, lifting his weight off the counter. "Don't hide from me, all right? Keep me updated."

I nodded. It was nice to be on his watch list.

"I gotta get back to dinner." He yawned.

"Save me some."

"You won't like it—it's spicy," he called as he went through the swinging door to the kitchen.

I smiled, thinking of that time we'd walked from school to the Thai restaurant and I'd let him order for me. He'd thought I could handle the panang at the three-chili level, but my heartburn was so bad, we'd had to call his mom to pick us up.

Alone again in the little office, I looked Clyde up on a professor-rating website. We all used it to dish not only about classroom experiences but also the character of our teachers.

Clyde had a great overall rating, and students weren't commenting on his personality except to say that he was helpful.

Well, some people left it all on the field at work and had nothing to give at home.

Autumn hadn't wanted Clyde for a brother-in-law, and his relationship with Selena was rocky. But they each had their own biases. I needed to track down another source.

X

Spies, Lies, and Alibis

The springs of Dr. Larsson's chair squealed like a hungry gerbil through the receiver of the front desk phone. The professor had been easy to find in the college's online directory but not as easy to catch at his desk. He'd finally answered on my third try.

Clyde had described Dr. Larsson as a friend, but like Clyde, he was a professor of literature, so I figured he must have been a classmate or a colleague at some point too.

The ethics of spying weren't cut-and-dry. Carl Jung had collaborated with U.S. intelligence during World War II, developing psychological profiles on enemy leaders. Genius that he was, he also foresaw Hitler killing himself.

But spying on a civilian, a college student not suspected of any crime, would be problematic, ethically speaking. If Clyde had asked this guy to do that, it would underline with a big black Sharpie Clyde's need to control the women in his life.

"Hello there," I said. "I'm a writer for the student paper at Carnegie Mellon, and I'm putting together a feature about Cl— Dr. Clyde Borough, and—"

"What a coincidence. I just got off the phone with an old classmate of mine and Clyde's." Dr. Larsson sounded genuinely pleased. He had a smooth, radio voice. "What's going on? Did the man win the lottery or something?"

"Uh, well, we're coming up on the anniversary of his tenure at the university." I had no idea when Clyde had been tenured, but it was a safe bet that we were within a couple years of some anniversary worth celebrating.

"A feature in the student paper, eh? Gosh, is there anything interesting to print about us old guys?" he said with mock surprise. He made small talk easily, like Clyde.

"I trust you can give me a juicy story or two."

"Well, sure—Clyde's a good friend and a real dynamo, too. We met in grad school, of course, a thousand years ago . . . under the shadow of these castle walls, actually."

A larger-than-life setup. I imagined him looking out his office window onto the school grounds, both hands cradling his head, perhaps.

"And what year would that be?"

"Aw, about 1982, I guess," he said.

"Thank you. So Dr. Borough is, of course, beloved by students. He's been called a gifted teacher," I said. "Did you see his innate brilliance right away?"

"Sure, sure. Always a smart guy." His tone was agreeable rather than decisive.

"Can you share a memorable example? Something pithy and inspiring for our readers?"

"Right. Yes. I . . . ." The sound of shuffling papers came over the line. "Let's see . . . just thinking through . . ."

"Take your time." I didn't mean it. It was just before dinner, when I would need to leave the desk for turndown service, so I didn't have all the time in the world.

"You know, let's come back to that one." Dr. Larsson cleared his throat.

"Okay. Next question. Our students are dying to know—how was Dr. Borough with the ladies?"

In my experience, dominating behavior was the prep school for a master's in abuse. Selena had said her father was controlling. If this guy could give me the name of a longtime girlfriend, she might be able to corroborate that story.

"Aw, well, you know, he dated a lot of girls. None of them too seriously."

I wished I could conduct this interview in person. Dr. Larsson was probably communicating paragraphs with his body language, but his spoken words left too much out. Was he hiding something?

"And his daughter goes to school there?" I asked. "Is she following in his footsteps?"

"Ah, oh, it's hard to say. She, um . . . I mean, Clyde actually had a point there where he didn't know what he was going to do either."

"He dithered at school?" Dithered? This historical environment was really getting to me.

"Mmm . . ."

"Please, go on. It might be encouraging to some of our students who add a major halfway through their program to hear that their hero professor didn't plow straight rows."

"It's not that he didn't take it seriously." His voice had gone higher and thinner. "It's just—he didn't have a great thesis idea. At first. His initial proposal was rejected by his committee while the rest of us were already well on our way. Then out of the blue, he had this lightning-rod moment, and well, you know the rest."

I waited for him to elaborate.

"Awards, fellowships, eventually Carnegie Mellon."

"Right," I said. It was a steep ascent from Covenant to Carnegie Mellon. That thesis must have been great. "And did you feel that he earned his success?"

"Sure, like I say, he got to work after the idea struck him, busted his rear to finish well. But he was always good at making connections."

The elevator dinged at my right, and Mr. Wollstone trudged past the desk on his way to dinner.

Almost time to start turndown service.

But Mr. Wollstone was always early to meals. He had to leave himself time to sit at the table and work up an abhorrence for whatever might be served.

"So Dr. Borough's daughter, she's following in his illustrious footsteps?" I asked.

"Well, she's only a sophomore. It can be hard for kids to find their niche, you know?"

If he couldn't say that she was doing well, then either she definitely wasn't or he wasn't spying on her. If she wasn't doing well, maybe Autumn was right about her instability. And if, on the other hand, Selena was mistaken about Dr. Larsson's interest in her, then she still looked unreliable. A touch of paranoid personality disorder, perhaps?

"And what about her mother—I mean, Clyde's ex-wife? Did you know her?"

"I think that's getting too personal for the scope of your article, don't you?" His tone was chastising with an edge of threatening, as if I were a student who had attempted plagiarizing.

"Oh sure, sorry. It's just I'm a big fan of Dr. Borough's, and I don't see how anyone could divorce him, do you?"

"No, no. Exactly right." Relief was evident in his voice. "Hey, what did you say the name of your paper was?"

Dagnabbit. For a millisecond I thought about running a quick search on the office computer. But even though Chattanooga had the fastest internet in the country, I couldn't get an answer quick enough to be convincing.

"What did you say?" I said, as if to someone nearby.

"I asked what the name of your paper is."

"Yeah, be right there," I said to my invisible friend, and then quickly into the phone, "Sorry, Dr. Larsson, there's a breaking story on campus—a fire, I think. Thanks for all your help."

I hung up and hoped he wouldn't return my call.

* * *

I rushed through turndown service. Since I wasn't feeling particularly drawn to any suspect beyond Clyde, the urge to snoop in their rooms for clues was easy to overcome. I shoved the flower-and-mint basket back in the landing closet and hurried down to the first floor.

There were many puzzles I had left to solve in this house, not least among them the purpose behind some of the weird equipment and rooms in the secret basement passage I had discovered last year. I would often find myself down there in the wee hours, perusing the books and letting my imagination run wild. Now I had to find a hidden way upstairs rather than down.

What was left of the original servant staircase was the one I climbed every day to get from the basement to the front desk, but according to Mr. Fig, it used to continue up to the third floor and even had roof access. During the conversion from house to hotel, it had been closed off somewhere, but I didn't know why . . . or what the space was used for now. More importantly,

I didn't know whether someone with evil intentions could have opened the staircase up again and used it.

And who might have known it existed? Only Clarista or Mr. Fig were that familiar with the former layout of the house.

Or someone who'd been here before the hotel conversion? Like *Clyde*.

As a guest of the Morrows, he would've had no reason to be in the service areas of the house, but by all accounts he was a smart guy, and if he had paid attention when he arrived at the hotel, he'd have realized that things were different upstairs, that there was no staircase now where there had been before. But would that late discovery have left him time to plan the murder before his and Renee's second night here?

Swells of Vivaldi reached my ears from the dining room. After two guests argued at the table last year, Clarista had decided classical music would ward off tension and had speakers camouflaged into the painted clouds on the ceiling.

The door to the old servant staircase was itself disguised from view by blending into the wall mural a few feet from the front desk. A simple push and I found myself on the other side. In front of me was a short landing and, if I had kept going, the long staircase to the cellar and dressing rooms, lit by wall sconces.

But to the left of the landing where I stood was the broom closet from which I'd fetched the mop on the night of the leak. If the staircase was blocked off, this would have been the place to do it, at the first floor before the staircase bent and turned up another flight.

I opened the closet door, which looked like any other door downstairs but felt light, as if it were of a cheaper wood than the heavy oak used for the original interior. Brooms, a vacuum cleaner, and other such paraphernalia huddled in the darkness.

I flicked on a light and stepped in to examine the walls. Two were just like the staircase and hall, painted white plaster. There was even a sconce, though unlit probably for many years now, on the back wall. I was on the right track.

The third wall, to my right, was Sheetrock. I ran my hands over the smooth surface and felt no crack or opening a person could have made as an access point. But could they have removed the whole piece of drywall? Pulled it out or something? I put my shoulder against it and pushed. It didn't give.

I looked around for something to use as a wedge. The metal dustpan would work nicely. I forced the hard edge in between the wall and floor, wiggled and applied pressure on the handle. But nothing moved. The wall felt solid as stone.

*　　*　　*

The grandfather clock chimed ten and, like a symphony crescendo, ended, leaving the entry hall more deathly quiet than before.

I stood behind the front desk and closed my eyes again.

"I owe you," Mr. Fig had said.

We'd entered the elevator, and he'd taken the master key from his pocket to unlock the strange, tiny cabinet full of keys. We rode down to the basement.

I watched him slide the document box from the storeroom shelf. He lifted the lid, and there it was in my mind—the blueprint book for the house.

I held my breath.

No, it was useless. I couldn't mentally bring up the original layout of the second floor, no matter how many times I walked myself through the memory. And I didn't have the key to the little elevator cabinet, so I couldn't get into the storage room without Mr. Fig here.

I could see pieces of the first-floor blueprint in my head. That's where we'd looked last year for the entrances to the forgotten passage. And no doubt the emotion I'd felt in the moment, the slightly heightened connection to the experience of my great-great-grandparents, had cemented the memory in my hippocampus. (I was learning about long-term memory storage this semester in my Biological Psychology course.)

I could see Mr. Fig's face at the moment he'd told me he had worked for my family. Why had he waited so long? And then, when I'd found the passage under the conservatory and it turned out he'd known the whole time—why? Why hadn't he told me about that either? Or that he knew I was a descendant of the Morrow family?

Before now, I'd chalked it up to him believing I wasn't ready, for some reason. But now the questions provoked me, against my will.

Because if there was another way upstairs, Mr. Fig would know it better than anyone. He'd worked here at the house decades before the remodel and for a dozen years now afterward.

But no—Mr. Fig didn't need a secret way upstairs. If he'd wanted to kill Renee—ugh, even thinking the words made my stomach turn—he could have done it when he brought the wine to her earlier in the evening.

So who else might have found a way upstairs? Clarista, possibly George, or another employee who'd been paying attention. In other words, a bunch of people who hadn't known Renee until she checked in.

I was so sick of hitting walls.

Some of our guests were watching a movie in the theater. Tom and Autumn had gone out after dinner, and I didn't know when they'd return.

The front doors were unlocked, though, and there was little chance of them needing anything at the desk on the way to their room.

Maybe I could leave the desk for a few minutes without an issue.

I needed those blueprints, so key or no key, I was getting into that storeroom.

* * *

Dr. Leonard Chaves stood across from me, his arms tightly folded against his gray turtleneck, his thin body angled away toward the staircase.

This was the kind of interview I hated. It reminded me of the stint I'd worked for the high school newspaper. I was great at talking to people and coming up with story hooks. Getting the words down in writing was the drawback, which was the reason I had quit—that and having to talk to people who, like Dr. Chaves, didn't want to talk to me.

I'd wanted to get him into the library, a disarming environment for a professor, but he had stopped in the entry hall seating area a few feet from the library door, clearly in a hurry to get this conversation over with.

Truth was, I didn't want to be talking to *him* now either. I wanted to be in the basement looking at old documents, but he'd returned from the conference just before I left the desk, and since he was evidently attending every single session of it, I had to take advantage of his momentary presence.

I sat down, hoping he would do the same, but standing seemed to be his way of conveying just how little time he planned to spend with me.

The man wouldn't even lean against anything, despite the sturdy grandfather clock being a foot away.

I was comforted by Mr. Fig's voice in my head. When the professor had checked in, he'd said, "*Chaves* is derived from *Flavius*, the family name of several first-century Roman emperors as well as Constantine's given name."

Leonard began to speak, and I had to step forward to hear him.

"So you said there's a problem with the payment method?" he asked.

Holy laurels. I *had* said that. Now how could I back it up and use it to milk him for information? "More of a concern, I guess. I wondered if you could help me. See, it's strange for us that the person whose credit card is on file has left the hotel but others are staying."

He shifted his weight and glanced toward the stairs. "I'm not sure how I can help with that."

I had a feeling Deena might be right about his general vibe.

"You've known Clyde a long time, right?" I said. "If you could vouch for him, that would go a long way."

"I've known him more than a decade."

"So you can put in a good word?"

"I could put in several words," he said.

I grinned mischievously. "But not good ones?"

His shoulders reared up in a stingy shrug. "I mean, he volunteered to front the cash for this whole stay, and you know more than I do what kind of money we're talking about there, but whether or not he's good for it, I can't say." He still wouldn't look at me. "If I were him, I would've picked the Holiday Inn."

Did Clyde actually have a lot of money to throw around, or was he overspending? "What kind of house does he live in?"

"Mount Lebanon, three stories, nice green lawn." He shrugged. "He used to take some of the department to a place in the Poconos, but I think he lost that in the divorce."

"He pays for those houses just by teaching?"

A short laugh popped from him. "Do you know what an average professor salary is in the U.S.? Sixty-seven thousand a year, according to Indeed.com."

That was freaky specific. "Okay. So how does he make his money, then?"

He shrugged. "Venture capital, maybe. Although I heard he'd sunk some money into a real stinker recently." He turned toward the window, and the sideways stream of light caught the divots of acne scars that deepened his wrinkles. "But he always seems to land right side up. Things fall into his lap. Opportunities, grants, all that."

Leonard stared at the floor while he spoke, lessening the dramatic effect of his widow's peak. His hands turned to fists in his pockets. "Case in point, I've published extensively on dramatic monologues, but Borough's the one who gets to teach on Browning."

"Robert Browning?"

"Yes."

Of course. Browning was a Victorian. So the book left on the front desk must belong to Clyde. "Everyone seems to like him. If I said he sounds like a modern-day Gatsby—"

"You wouldn't be far off. At least until recently."

"Recently?" I said.

"Someone seems to have it out for him. Vandalizing his house, that sort of thing."

That was right. Clyde had mentioned as much at his hotel. "So why don't you like him?"

"Who says I don't?"

"Come on."

The theater doors swung open, and guests flooded the hall—Parker Rogers and his dad Furnell, Velvet and Deena linked arm in arm, Mr. Wollstone, plus a young couple I didn't recognize, and a family of five I'd checked in Tuesday night.

Deena and Velvet still wore the fabulous dresses they'd put on before dinner tonight. Deena's was an emerald-green ballgown that matched the feathered purse she carried, and Velvet's was full-length ivory silk with a flattering cinched waist and black lace accents.

On their way to the dining room earlier, I'd asked them where they got their fabulous outfits, and Deena had said Velvet borrowed them from the drama teacher at her old school. If only all our guests were so well connected, this place would feel every bit as historical as Clarista wanted.

Leonard glanced their way and then moved closer. "Look, is this about Renee?"

Blast. He was onto me.

"Why would you say that?" I gave myself some time to change tactics.

"I'm just not buying your story. Why not simply run Borough's credit card and be done with it?"

"Okay, you've got me. What can you tell me about Renee?"

He sat down on the green velvet sofa opposite me. "She was a lovely person."

How interesting that he became invested in the conversation as soon as he discerned that it was about Renee. He must have been genuinely fond of her, and that went a long way coming from someone who seemed as emotive as a pet rock.

"But I've told the police everything I know about that night, which is almost nothing anyway," he said.

"I get the sense that Renee wasn't very sure of herself."

"Well, no, how could she be with a sister who second-guessed every choice Renee made? And Borough . . ." He shook his head.

"What about him?"

"God, did you see the way he treated her?" He finally looked up at me.

"Like a child." I frowned and nodded.

"Yes. Between Clyde and Autumn, Renee was hardly able to think for herself."

I inched closer to him and lowered my voice. "You sound like you have some personal stake in the situation."

He twisted his head awkwardly, as if my question put a kink in his neck. "I only wanted to be friends with her."

"And Clyde didn't like that."

Leonard kept his focus on the pattern of the rug beneath his feet. "Exactly."

"Thank you." I had one more question for him. "I wanna go back a second to Browning."

He glanced at me from the corners of his eyes. "Yes?"

"Did you lose a book of his poems somewhere?"

"No." He stared into space behind me, considering something, each new thought changing his face by a degree. "I need to go now."

"I can show you the book I'm talking about."

He stared at the floor again and shook his head as he moved toward the stairs.

Outside the theater, Deena glanced up as Leonard walked away. She had been reapplying her lipstick and perusing a painting of Virgil reading the Aeneid to Augustus Caesar, which wasn't my taste and hadn't attracted my interest at all until last year, when Mr. Fig had told me what it meant to my family.

I caught Deena's eye, and she waggled her eyebrows at me as if to say, *See?*

I wondered whether to believe all that Leonard had said about Clyde or if I should take his comments with a grain of simple psychology. It was possible he suffered from an inferiority complex. Or maybe avoidant personality disorder, which included feelings of incompetence and self-consciousness. People with APD often came across as stiff and distant.

But the more psychology classes I took, the more I began to realize how much work went into a diagnosis like that. Playing around with labels wasn't as fun for me now as it once had been. Ignorance is bliss, as they say.

Now that Leonard had brought up the poetry and reacted a bit strangely to my mention of the book, I couldn't shake the idea of the Browning poetry being relevant, but I had no time for sifting through poems looking for clues like a literary conspiracy theorist.

Still, I wondered if he was simply afraid to admit the book was his. And if so, why?

XI

Grave Digger

∽

When everyone from octogenarian skinny-dippers to intro-verted English professors had finally drifted upstairs, I put the *brb* sign out on the desk and pushed the golden down arrow outside the elevator.

The doors slid back soundlessly, and I rustled inside, careful to pull my wide skirt clear of the threshold.

In a moment I was alone in the gilded box. From the deep pocket of my dress, I unsheathed the screwdriver I'd swiped from the emergency toolbox in the office.

There was a bump, and then the elevator creaked slowly down to the basement. I slipped the flat end of the screwdriver under the crack of the small door in the elevator wall in front of me. To the uneducated eye, it was a control panel, but when I applied a little pressure, the door popped open and revealed several rows of ancient-looking skeleton keys on pegs.

I didn't have a great plan for how to close the panel again. There were zip ties in the office. That would probably do it.

I held the close-door button while I examined the rows of keys. Mr. Fig, or some caretaker before him, had labeled the pegs with tiny symbols—a piano, a bathtub, a book, a bed, the letter *A*, and so on.

I couldn't relate any of the symbols to the door marked *Storage* besides the *S*. I grabbed the key under that peg and hoped it was right.

Thankfully, the storage room lock opened without complaint. I flicked on the bare bulbs overhead, and the memory of being here with Mr. Fig was so tangible that I teared up.

Although he and I had talked some since about the things in this room, I hadn't been back down here. I told myself it was because I wanted to behave more like a regular member of staff and not bother Mr. Fig with too many requests for special treatment. But I wondered if some part of me was avoiding looking at anything to do with my mom.

I went back to the same green metal box Mr. Fig had lifted from the shelf last year, the one labeled *MCMX–MCMXIX*. It was heavier than it looked. Inside, I found the original blueprints once again, handling them as if they were Dead Sea Scrolls. Mr. Fig might've preferred that I wear white gloves, but I didn't have any handy.

When Clarista purchased the hotel, all of these old things in storage would have been sold along with it, right? Or did I have any claim to them as a descendant? If she didn't know all these old documents existed, would she even want them?

I knew as little about the answer to that question as I did about quantum physics, but I sure wasn't going to tell Clarista all this was here for a while longer. Anyway, there was a good chance she already knew.

I flipped open the beautiful cover of the bound blueprints with its gold-embossed sketch of the hotel and past the page of the first-floor plan. The Achilles, on the second floor, was easy to pick out because it was a good 30 percent larger than the other rooms—and of course because of the helpful *Achilles* written in fine, slanted cursive in the white space.

I could see the marked openings for the room's entrance from the landing and the doors to the bathroom and closet.

And then there was a smaller opening marked *D* along the interior wall of the room. But why? Why an opening in the wall, and how could it be accessed? Was it simply a niche to hold a small sculpture? Or perhaps a narrow laundry shoot? Judging by the scale, this opening took up no more than half the width of the room's other doors.

Whatever it was, I was going to find out.

* * *

Moments later, as I climbed the stairs back to the first floor, I thought I heard some kind of music in the air, too faint for me to identify either the tune or the instrument. Maybe a guest was playing it from their phone.

Like swimming in the pool, music late in the evening wasn't expressly forbidden, but if the noise kept up much longer, I'd need to put a stop to it just to protect the peace and, selfishly, to help people fall asleep. The earlier they did, the sooner I could leave the desk and get back into the Achilles suite.

The sound had stopped by the time I reached the desk, so I sat down in the office to catch up on paperwork and pass the time.

In a few minutes, I heard voices, and the music started back up. Both came from the direction of the drawing room. The thin somber whine of a violin was easy to pick out now.

On the drawing room bookshelves, where most inns might keep board games, Clarista displayed old instruments. I knew she'd put a sign on the grand piano when she'd moved it into the drawing room at Christmas that said, in Clarista's typically drawn-out way, *Dear guests, please kindly refrain from playing the piano unless you know how and have received the express permission of the staff beforehand. Sitting on the piano bench without using the instrument is also discouraged.*

(I'd started to wonder if she used so many words because she thought it seemed more old-fashioned.)

But there was no sign by the violin, trumpet, or other instruments on the shelves. I'd assumed they were mostly decorative, too old to be put to use, but maybe someone had decided to give it a try.

The playing continued for another quarter hour, and as much as I was enjoying it, it was almost ten o'clock, and my job required that I make it stop.

From the doorway of the drawing room, I could see the violinist. He sat facing the fireplace with his chin angled to pinch the end of the violin, so all I could see was the back of his slender head, clipped in a fade that revealed the deep golden brown of his skin. It was Furnell Rogers, Parker's dad.

I couldn't place the melody, although I'd heard it before, but I could tell by the way he played that he was on a first-name basis with the piece.

Now that I was close, the music was liquid glass, too beautiful to be interrupted.

Furnell must have heard the swish of my dress, because he paused and turned toward me. "Sorry, is this all right?"

"Please, yeah, go ahead," I answered on instinct, then thought better of it. "Well, actually, sir, you should probably stop in a few minutes. We try to have quiet after ten o'clock. Your playing makes me wish that wasn't our policy, though."

His lean face drew up to a smile, and he nodded toward the middle of the room. "That's all right. Just killing a little time while my son sketches."

I took a few steps forward.

Parker sat on the floor using the coffee table like a desk. Was this the moment I would catch the little Banksy, crayon in hand?

Although I got close enough to look over his shoulder, he didn't look up at me. He wasn't coloring, though—he was indeed sketching, as his father had said.

I was the weak link in a family heavy with artistic talent, so I was far from being a critic, but to me his drawing was pretty impressive, a realistic representation of an overhead view of the rear garden and the river. The perspective from their room on the third floor, I realized. The confidently sketched shadows of the statues lay on the lawn at convincing angles, and everything was detailed and in proper proportion.

Nothing like the cartoonish, simplistic pictures I'd found on the walls.

"Does he always work in pencil?" I asked his dad.

He laid the violin on the sofa table behind him, a tall, narrow thing with fat, shapely legs. "Eh, sometimes pen, sometimes whatever they require at school."

"I like your work, Parker," I said.

He murmured back without lifting his face from the drawing.

"He's a man of few words, you may have noticed," said Furnell. "Parker is on the autism spectrum."

"Okay, cool." I nodded. I understood the kid's behavior a little better now. "It's nice that you could bring him along with you for the convention. I mean, a lot of kids would complain about being here, right?"

"*Hmph*, other way around, actually. He brought me with him."

"Ha," I said.

"No, seriously. He's the graver. I'm just his chaperone."

"Oh, wow. Graver, huh? I haven't heard that term."

"Taphophile," said Parker. "From the Greek *táphos*."

He was an adorable nerd. I wished we could keep him around.

"Yeah," Furnell continued, as if agreeing with my unspoken thought. "We had no idea how interested he was until he started checking out books only about graveyards and tombstones and drawing all these pictures. Went and found 'em in his room one day, and I was like, this kid is obsessed!"

"So what do you do while he's in the conference all day? You go with him?"

"I check in between sessions, but otherwise, I'm a free man." He stretched his arms and put both hands behind his neck.

I had to appreciate the hard work that put those muscles in his arms. "Good. How have you been occupying your time?"

"You know we've been here since early Wednesday, so I've been to all those shops and stuff at the Choo-Choo and down Main Street, I went hiking and hang gliding off the side of one of your mountains, and tomorrow I'm going stand-up paddleboarding."

"You're high-energy. But tomorrow's the last day, right?"

"Yeah, there's some big party that goes on kinda late Sunday night, but we probably won't do that. Parker's not much for parties."

Hmm. So he skipped out on club activities and he had a sporty physique. Could he have climbed up to the second floor somehow? "Did you take the tour with the group around the hotel's gravestones Thursday night?"

"I did."

So much for that theory. "Did everyone stay the whole time? Or did you notice anyone getting bored and drifting off?"

He shook his head. "Nope. Can't say I did. Clyde seemed to hold our interest pretty well."

But I already knew that Deena had slipped away for a bathroom break, and if Furnell hadn't seen her leave, then couldn't someone else have disappeared without the group noticing too?

"How 'bout you, though?" Furnell said. "You must like this kind of stuff—working at a place like this."

"Um." It was hard to respond without knocking his son's interest. "I like history. I'm probably only interested in graves of family members, though."

Actually, they hadn't been an interest either until this group had showed up and rubbed off on me.

I had taken the time before falling asleep early this morning to look for my grandparents' obituaries in the online archives of the local paper. I'd prepared myself for disappointment, but when I found each of their write-ups, they had left me more mystified than sad. Both obits talked briefly about basic facts and accomplishments, but neither listed any surviving children. My mother would have still been in town during those years. Had she sent in the copy to the paper and purposefully left herself out? And if so, why?

"*Monuments are for the living, not the dead*," said Parker. "Frank Wedekind."

Furnell shrugged, as if to say, *See?*

Whoa. I didn't even know who Wedekind was, and this kid could quote him. I wondered if Parker had also cataloged the graves out back. "Hey, Parker, while you were checking out the graves here, did you happen to see any with the names Hortensius Morrow or Mary Quinn Morrow?"

"No," he said.

If I hadn't found those headstones and he hadn't found them, maybe they simply weren't here. Did that mean something?

I shoved down my questions. "Well, I'll get back to work. Good to see you again, Parker."

Although he didn't look up, he craned his head in my direction, and I knew he was getting ready to speak to me.

I waited.

"Where will they bury you?" he asked.

A chill skipped down the backs of my arms. I didn't have an answer for him.

XII
What Ivy Found There

∽

I locked the door of the Achilles behind me and tiptoed through the alcove into the heart of the suite. The house had been built sturdily, but a singing floorboard here or there wasn't entirely out of the question. I was much more aware now than I'd been the night before of the rhythmic rush of my breathing after climbing the stairs.

I had to be extra careful tonight. If Renee's killer was the intruder who had found me in here before, they might already suspect I was on their trail. Whether they had watched and followed me into the room last time or if our simultaneous presence here had been merely coincidence, I didn't know, but if we met again in the dead of night, well, who knew what they might be tempted to do.

I understood well enough from last year's experience that murderers didn't have scruples about little things like killing again.

I estimated that the mystery opening I'd spotted on the second-floor blueprint was seven feet ahead of me along the right wall. The burgundy settee and matching armchairs were at my left in front of the fireplace, and straight ahead was the bed on the far side of the suite.

Glancing to my right, I saw an obvious problem. The heavy armoire in which I'd hidden last time spanned five feet, and it was pushed right up against the flocked wallpaper. I swooped past it and checked the wall on the other side. No, there was nothing but a framed picture that wasn't nearly large enough to conceal an access point.

I rechecked the picture of the blueprint on my phone and measured the wall by walking toe to toe along the baseboard.

It was impossible.

Maybe the room had been built with some kind of opening here, but I couldn't see how Renee's killer could have used it.

Unless . . . what if the intruder who surprised me in the armoire had indeed been the killer, and what if their reason for opening it had had nothing to do with me?

I grabbed the knob of the massive door and nearly pulled it off its hinges in my eagerness. Leaning inside, I could just reach the back wall of the armoire if I extended my arm under the half-dozen empty hangers. In the light of my phone, the wood was one solid piece, but I ran my fingers across the cool grain, and my fingernail caught on a crack.

I sucked in a breath and followed the crevice until it turned ninety degrees three times and my hand was back where I started. The crack formed a long rectangle about four feet by three. A tiny drop of hardened glue glistened in the left corner.

This had to be it. This was the killer's access point.

I knelt inside the armoire, put both palms against the wood, and shoved. With a pop, the rectangular panel broke free of its gluey hold. All hail Ivy Nichols!

I couldn't stop the panel from dropping into the dark valley between the armoire and the bedroom wall or the resulting thud and smack of wood. I feared the noise would wake Mr. Wollstone in the next room, but my risk paid off when the light of my phone revealed a small sliding door on the wall behind the section of armoire I'd removed.

Mr. Wollstone in the next room. Could the rats he thought he'd heard on the night before Renee was murdered actually have been the sound of the killer sawing this panel? Or of someone moving around inside the wall behind it?

The door I'd revealed was set in a gilded frame in the wall, some kind of cabinet, I supposed, and judging by the acacia—no, acanthus—leaf carving on the frame, whatever it was had to be original to the house.

I reached through the hole I'd reopened and slid the door to this strange, new cabinet upward, shining the light from my phone with my other hand. But behind it was just another wall.

No, a shaft. What was this? A laundry shoot? Only someone in impeccable shape could scale this. A barefoot Bruce Willis came to mind.

I leaned forward with my light again and shined it into the box. Maybe the killer had stored something here . . . the murder weapon, perhaps?

The light caught on a thick rope that ran vertically along the left wall of the shaft down into the darkness. I reached out and plucked at it with a hand. It was sturdy and tight.

I sat back a second, puzzled. The blueprint had marked the hole *D*.

And it came to me. It was the dumbwaiter. The same one George used in the kitchen to get crates of vegetables up from the cellar.

There must be some kind of control here. In the kitchen, it was a button in the frame. I felt around the trim and found it, pushed it, and the ropes began to move. Somewhere up above was a pulley, but I wasn't sticking my head in this hole to see it.

Could Clyde have known this was here? Could he have seen this room when he visited the Morrows so many years ago?

The box of the dumbwaiter stopped in front of me with a click.

A person could fit inside it if they curled up. But could it be operated that way?

Getting in was too dangerous. I'd seen George load it up pretty full with vegetables from the cellar, but how many onions did it take to equal the weight of a person, even a smallish person like me?

Well, I didn't feel like endangering myself to prove it would hold my weight. A theoretical knowledge of the killer's method of entry was enough for me, thank you very much.

But who would have been clever enough to use this method of entering the room? Who had returned to find me hiding here? I was sitting in the same spot where I'd been found, and I let myself trace over the memory. As the panic had taken over, I'd searched for sensory details to ground myself, and there'd been no particular smell in the air. Clyde and Selena were both smokers, so that seemed to rule them out, and Deena's perfume was heavy, so surely I'd have known if it had been her.

I traced my steps back to the door, still pondering, and turned the key to unlock it, but a heavy thudding on the stairs stopped my hand.

Tom's moose-ish footsteps?

"Shh," said a voice from the gallery on the other side.

"What?" said another.

I was right. It was Tom on the landing, accompanied by his wife, back from dinner.

"I heard something," said Autumn.

"You're just being paranoid again," said Tom.

His speech was even more mumbly than before. I could hardly make out what he said.

"Clyde's paranoid. I'm not," she said, like a slap across the face. "Not now *or* at the restaurant when you kept sneaking off. I know something's going on with you."

"I wasn't sneaking," he said.

I heard the rattle of a plastic bag and realized he was snacking again and talking with his mouth full.

"I saw you from the balcony," Autumn said.

"What?" he said.

"Talking to Renee again. The day she died."

He paused. "I was just . . . hassling her about the money."

"You still think she knew who's stealing from me?" Autumn said.

"She was the office manager—sure she did."

"Clyde saw you talking to her too," she said.

"So?"

"So what if he made something of it? You know how jealous he gets."

"Den he's an idiot," Tom said. "Anyway, listen, don't worry about the money. We'll figure it out when we all get home."

She took a long pause. "Maybe Clyde shouldn't get home."

"Darlin', it's just money. We'll figure it out n'at. C'mon, let's go to bed. I'm beat."

"I'm not talking about the money." Her voice shook. "I'm talking about Renee. Whoever killed her is going to answer to me."

"You be careful."

Their voices were moving off in the direction of the staircase.

"And why are you so tired?" Autumn said. "You slept half the morning."

Tom's unexplained sleepiness and constant snacking sounded like side effects of something.

I stepped closer to hear his answer, and the floor squealed.

"Tom—someone's in there."

"Prob'ly a maid—"

"Who would be in there *with the lights off,* Tom? I'm going to find a key at the desk. I'm getting in there."

Her quick footfalls backed up her words.

I had one key to the room, but she was right that there was another at the desk.

I couldn't let them find me in here. Now suddenly seemed like as good a time as any to see if that dumbwaiter would function as an elevator.

I went back through the armoire and shuddered. This would either be a joyride or the Tower of Terror.

From inside the dumbwaiter box, I reached my hand around to push the button.

The thing was surprisingly quiet as it began to glide down, except for a squeak here and there that might have sounded a bit like a rat to Mr. Wollstone.

I watched the brick wall slide upward in front of me and released the breath I'd been holding.

A moment too soon.

The small box creaked to a halt, and the hole wasn't aligned with another door. I only saw wood studs and more brick in front of me.

I tried pulling the rope that ran vertically along the inside of the box, put it was too tight and wouldn't give at all.

There had to be a way to start this thing moving again.

My heart began banging in my chest.

I was sitting and crouched as it was, but I managed to lift most of my weight from the floor of the box and drop myself down hard again.

The box shook but didn't move.

This was terrifying, and I didn't even suffer from claustrophobia. The walls were just inches from my skin. If I couldn't get myself out of here . . .

I lifted my weight again and slammed my body into the floor below me.

Something snapped overhead.

The box began dropping again. It moved slowly at first, then picked up speed.

Too much speed.

How fast was I falling? And how far down?

The rhythmic squeak of the mechanism overhead picked up its tempo.

I stomped the rope against the side wall, using my foot as a brake. The friction made a horrible, droning sound.

My makeshift brake seemed to be working, but in a second I felt the rope burning the sole of my shoe. I kept pressing and cried out from the pain and the effort.

The dumbwaiter crashed to a stop. The jolt of the impact shot through my tailbone and up my spine. I was thrown off-balance. My back smashed into the wall behind me.

From where I sat, the noise was deafening, and I hoped I hadn't woken the whole house.

I took a breath and checked the bottom of my shoe. The rope had worn clean through my thin Chucks and my sock, leaving a nasty strawberry on my skin. I'd need to treat it with the first-aid kit at the desk.

I slid open the door panel and found myself in total darkness, except for the light my phone gave off. I shifted my legs out and felt the cold, stone floor through the hole in my shoe.

The air smelled of earth and spice.

I'd hoped to land in the kitchen, but this was the cellar, one floor down.

I shined my phone flashlight briefly around. I was sure I was alone, and yet the deep, total darkness of the windowless room freaked me out.

My light caught inside the dumbwaiter box on a patch of color, a piece of deep-green-and-blue plaid caught on a nail. I pocketed it and headed for the door to the servant hall.

As soon as I laid my hand on the knob, I remembered that it would be locked. The cellar was always locked. The knob didn't turn at all.

Perfect.

Thank God Clarista had allowed me to start carrying my phone. Otherwise, George might've found another corpse next time he came down to restock the kitchen.

I called Dad first. "Hello?" he said.

"Dad," I answered.

"Hello?" His voice came through spottily. "Ivy?"

"Can you hear me?"

"Ivy, are you there?" His voice faded.

We circled through the dance a couple more times before the sound died completely. I stomped, then reeled and sat down. I'd used my sore foot.

I sent a text to Dad, hoping to ease his mind but not knowing if it would get through on the poor signal. I tried calling George next, but the connection was even worse.

I stared at the heavy door in front of me. There was supposed to be some way to open a door with a credit card, but I didn't *have* a credit card handy.

Thankfully my turn-of-the-century hairdo meant I had a wealth of bobby pins at my command.

I had two bars of Wi-Fi signal. I did a little Googling and figured out this old lock was a mortise style, so picking it was different than the technique featured in nearly every spy movie ever, although it still involved a couple of hairpins. I found an instructional YouTube video, but it wouldn't play at all. I finally pulled up a locksmith's blog that loaded onto the page in fits and starts. Holding the light and working the lock together turned out to be too difficult, though.

I tossed the warped pins aside and sat back, half exhausted and frustrated with my lack of skills, my lack of progress on this case. I touched my foot and winced.

When I had time after all this was over, I would practice lock-picking and all manner of spy abilities. But calls for help didn't come when you were prepared for them. I hadn't known I'd be taking this on.

Anyway, the most immediate thing in my way was this massive, ancient door. I glared at it.

The hinges were on my side. I did a little more research, located a mallet and screwdriver that George used for opening and closing barrels, and wedged my phone between two heads of hanging garlic to give me light.

Hammering away in the darkness, I couldn't see how much damage I was doing to the old door. Mr. Fig would be appalled when he made it back here.

My phone battery died halfway through the process, but I was able to finish beating the pin out of the top hinge by feel.

As I hobbled up the stairs, I processed Autumn and Tom's conversation. Clyde had been pressuring Autumn for money at his cottage on the mountain. She'd said someone was stealing from her. And Tom had been hassling Renee in the conservatory because he thought she knew something about it?

I wondered along with Autumn what Clyde would have made of seeing Tom alone with his girlfriend. According to more than one source now, Clyde was a jealous man.

Back in the entry hall, I took off my holey shoe and sock and grabbed a Band-Aid from the first-aid kit. I heard the door from the morning room to the conservatory, a very particular creak that I'd hardly notice at any other time of day. I tiptoed, one foot bare, to the dark morning room. All was quiet here, but I could see a flash of movement in the barely lit conservatory through the windows.

I focused in on a head of blond hair. Selena was crouching at the foot of the bougainvillea vine. She stuffed something in the purse she carried, shot up, looked around, and dashed out the nearest exit.

Was she stealing from us? But what and why? I didn't take her for a botanist trading rare plants on the black market, and it wasn't as if we had garden gnomes nestled around the conservatory that she might nab as some college prank.

She'd come across to me as a kid with a bad attitude and daddy issues, but like her father, she had secrets.

She wasn't going to like me digging around in them.

XIII

Second Fig

∽

I had a restless night's sleep with the throbbing pain in my foot, all too familiar after what I'd done to my arm. I woke repeatedly from nightmares that my feet were being crushed by an elevator with prehistoric-looking teeth lining its sliding doors.

But unlike the burn on my arm, this injury had been acquired while I was up to something good. Clearly, I was maturing by the hour.

In the morning, I sat with my plants on the balcony of our apartment and drank black tea to try to get going. I thought of Mr. Fig. What was his usual morning beverage? And what were they giving him in jail? Water? Anything?

I wished I could smuggle in something good for him.

Knowing how the murderer had accessed the Achilles surely narrowed down my list of suspects. At five feet five inches, I had fit fine into the dumbwaiter, but some on my list would not. Tom was too tall and wide, and Clyde was really pushing it. But I could see him cramming in, if he was flexible. Selena would definitely make the cut.

Then again, there was the possibility that Tom and Autumn were in it together, or that Clyde and Autumn were. I hated to think anyone would do in their own sister. It was easier to believe that of a romantic partner, although I didn't like admitting that either.

I rubbed the back of my neck and drained my teacup.

I decided to visit Selena Borough. As hotheaded as she was, she might *want* to dish about her dad. And if I could figure out what she'd taken from the conservatory, that'd be a win too.

Unfortunately, it was Sunday, and students at a Christian school like Covenant would be at chapel at this hour.

A burning dread gnawed at my insides. There was someone else I needed to question who would find himself with nothing in particular to do this morning.

Two parts of me warred against each other. I had to talk to Mr. Fig again in order to get him out of jail. But talking to him required going back there, and seeing him in that place again was the last thing I wanted to do.

* * *

I drug my feet up the steps of the county jail as if I were pulling a body behind me.

Once I'd passed security, I made my way down the hall. I smelled the men before I reached the holding cell this time. The acidic odor of vomit and unwashed bodies invaded my nose, and I thought I'd never feel hungry again. I didn't know if this place was dirtier than before or if I simply felt worse about it.

I found Mr. Fig crowded in with mostly the same group. Neither busy nor resting, they leaned and shifted and lay down tensely. One man was on the phone, yelling. Others talked only to themselves.

Mr. Fig had managed to win a spot on a bench, but he gave it up when he saw me and wove through the other men to stand on the opposite side of the bars from me.

The circles below his eyes had darkened, and his silver stubble had filled in, making him seem older and somehow helpless. And was it possible he'd lost weight, or had his suit simply gone limp?

"I'm still so sorry you're here," I said.

"I know. Thank you." The spark and confidence that were so much a part of his usual expression were completely gone.

I could understand him being depressed, but I still worried.

I swallowed hard and got right to the point. Maybe giving him something else to think about would help. "Someone cut a hole in the Achilles' armoire to get to the old dumbwaiter opening. That's how the killer got to Renee without you seeing them."

He opened his mouth, closed it, and shook his head. "I'm sure there's not time now, but someday I want to know how you came to this realization."

"You may not like my methods."

He smiled—well, something that was almost a smile. "I hadn't thought of the old opening, since that armoire is too heavy for any one person to move. The dumbwaiter was used often when that suite was your grandparents', but the bathroom in the suite was expanded during the hotel conversion, so they needed to block the dumbwaiter with the armoire."

"I figured it was something like that. So anyone working at the house in my grandparents' day would have known about it?"

"Oh yes."

"Clyde told me he visited the hotel when he was a student, I mean before it was a hotel. I think that would have been in the eighties, maybe. You worked for my family then, right?"

He hesitated. "Yes, but I'm afraid I don't remember him, if that's what you're asking. He may have been to one of the student dinners Mr. Morrow liked to host."

"Okay." I nodded, making mental notes. "Also, my dad says the leak the other night was probably purposeful. I think someone was trying to get me away from the desk long enough to try out the dumbwaiter from the kitchen without me realizing."

"Yes, that would have been the easiest way to access the dumbwaiter in the middle of the night. From the kitchen." Mr. Fig stared through me for what felt like a long moment. "Tell me again about the drawings."

"The drawings?" What a non sequitur. "The ones I found taped to the walls?"

He nodded.

"Well, the first one had kind of a blue background, a sky, I guess, and some orangy-tan vertical lines and upside-down horseshoes—"

"Could they be arches?" he asked.

"Like doorways? Yeah, I think so."

"And the second?"

"It had kind of some big, gold rectangles and a blue strip in the center with a wider arch through it."

"The bridge over the Grand Canal," he muttered, and looked at me sadly, his mouth a rigid arch too. "I don't think the leak is related to the dumbwaiter. I think it's related to the paintings. And if I'm right, there's someone at the hotel, other than the murderer, who is a danger to us."

"What? Who? Tell me."

"I will, but—oh—" He rubbed his stubbly jaw with a hand. "Miss Nichols—it will change everything between us."

Impossible, I thought.

He folded his hands together in front of him and stared at the floor.

Mr. Fig wasn't a man of hesitation. Confidence radiated through everything he did, from running a meeting to firing an employee. But he was clearly afraid of something now. What was it?

"I'm sure you know this already, but I have all the respect in the world for you," I said. "I've never had a boss I liked so much. But no, that doesn't cover it. I like you as a person—"

"Please let me stop you before you give away any more words you'll want to take back."

I needed to see his eyes, but he looked away from me. "Mr. Fig, just what are you about to tell me?"

"I think someone has come to the hotel to haunt me. Unfortunately, if I'm going to help you understand who it is, you'll also have to hear about the worst thing I've ever done."

"It'll be okay," I said, but I wasn't at all sure.

He made a soft noise of disbelief in his throat. "I wish that we could sit down somewhere private at least."

"Me too. But whatever it is, I won't hold it against you."

"I appreciate that. I don't expect you to believe this, but I truly intended to tell you the whole story one day, when the time was right."

This was sounding more and more ominous. "Well, I'm sorry that you have to tell me now."

"What I give you, I surrender willingly."

The skin of my arms felt raw and cold. "I'm listening."

Dread and doubt crept into his eyes as he started speaking. "One day, when I was a young man working for your grandparents at the Morrow house, the kitchen plumbing began to leak.

I called a plumber, just as I did when you discovered the men's room leak a few days ago."

He swallowed. "The man arrived later that afternoon. I was unfamiliar with his company, but he wore a uniform with their insignia and seemed capable as he assessed the leak.

"I've gone over these moments so many times in the last few decades and agonized over my decision to trust him. If I had looked closer at his patch, would I have seen he'd sewn it on himself? If I had inspected his van, could I have known that he was not the man he pretended to be?"

"I shouldn't interrupt, but I think the answer to all of those questions is no," I said. "You couldn't have known. It sounds like you've been blaming yourself for something—whatever you're going to tell me next—that you had no control over."

"You've not heard the whole story yet."

"Okay, lay it on me." I began to think this event was one of those things Mr. Fig measured differently than most people, and I felt my chest relax. Whatever guilt he'd felt all these years, it was a result of his extremely exacting standards.

"The plumber began a conversation with me about baseball," Mr. Fig went on. "I realize now I should never have engaged in chitchat with a fellow service person, but I was less discriminating then.

"We talked about the season the Braves were having. Soon we were 'cutting up' like old friends. It was late by the time he finished replacing the section of corroded pipe, and I had chores to finish upstairs. He said he needed to get into the boiler room.

"And so"—he sighed heavily—"and so I lent him my keys and told him to see himself out through the service entrance when he finished. Later, I reached for my key ring to let myself into the wine cellar."

At this point, Mr. Fig paused, crossing his arms and uncrossing them again. "And I realized he'd never given them back."

Where was all of this going? "He stole your keys? And they would let him open anything in the house?"

"Yes, but I couldn't admit that to myself right away. I was anxious over having been careless but hoped I would find them lying around somewhere later. It was purely embarrassment that kept me from reporting the loss to my manager or anyone else.

"Then the next morning, without any sign of a break-in, the family discovered a dozen paintings were missing from their walls."

"The plumber used your keys to get in and steal the paintings in the middle of the night?"

"I believe so."

A dozen paintings. Judging by the quality of the work the thief had left behind, the ones they took must have been worth hundreds of thousands of dollars, maybe millions altogether. "But it wasn't your fault he stole your keys. And surely the thief would have found a way inside the house anyway."

"Perhaps, but I haven't told you the worst of it yet, and you see—the theft was a perfect crime," he said. "With no sign of forced entry, the only suspects were members of the household and their employees."

"So they thought it was *you*?"

He shook his head. "I wish they had. If my own neck had been on the line, perhaps I would have done what I should have and told the investigator everything I knew. Instead the family suspected a young maid. They had no proof to make an arrest, but your grandfather fired her, and I've carried that guilt too."

My lips parted, but I had no words ready to come out. Mr. Fig was telling me he had been . . . dishonest. It was hard to picture him as a young man, as anyone less whole than his current self. But a woman was fired because of his lies. And besides that, what if telling the police what he knew about the theft could have helped the family track down the thief? How many future thefts might have been prevented?

"What happened to the paintings?" I asked.

"They were never found, and I'm sorry to say that their loss cost your family dearly at a time when the Morrow fortunes were already falling."

I thought of my grandparents' faces, pictured them staring at the blank walls where their paintings would have been, feeling betrayed by their own staff, unsafe in their own house. Mr. Fig could have saved them that heartache.

"I know it was wrong, and I don't expect you to forgive me, Miss Nichols. At the time I wondered if perhaps God had given me a clean slate. I thanked him and vowed that if he let me continue to live as a free man, I would earn enough to repay my debt to the Morrows."

"And did you?"

"Unfortunately, no," he said. "They were already in dire straits financially, and I'm sad to tell you that in the year following the horrible incident for which I am responsible, your grandfather suffered a mental break. Your grandmother took over for him, when it came to business matters, but it was ultimately a lost cause."

"Why? She wasn't any good at it?"

"Ms. Mary managed quite capably with the investments and the business still remaining in the family's hands at the time. However, three years after your grandfather's lapse came Black Monday."

"What's Black Monday?" I asked.

"October 19, 1987, the stock market crash. I believe the family lost everything then. Your grandfather suffered a heart attack the next day. He never recovered."

I knew Mr. Fig was not responsible for the stock market crash or my grandfather's heart attack, but hearing the details linked together this way faked a causal relationship for a moment in my heart, as if my grandparents would still be here if Mr. Fig had simply confessed what he knew about that plumber.

My stomach turned over, and I couldn't look up at Mr. Fig again. "So . . ."

I had to reach to remember why he had begun this sad tale. "So, you think the painting thief is back, starting the leak and leaving those pictures for you? Why? To torment you?"

"*Paulatim ergo certe.* Slowly, therefore surely. The drawings are meant to represent two of the stolen paintings, capricci of Venice by Francesco Guardi."

"That's clever. But why now, after all this time?"

"I imagine the money he earned from the sale of the paintings on the black market dried up long ago, especially if he split it with his associates. He's going to blackmail me."

"But who would care about this secret besides me? Who would this thief out you to if you refused to pay?"

"That's exactly why I had to warn you," Mr. Fig said. "He must be aware that you are the family's descendant."

It made me sick to consider it, but I wondered if this blackmailer's goals, in part, aligned with my own. He also needed to clear Mr. Fig's name if he expected to be paid.

"These people rarely operate only one con, Miss Nichols. I wouldn't be surprised if he reached out to me or you in the next day or so offering to reveal evidence that would point the finger elsewhere if I pay up. He'll make money any way he can."

My shoulders had taken up residence beside my ears. I lowered them with effort and took one slow, deep breath.

Mr. Fig was usually right about things, whether due to his sensitive moral compass, some innate wisdom, a lifetime of experience, or some combination of the three. If he thought this person was present and a threat to us, I would aim at least part of my attention in that direction.

"All right, tell me everything you remember about that plumber."

XIV
The Spell Begins to Break

∾

Mr. Fig's confession simmered in my thoughts as I drove up Lookout Mountain again. He had, at least in some small way, betrayed my family, but I hated that his mistake had weighed on him for so long. I realized now that I'd considered Mr. Fig faultless all this time, which was naïve and stupid of me. He was capable of miscalculations, like anyone.

I remembered how, standing in the snow a few nights before, he'd warned me about digging into the histories of people I loved. He couldn't have known at that moment that he'd have to tell me this story in a few days' time. He couldn't have been talking about himself . . . unless, like he said, he'd already planned to tell me one day when the time seemed right to him.

Still, I found myself wondering, over and over, if anything would have been different for my family had the paintings been recovered, had the investigator known which direction to look.

I wished I could ask my mother how the change in the family's fortunes affected her. How it had felt to lose her father at a young age.

Eventually the crenelated tower of Covenant College's campus rose above a hill on my right. The historic main building had been a magnificent hotel itself from the late 1920s to the middle of the century.

I drove a little farther down the road, parked by the newer brown-brick student apartments, and found Selena's dorm. I'd called in a favor from an old coworker who was a Covenant student to get her room number.

Selena had reasons to hold me at arm's length. Not only was I showing up here without warning, but she'd caught me spying on her dad too.

We were of the same generation, but in the last year of my twenties, I was supposed to be at a different life stage than her, and I wasn't.

Given those gems, I was pretty sure we weren't going to strike up an automatic friendship.

My only hope was to take her side when it came to the conflict with her dad. And given all of those same gems, I had a handle on how to do that.

Selena's face showed neither surprise nor suspicion when she answered the door. "Ivy, right?"

She left it wide open as if to say *Come on in*, so I did.

Her eight-by-ten dorm room was decorated mostly in green and white with a simple quilt on the bed and some signs with words like *Resist* and *Rise Up* tacked to the walls. It smelled of vanilla body spray and was disappointingly boring for a girl who was supposedly unstable and hostile toward her father.

She had no teakettle or coffeemaker, so there was nothing she could offer me, even if she wanted to, and that made things awkward. How I craved something to hold.

She sat down on the bed, leaving me her desk chair, I supposed. It sat at the foot of her bed, piled with papers and books. "Mind if I move these?"

"That's fine." Her words were monotone, as if she seemed uninterested in me or anything I was doing.

There was hardly another place to put the stack. I commandeered a suitcase in the corner. "Are you going out of town soon?"

"No."

Her phone rang. She pulled it out of her back pocket, silenced it, and turned the phone facedown on the quilt beside her.

I got things moving. "I wanted to come talk to you because I'm looking for help."

Always appeal to the heart. People wanted to help. Most people. Probably even the ones who didn't offer you places to sit down in their dorm rooms.

"All right." She stood and walked over to her desk.

Her back was to me, but I heard a drawer open and the crackle of plastic.

She took a sip from a water bottle and threw back her head. "You okay?" I said.

She turned around, nodded, and sat back down on the bed.

I began explaining to her that Mr. Fig was a good friend and that I was trying to prove his innocence.

She listened with her eyes, but there was little compassion in them.

"I know Renee wasn't a good person." I really didn't. "But Mr. Fig is, and I think you may be able to give me information that would free him."

"I'm not sure how I can help, honestly."

"Well." *Easy now. Don't spook her.* "I'm sure your dad isn't perfect. No one is. But I don't know him. I'm sorry if this isn't cool, but do you think . . ."

The twist of her mouth told me she'd gotten my gist. She looked thoughtful but not offended by the suggestion that her father might have killed someone.

Her phone vibrated this time, and she checked it but didn't answer or text back.

"I mean." She shrugged, eyes on her phone. "I don't know if he's a murderer, but he's a liar. He promised me he wouldn't marry her, and then he proposed anyway, and he didn't even tell me. Autumn did."

Now *that* was suspicious. It seemed intentionally hurtful when Autumn must have known the news would upset Selena. And what other point would there be in telling her if Renee had turned him down?

"I'm sorry," I said. "That sucks."

She typed something into her phone with her thumbs. "He made me come to school here too. He loves this place."

"Has your dad ever said anything negative to you about Renee?"

"No. He wouldn't. He was trying so hard to get me to like her." She glanced at the bathroom door and back at me. "He's been so paranoid lately. First, thinking my mom is vandalizing his house, and then the thing with Dr. Chaves, and he keeps talking about how he can't say anything anymore."

"Wait. Leonard Chaves?"

"Yeah. Dad thinks he's after his job." She put her phone down again and swallowed hard.

"And what do you mean that your dad can't say anything?"

"Like the way he's so upset that he has to use words like *member of Congress* instead of *Congressman*, or how he doesn't understand why some people don't want to celebrate Columbus Day."

"Oh, yeah, I get it. *Okay, boomer.*"

"Exactly." She raised her voice, excited. "I try to tell him he's not in the Bible Belt anymore."

"And that he's not in the twentieth century anymore."

"Oh my God. *Yes.*"

Now I had put myself on her team. I could dig in. "So did you visit him at his hotel room? I mean, at Hotel 1911 . . . before the murder?"

"Uh-uh."

I wondered if she'd admit to whatever she'd been doing in the conservatory last night. "So you haven't been to the hotel at all then?"

"No." She shrugged.

She was a good liar. But the hairs I'd found in the Achilles room didn't come close to matching anyone else. I had brought them with me. I just had to find a way to compare them to hers without being really creepy.

"Has your dad ever threatened to hurt anyone?" I asked. "Is he jealous?"

"I mean, no, he hasn't threatened to hurt anyone specifically, but he's definitely made some people uncomfortable, like if my mom talked to another man. I don't want you to think she's perfect either, but she's justifiably angry." She got up, grabbed her water bottle from the desk, and leaned against the wall.

"About what?"

"I didn't—" She blinked hard and swallowed again. "I just mean like any other ex-wife who stayed a little too long, you know?"

"Yeah, I think I do." I didn't want to make this about me, but I couldn't help thinking of my mother, who hadn't stayed. "So your mom was angry, and your dad said someone's been tearing up his house."

"It couldn't be her, though, because at least one of those times she was here, staying with me."

I nodded. I believed her.

"Anyway," Selena went on, "Renee probably had plenty of enemies."

"Why?"

"Like I said. She was horrible." Selena rubbed her head and let it rest on the wall.

"Are you sure you're okay?"

She swatted away my concern. "Renee does the hiring, *did* the hiring, for Autumn's company, and she exploited undocumented workers."

"Oh, I see. It's some kind of security that Autumn does, right?"

She scratched one arm. "Like security guards for businesses and stuff, not cybersecurity."

A twinge of doubt pricked my thoughts. Selena was really forthcoming about everyone other than herself.

I set it aside for now and thought of the mysterious money Clyde had hassled Autumn about. "Does your father have anything to do with Autumn's company?"

"Autumn was a student of his, and then when she started her company, he became an investor. That's how Dad met Renee, actually."

"Oh. So that's why Autumn owes your dad money?"

She shrugged and took a sip of water.

"And why did Autumn fire your mom?"

"Autumn accused Mom of stealing, but my mom wouldn't have done that. In fact, I have it on good authority that Renee had something to do with it."

Hmm. If Selena's mom was fired for something Renee was guilty of, would Selena have sought revenge? Or maybe Selena and her mother were in on it together. "Is your mom in town now?"

She shook her head.

"What about Autumn? Do you like her?"

"I don't know. We kind of bonded over my dad, I guess."

"Because neither of you wanted him and Renee together?"

"Yeah. I think Autumn couldn't stand to let Renee live her life without her constant input. She loved finally getting to be her boss for real." Selena lifted her weight off the wall, and her long hair swung forward as she lost her balance and tipped forward.

I reached out instinctively to catch her, but she got her feet under her and fell back against the wall again.

She covered her mouth. "Sorry."

"Are you sick? Do you want me to leave?" I said.

She looked back at me, narrowing her eyes as if she didn't understand what I was saying.

"Are you okay?" I said. "Should you lay down?"

Without answering, she stared at the bathroom door.

I wondered if the suitcase belonged not to Selena but someone else. And if that someone might be hiding in the bathroom.

Keeping an eye on her, I leapt up and threw open the bathroom door. There was no one inside, not a mother from Pennsylvania nor a cousin from Tahiti. I closed the door behind me and checked behind the shower curtain. Empty there too.

I came out of the bathroom, and Selena seemed unfazed by my behavior.

Standing in the middle of the room now, she wore the strangest blank expression.

"Selena?"

She turned her head toward where her phone lay on the bed, took a step, and her body crumpled to the floor.

"Selena!" I yelled.

She lay facedown without moving.

I dropped beside her and rolled her onto her side.

Her eyes didn't open.

I shook her gently.

She still wouldn't wake.

Her mouth opened, and a rust-colored flow puddled onto the carpet.

I snatched my phone from my bag and dialed 911.

* * *

After I told the 911 operator where to find us and made sure Selena was still breathing and lying on her side where she couldn't choke, I turned to her desk.

From the sound of the plastic when she'd stood here and the way she'd thrown her head back, I was sure she must have taken something.

I opened a couple of drawers before I found a sandwich bag of white pills.

Was she on something for her mood? And if so, why didn't she have a prescription bottle?

If she hadn't come by these pills legitimately, the drug might have been tainted with something that had made her sick. Or she might have taken too much.

The pills were too generic looking for me to identify.

Next, I went for her phone.

The screen was locked.

She'd silenced it twice and looked uncomfortable doing it. I didn't want to pry, but if this had anything to do with Renee's death, I had to know. And I wouldn't know until I pried.

I took a bet that the phone was protected with facial recognition, pressed a button, and held it up to Selena's face.

Bingo. I was a wizard.

Her last two calls were from *Tom*. No last name. Tom Truman?

I thought of his wife's suspicions about him when they talked outside the Achilles room the night before. Plus there'd been the name Truman on Bennett's office calendar and the enormous footprints outside Clyde's cottage window.

Was the eavesdropper a literal peeping Tom? Had he been at the cottage because Selena was there? Watching her? Or waiting for her? And why?

We had only minutes until the ambulance got here. I put Selena's phone in her pocket and took from mine the hairs I'd found in Clyde and Renee's room.

I stretched a couple of blond strands out beside hers. The color matched well enough.

But they were too long. Unless she'd had a haircut in the last two days, they couldn't belong to her. I sat back, mystified.

I heard a siren outside before much longer, and I met the paramedics at the door, handed them the bag of pills from Selena's desk, and told them everything I knew.

I was allowed to ride in the ambulance as it sped her to the hospital, but when they took her back to a room, I had to stay behind in the waiting area. It was strange to be back here after only a few days.

In half an hour, they let me go back and see the patient. The door was propped open. A nurse at the bedside took Selena's temperature and made notes on a chart.

Selena was pale, kind of greenish, but otherwise looked normal, sitting up and texting. Cords stretched from her to a couple of screens nearby. Their regular beeping was probably a good sign, but it unnerved me like the shriek of an alarm clock. *Eek. Eek. Eek.*

She spotted me standing inside the door. "Oh, hey. Thanks for calling 911 or whatever."

"Yeah. Glad to. Are you feeling better?"

"I'm fine." Selena was especially calm, considering what she'd just been through.

"Do your parents know you're here?" I asked.

Before she could answer, a voice behind me said, "I'm glad you were with her."

I nearly jumped out of my skinny jeans.

Clyde came out of the adjoining bathroom. His sleeves were turned up, and a coffee stain marked the front of his shirt. I imagined him holding a mug in one hand and answering Selena's call with the other.

"Hey, Dad, don't freak out, but I'm in the ER," she would've said.

Exactly the kind of call I was used to making.

Selena's attention turned to her father. An almost physical anger bonded them across the room.

I seemed to have interrupted their latest battle.

Selena lived more than five hundred miles from Clyde, but if she had wrecked her car just to stick it to him, as Autumn had said, then maybe Selena hadn't done a great job of individuating from him.

Individuation was a hundred-dollar word I had learned in therapy. (I may have overpaid.) Jung talked about it as the process of merging the conscious and unconscious minds. When it came to controlling parents, individuation was more about a child's process of defining the self apart from the parent, often by delineating boundaries.

I backed toward the door, positive that my presence was unwelcome. I would probably hear them outside the room anyway.

"Don't leave, Ivy," Selena said. "You'll miss Dad yelling at me again."

Clyde shook his head and huffed. "You're playing with fire, little girl."

"I'm not a little girl." Selena jabbed the words at her dad. "*You're* just mad that I did something without your approval."

"And look where it landed you."

"I have anxiety!" she shouted. "I have to take something for it. You want me to just ignore it and pretend it will go away?"

Oh, I could see it now. The pills probably caused the apathy I'd seen from her, and the prickly attitude was likely a defense mechanism. I felt for her. This thing we shared was all too common.

He stepped toward her bed and aimed his finger at her like a pistol, firing off each word emphatically. "*I* want to know what *happened*. You did this to get back at me, so at least do me the favor of telling me what I did this time."

"Oh, right, like I overdosed on purpose." She threw a hand in the air. "Why is everything always about you?"

"Listen, we all have passive-aggressive moments." He'd shifted his tone now. It was softer, conciliatory even, but a sorry attempt to hide his anger. "And it's not surprising, given the way your mother handles conflict—"

"No. You're the one who justifies hurting people to make them do what you want. What you think is best for them." Selena turned onto her side away from him, or as much as she could with the cords attached to her.

"You're not thinking straight." He stood, his upper lip snarled. "I'll come back when your pills have worn off."

She pushed herself up halfway to sitting. "You can't deal with the world leaving you behind. You can't deal with Mom leaving you. Is that why Renee had to die? You couldn't control her either? And what will you do when you finally realize that you don't own *me*?"

"That's enough!" Clyde ushered me toward the door. "Ivy, wait outside for me."

Bossy, I thought, but I left just like he'd said. I needed to stay on the man's good side.

We were finally getting somewhere. He seemed in a mood to talk, and if so, I might finally find whatever was at the bottom of his story.

I played around with my phone in the hall, hoping I might hear something of their father-daughter exchange.

Surely, if Selena's mother were in town, she'd have been here now too. Unless she had some reason to hide from everyone—say, if she was guilty of a crime. I kept thinking about that suitcase in Selena's room. It seemed like Selena had simply been looking at the bathroom because she felt sick, nothing to do with a visitor.

In a few minutes, Clyde slipped out of Selena's room and headed for me. He couldn't stand still, jamming his hands in his pockets and looking like whatever he had to say was stuck in his throat.

"So do you really think she OD'd on purpose?" I asked. "Or was this purely accidental?"

He stared darkly as if a threat were waiting down the hall. A fluorescent light flickered over his head. "I need to make Selena safe."

It was like he hadn't heard me. "Clyde."

He glanced at me.

"Help me make sense of this," I said. "Was there something wrong with the pills she took, or—"

"They weren't on my insurance." He shook his head. "She couldn't have gotten them from a doctor. I don't—yes, there's probably something wrong with them."

"So she won't say where she got them?" I said.

"She's—" Clyde stopped speaking as a doctor passed us. "No, she won't say. I don't know if she's protecting someone else or herself."

"Or if whoever gave her those pills was trying to hurt her?"

He crossed his arms and clenched them until his hands went white.

"Or hurt you?" I said.

"I . . ." His face contorted.

"Are you hurting . . . for *money*, Clyde?"

I'd hoped to catch him off guard, but he merely looked confused.

"Divorces are expensive, right?" I said.

He turned away by a degree.

I reached into my bag, pulled out the book of Browning poetry, and thrust it at his stomach.

He started as if waking up and looked back and forth from me to the book. The muscles of his face contorted as if from fear, and he stepped back. "What is that?"

"That's what I'm asking you, Professor."

He shook his head but still wouldn't take it from me. "Where'd you get it?"

"Is it yours?"

"No!" He threw up his hands.

"It's about time to fess up, don't you think?"

"Confess? To what?"

"I think I can find out who did this. But you have to come clean. Tell me what you know."

He took the book from my hands gingerly, opened the front cover, and relaxed his shoulders an inch. "I guess it was only a matter of time before someone made this connection."

He thought I knew more than I actually did. That book was somehow incriminating for him.

Tread carefully, Ivy. "I finally put the pieces together."

"But how? I fixed it." His chest convulsed and chopped his breath into pieces.

If he wasn't a guilty man, then I wasn't Ivy Nichols. But guilty of what, exactly? "Yeah. I thought so. When you came back from the tour?"

He screwed up his mouth in acknowledgment, but he clearly wasn't proud of what he'd done. "It only took a second."

Turning from me, Clyde began his pacing again. "But I only did it because I was framed. I would've been arrested! You've got to understand that."

"Of course." What had he done that "only took a second"?

"This whole thing is a . . . a show," he said. "The wig, the poem, the fire. It's all meant to point to me, to my work."

The wig? The one Bea had found in the men's room? Was it connected to the blond hairs I'd found in the Achilles? But which poem? And what did he mean "the fire"?

"Your work?" I asked.

"Yes. My dissertation."

"The dissertation that everyone loved you for? But that had to be, what, thirty years ago?"

"Almost forty."

"So who framed you?"

"I . . . I don't know . . . I—I saw Tom and Renee in some kind of heated discussion the day before she died. But he's too stupid to frame me like this."

Was Tom really too stupid? Or was he smart enough to play dumb? "Is there some reason that Tom would be calling Selena? Are they close?"

Squinting at me, he said, "He was calling her? You're sure about that?"

"I don't know. It might have been some other Tom."

He took a long breath, turning one way and then the other, like he was desperate to do something but didn't know what it should be.

The only thing keeping me from feeling sorry for him was the idea that this might all be a con.

He looked at the poetry book in his hands, then held it up like he might hit me with it. "Where did you get this?"

"Someone left it for me to find."

A door opened at the end of the hall, and a monitor's alarm assaulted the air.

"Well, there's your answer. You find that person, Ivy, and you find the person who framed me, the person who murdered Renee, the person who knows you're on their trail."

I held my breath. I could see where this was going. "Whoever put that book on my desk was pointing me to you."

"Yes, and if you don't take the bait, Ivy—" He stepped closer and stabbed a finger toward me to enunciate his words. "If you don't look like you're on my trail and no one else's, you may be in serious danger."

XV

Back on This Side of the Door

~

Clyde said he was stepping outside to smoke and left me in the hallway. I was still thinking about Selena's anxiety and what I'd learned about myself that might help her.

I knocked softly on her door and, when there was no answer, peeked in to find her sleeping. I jotted a few quick resources down—websites and my therapist's info—on the hospital stationery along with my phone number and a few well wishes for her.

It was noon by the time I walked out, and seeing the lines of cars in the parking lot, I realized I didn't have a ride . . . or a plan.

Going back to the hotel was always a good idea, but I'd have to hoof it, and the sole of my foot was already smarting despite the Band-Aid and thick sock I'd put on over the strawberry this morning. And the pain from my stove injury had me feeling like one of the hotel statues that had a hairline crack cutting through one arm.

The day had turned overcast along with my mood, and maybe that was the only reason I had a growing sense of being watched as I weaved through the parked vehicles toward the road.

It was more obvious now than ever that the killer, whether that was Clyde or someone else, knew I was hunting them. If Clyde was guilty, he thought he'd misdirected me with the attempt on Selena's life and the story of being framed. If the killer was anyone else, they needed to believe I thought Clyde was guilty.

"There you are," said a tall, dark-headed man several yards away.

I started, then realized it was only George. "Hey!"

His face began to relax as he picked up his pace to reach me. "So you're not hurt?"

"No, Selena Borough was. How'd you know I was here?"

"I overheard Tom Truman taking a call in the dining room. He said enough for me to understand that you and Selena had ended up here."

Hmm. Had Selena called him back? "What was he doing in the dining room? You haven't started serving lunch or something?"

"No, he was working on his laptop."

"Laptop?" I blinked. "Doing *what*?"

"I don't know. It looked like a bunch of Excel spreadsheets, maybe for his personal budget or taxes . . ." He clicked his key fob, and the lights flashed on his new gray Toyota Highlander that had replaced his old gray Toyota Highlander last week.

I actually missed the familiar smell of the old one. I caught him up on what had happened at the college as I got in and buckled up.

"What do you think about Tom?" I said.

"Well, I don't like anybody who brings a Hostess cupcake into my dining room."

"I thought he was kind of slow, but now I wonder."

"He's quiet," George said. "But that's not the same as simple."

"I agree. And Autumn seems too smart to have married a dummy."

"Do we believe Autumn about Selena?" He turned the key in the ignition. "Because if we do, Selena's a mess, and she had reasons for wanting to hurt her father."

"You think she may have overdosed on purpose? That's what Clyde said too."

"I don't know her, but . . ." He shrugged.

"Hey, do you mind driving me over to the police station? There's something I think Bennett needs to see."

"Yeah." He aimed the car in that direction as we pulled out of the parking lot.

De Luna's complete absence from this case still rankled. I wished there was someone there I could trust. But all I had was Bennett.

While we drove, I explained how I'd found the dumbwaiter and the torn piece of plaid. At home, I'd written out an explanation for Bennett and signed my name to it, thinking even as I did that he was so biased against me I might as well throw it in the trash myself.

When we got to the station, I took out the envelope where I'd sealed the fabric and the note.

"You're sure you shouldn't hang on to that?" George said.

"I have a picture of it, and if there's DNA on the material, it could benefit Mr. Fig, and that might be the only hard evidence I find. The police probably can't use it, officially, but it might at least prove something to Bennett, if he's willing to listen."

"That'll be a long shot," he said. "What about De Luna?"

"On vacation." I sighed.

Inside the station, I handed the envelope to the officer at the front desk, and when I came back outside, I spotted George at a popsicle stand in the next parking lot over.

I walked to meet him, noticing that on the horizon, gray clouds were building a bridge between Lookout and Signal Mountain.

George turned around with two pale yellow pops in his hands and passed me one.

"Mm. Thanks. Orange?"

"Pineapple saffron."

"*Of* course."

We strolled toward the car.

"Ugh," he said. And turned his head to pick his teeth.

I looked away.

"Sorry," he said. "There was, like, this one long yellow string of pineapple wound through my teeth."

My ears pricked, and I didn't know why. I stopped and looked around.

"What?" George said.

"What did you just say?"

"There was pineapple caught in my teeth." He took another step toward the car.

"No." I grabbed his arm. "You said, 'one long yellow string wound through your teeth.' "

"Okay." He looked at me like my popsicle had been spiked with something.

"That's it. Oh my word. That's it, George."

I pulled the book of Browning's poetry from my bag and flipped through.

" 'Porphyria's Lover,' " I said aloud, and the whole picture flooded my brain. I sat down on a parking block.

The narrator waits for his lover in the dark. Porphyria comes in out of the rain, lights a fire in the hearth, and sits down with him.

I scanned the open page on my lap and read fast and loud.

That moment she was mine, mine, fair,
Perfectly pure and good: I found
A thing to do, and all her hair
In one long yellow string I wound
Three times her little throat around.

I paused for dramatic effect. *"And strangled her."*

"What's going on, Ivy?" He studied my face like it had sprouted polka dots.

"This book was left for me, George. Someone wants me to know that this murder was meant to look like the poem."

"What?" George said.

"We read it in sophomore English. Do you remember?" The class had kinda loved it because before that *some* of us had thought poetry was all lovey-dovey nonsense. (Okay, me. I thought that.) "The long blond wig. The fire. The Victorian poetry. The strangulation with a soft, broad garrote. It all fits."

"You're saying this was some kind of . . . literary copycat murder?" George cocked his head.

"Yes!" I bounced back up to standing. "It's why Clyde said he'd been framed. He teaches Victorian poetry."

"Weird," George said slowly.

"Yeah. And he admitted to tampering with the crime scene before the police arrived. I think he took the wig to keep anyone from making the connection."

"*Would* they make the connection, though? Bennett's not that insightful."

"I don't know. Maybe anyone so wrapped up in their field that they would stage a murder like this wouldn't see that the metaphor isn't obvious to everyone. For instance, I happen to know this chef who throws around terms like *coulis* and *remouillage* as if they aren't obscure culinary jargon." I threw him a pointed glance.

He laughed. "Busted. But what about the framing aspect? Is there any reason to believe Clyde on that?"

"Only that he led the tour, so he's the least likely of all the gravestone society to have been able to get away at the right time."

"And why would the killer commit the murder at a time when Clyde is the least likely suspect if their goal was to frame him?" George said.

"Your popsicle's dripping."

"It's a *paleta*."

I rolled my eyes and took another bite of mine. "Because it wasn't supposed to be him leading the tour."

"And they couldn't change plans once they realized Clyde was substituting for him?"

"Maybe." I said. "Or maybe the killer decided Clyde's iron-tight alibi actually added credibility. In other words, *wouldn't* Clyde plan ahead of time to cover his tracks?"

"To make it seem like he wasn't guilty? Yeah. Smart."

"I am smart." I grinned annoyingly in his face. "Unfortunately, now I have to consider not only who would want to hurt Renee, but also who had a vendetta against Clyde."

"Our suspect list just doubled."

"And the gravestone convention ends tonight," I said, eyeing the faraway storm cloud. "They'll all check out tomorrow."

A distant peal of thunder punctuated my words.

* * *

George and I left the police station for the convention center. It was a newish building adjoining a Marriott off the interstate downtown. And it was where the Association for Gravestone Studies, including the Gravestone Friends of Greater Pittsburgh, would be right about now.

Tom Truman's name had popped into three separate conversations today, and I wanted to talk to him.

We followed the long hill of Fourth Street down to the City Center. Besides those thunderheads threatening in the distance, it was a lovely day, maybe the first nice weekend of spring, and that meant the sidewalks were crowded with merrymakers breaking free from the gloom of the long winter. Every time we stopped at a light, pedestrians crossed in front of us, some of them wearing flip-flops, as if their choice of footwear would bring on summer faster.

George parked the Highlander on the street behind the city library, a 1970s, modernish block of concrete and glass. He paid the meter, and we walked the block to the convention center, the sidewalks humming as we got closer with people enthusiastically carrying notebooks and laptop bags.

Inside, a mass of taphophiles chattered in the lobby—or what would be a better collective noun for grave enthusiasts? A cemetery of taphophiles? A graveyard of taphophiles?

Scaled for a city as small as Chattanooga, the building would be dwarfed by the convention centers of New York or even Atlanta. But this beautiful vestibule was so spacious that it made me feel like I wasn't in my hometown anymore. The roof, which had to be thirty or so feet high, was supported by a long row of metal trestles. Dozens of strategically placed windows overhead filled the room with natural light.

Booths set up for the conference along one wall advertised ground-penetrating radar services, sold books on mapping and preservation, and offered bumper stickers that read *I brake for old graveyards*. The "Visit Chattanooga" tourism people were well represented too.

A café cart was set up in the lobby, its espresso machine's roar accompanying the conference babble.

"They must be between sessions," George said. "Maybe that will make it easier to find Tom."

I'd told him on the way here about the mysterious calls to Selena's phone and that I wanted to find out what Tom was up to with a woman less than half his age.

The conference commotion rivaled my own stir of thoughts. Were we getting closer to the truth or farther away? I couldn't tell. We had so little time left, and I didn't want to waste it.

George raised his voice over the noise. "We should split up."

"But we're not even dating." I winked.

"Very funny, Tina Fey. You go one way. I'll go the other. We'll find Tom faster that way."

"Right, of course." I stepped back to accommodate two women carrying a clear acrylic box with an ancient-looking tombstone inside.

"I'll text you." George nodded a good-bye and disappeared into the crowd.

The conference center had a fancy map in the lobby, and I began to peruse it.

"Program?" someone said beside me.

It was Leonard Chaves, holding out a pamphlet and looking entirely unsurprised to see me. Set against the noise of the convention center, his voice seemed even softer than before.

"Uh, hi." I took the schedule from him. "Thanks."

"Did you get curious about our goings-on?" He wore a lanyard covered in smiley faces to hold his name tag.

"Yeah, I guess so. I've never known any gravers before."

He didn't reply but didn't walk away either.

"You know I'm trying to figure out who murdered Renee."

I didn't know why I said it. He just seemed trustworthy.

He nodded and looked down.

"Do you know anything about the leak on Wednesday night?" I said. "It was about nine or ten o'clock."

He shook his head.

I thought back to that night. "You ate in the dining room that night, didn't you? And then you hung out in the drawing room a while."

"Looking at the art, yes. You have some very fine nineteenth-century oils in there."

The crowd had thinned around us, drawn like mourners to their next sessions.

"Have you seen Tom Truman this afternoon?" I asked.

He shook his head again, the dark widow's peak making the movement more pronounced than it should have been.

"Well . . . thanks anyway," I said, and walked away, flipping through the paper he'd given me.

There were lists of exhibits and daily schedules of presentations and classes, including evening lectures. It was nearly two o'clock, which meant the sessions on "seventeenth-century symbology," "cast-iron gravemarkers," and "cemetery mapping with aerial drones" were about to begin.

Yawn.

Where would I find Tom? He didn't seem the academic type.

On the conference map, a stone-carving room was indicated well away from the lecture area. Tactile labor seemed just the activity for a burly guy.

Once I started down the right hallway, the room was easy to track down. I followed the stream of tap-tap-tapping, which I imagined was the sound of a hammer and chisel. There was a high-pitched roar as I got closer, too, like a vacuum.

I peeked through the glass in the door.

The source of the roar was a cylindrical machine in the corner with various fat, corrugated tubes running out to what appeared to be gravestone-carving stations.

I guessed they'd be called carving stations. Funny how different the meaning of that phrase would be in the context of a Golden Corral.

The workshop was empty of people except for a thin woman wearing a dust mask and safety glasses, leaning over a work bench. She turned to aim her chisel in a different direction on the headstone in front of her, and I recognized her as Autumn Truman.

I considered my options.

I'd had a plan in mind for talking to Tom, but not her. I didn't think she had killed her own sister, but I had to admit there was a chance, and based on Clyde's warning at the hospital, I couldn't afford to stir up her suspicions against me.

She took a small, dry brush and swept off the stone, stood back to examine it, and then picked up her hammer and chisel again.

Heavy footsteps sounded at the end of the hallway.

It was Tom himself coming toward me and taking a bite of some kind of wrap or burrito he held with one hand.

I stepped away from the door and tried seeming nonchalant.

A look of recognition rather than suspicion crossed his face, and I felt relieved. "Hi, Mr. Truman."

He nodded wordlessly.

"It's Ivy." I smiled.

He grunted and grabbed the door handle.

"I have some bad news for you, unfortunately," I said quickly.

Tom turned around, clearly interested.

"It's about Selena," I said.

Tom lowered his eyebrows, more confused than concerned.

"I just came from the hospital with her," I said. "It looks like she took some bad pills."

Tom went rigid, and a deep wrinkle split his wide forehead in two. "She okay?"

The door opened beside us, and Autumn stepped out into the hall, hammer and chisel still in hand. "Ivy?"

She pushed her safety glasses back into her stone-dusted red hair and looked at Tom. "What's going on?"

He shrugged.

"Selena's at the hospital, and Clyde is with her," I said.

Autumn watched her husband's face. "And why are you talking to my husband about it?"

Her harshness intimidated me as much as his size. But I had to go for it. "Did you know Tom was at Clyde's cottage at the same time you and I were yesterday?"

Her gray eyes flickered with alarm.

"And did you know that Clyde's been threatening your wife about the money?" I asked Tom.

She stepped toward me and pushed the hammer into my chest. "What do you know about the money?"

I backed away from her and right into the privacy of the stone-carving room. My blood was a whitewater rapid in my veins. "I just mean his investment."

She followed me into the room, small but menacing, and Tom loomed behind her, blocking out the light of the hall.

"Whatever Selena's told you, it's all lies," he said.

"So why were you calling her?" I asked.

Autumn glared at him, even more interested in the question than I was. "Were you at the cottage to see *Selena*?"

"Look, she's tryin' to blackmail us," Tom spit out. "Linda was mad when you fired her, and she told Selena that Renee was hiring illegals."

Autumn stiffened, and horror overtook her face. "Illegals, Tom? Why didn't you tell *me*? Renee said all their paperwork was good, and I . . . I didn't check. I just believed her."

"I'm sorry." Tom couldn't meet her eyes. "I was gonna tell you."

"So she's threatening to report me to ICE?" Autumn said.

Tom nodded.

"And you were negotiating with her?" Autumn said.

He nodded again, his gaze still on her feet.

"But what leverage do you have?" Autumn dug her head forward.

"Look, I don't have a plan really." Tom shrugged. "I just knew I had to try to stop her."

"Didn't you fire Selena's mother because you thought she was stealing from you?" I asked Autumn.

Autumn backed up and lowered her hammer by her side. "I wasn't happy about that, especially because my sister and Clyde met through the company—but the embezzlement had to be coming from someone in the office. Linda was the office manager."

"But the stealing continued?"

"Yes." Autumn gritted her teeth.

"Do you think Linda would hate Clyde or Renee enough to have committed murder?" I said.

Autumn threw up a hand, exasperated. "Look, I've been lying awake at that hotel every night, asking myself all these questions. I don't know about Linda. I don't know who's responsible."

She didn't break down and cry, but something in her face, set even more rigidly than I'd seen it before, made me buy that she was actually upset. Maybe she was doing all of her grieving in private. Some people had their emotions tightly reined in like that, but feelings as strong as the grief and rage she probably harbored had to come out eventually.

"Well," I said. "what I know is that the police have arrested the wrong person for your sister's murder, and that means the real killer is walking free."

"C'mon." Tom pulled her back by the shoulder, glaring at me. "Let's go get something to eat."

Eat? He had just downed a burrito. And why was he in such a hurry to get her away from me?

Autumn kept her eyes on me. "I'm sure there's nothing we can do that the police haven't."

I worried that she was right, but I tightened my jaw. "Maybe, but I'm not giving up until I've tried everything."

She didn't respond but let her husband lead her out of the room.

I stood there, frustrated that I couldn't get the answers I wanted.

I texted George that I'd found Tom and was headed back to the lobby.

Before I left the room, I took a peek at Autumn's work on the headstone. She'd carved a design at the top that looked like two overlapping infinity symbols. Below was Renee's name and the years of her birth and death. And under that was a simple line drawing still in progress, a pair of curved animal horns if I was right.

Before going to meet George, I took a picture with my phone in case there was some important symbolism here that would enlighten me later.

XVI
Dead Men Don't Wear Plaid

❧

There was more I needed to see now at the hotel, so George drove us there next.

He pushed a button on the dash. "Hey, you should pair your phone to the car so your music can play in here."

"Yeah, I guess I should." We both knew I was the one with the better music collection. I smiled and got out my phone. "Listen, I need to tell you something that Mr. Fig told me at the jail."

He eyed me seriously. "Is he retiring?"

"No," I said, a little too defensively, and then relayed the story about the theft of the paintings, noticing the whole time how I finagled the narrative to make our manager seem less suspicious. I felt protective of him even with George.

"Well," George said, "we always knew he had to have some skeletons hiding behind that freshly painted closet door, right?"

"Yeah."

He was right, and he was somehow able to look at Mr. Fig more objectively than I was. I realized I'd idolized Mr. Fig like a child would a parent, like when you're unwilling to see a person you love as fully human, as inevitably flawed.

"And now I have to figure out whether the killer started the leak to get me away from the desk so they could get to the dumbwaiter," I said. "Or whether Mr. Fig is right that the painting thief has returned and is trying to make him squirm."

"Do you think there's any way Clyde could be the painting thief?" George said. "He changed his story about being at the hotel when he was a student, right?"

I shook my head. "He seems too young for that. Mr. Fig said the thief was roughly his age and named Bob, but he doubts that was his real name. It's definitely suspicious that Clyde's lying, though."

"But who's not suspicious, honestly? Bunch of weirdos."

I laughed. "Yeah. According to Tom, Selena is trying to blackmail Autumn's company because her sister Renee was hiring illegal workers. Autumn owes Clyde money she can't pay, and Tom's hiding all kinds of things from his wife, I think."

George raised one eyebrow at me. "Pot, kettle."

"Well . . . yeah, I know all about hiding things, don't I?" I didn't let just anyone call me out on my faults, but George had earned the privilege.

The deeper I got into these people's lives, the more overwhelmed I was by signs that all seemed to point me in different directions. Who had given Selena those pills? Was one of the gravestone guests the thief threatening Mr. Fig? And did the thief have anything to do with Renee's death?

"So who was around the night of the leak?" George put on his blinker and turned onto Third Street.

"Right. That's a good question . . . Let's see, it happened just before Clyde and Renee and the Trumans—Autumn and Tom—checked in. Furnell Rogers and his son Parker got here earlier that afternoon, and so did the two older women—Velvet and Deena. I think Mr. Wollstone was already here too, and a family with kids . . . I can't remember their names."

"That's already a long list," he said.

"And then you can't rule out the people who aren't staying at the hotel, like Clyde's ex-wife or Selena. Either of them could have snuck in to create the leak." There was a hidden passage leading from the drawing room to the men's room. It had been secret at one time but was known to pretty much everyone now as one of the eccentricities of the place.

"Sneaked," he said.

I rolled my eyes emphatically.

"That's a lot of possibilities." He sighed.

"Do you think I can even get to the bottom of this?" I said. "They're all going home tomorrow. I won't be able to find out much more after that."

"You'll do it," he said. The way he said it, I believed him.

* * *

When we reached the hotel, George parked in the staff lot, and as we cut through the line of trees edging the eastern garden, I realized that I no longer thought of my mother every time I came this way—the numbing force of repetition, perhaps, or maybe a result of the work I'd been doing in therapy. Was it ironic that in realizing that I wasn't thinking about her, I was thinking about her?

We passed Mr. Zhang, on his knees, dividing the feathery hay-scented ferns that edged the tree line.

"Hang on a minute," I said to George.

"That's all right. I need to check something in the kitchen. I'll meet you in the storage room."

"Perfect. You can bring me back some kind of snack." I knelt down by the gardener on the gravel path. "Hi, Mr. Zhang."

The old man grunted, and his ears moved as if they too were disturbed by my interfering.

"I hate to interrupt," I continued. "But I wondered if you, as the person around here who spends the most time in the garden—"

He glanced up.

"—if you've seen graves with the names Hortensius and Mary Morrow?"

"Graves?" He stabbed his trowel into a clod of roots and soil.

"Yes, you know, the memorials? The inscriptions on the statues?"

"Mm, no. I don't pay any attention to the names. *The life of the dead is set in the memory of the living,*" he said ardently.

"Cicero?"

"Yes."

Ha. I was finally catching on. I was sure Mr. Zhang was pleased, but he only grunted as I said good-bye.

The phantom of Mr. Fig had lingered in every room of the hotel ever since his arrest but haunted the servant hall especially as I made my way to the elevator.

At the jail, he'd said that the Morrow family used to host special dinners for college students, something about fellowships or scholarships, and that there were a lot of photos of that kind of thing in the storage room.

He'd also told me where to find a key to the elevator's key box and therefore to the storeroom, not knowing I'd already had to break into the elevator box once.

Now that I thought about it, I didn't feel guilty about keeping that one detail from him when he'd kept so much from me.

His many charming mysteries, which I had always interpreted as stemming from his care for my family and the estate, looked like plain old secrets at the moment.

And yet, I wondered if that was just my disillusionment talking.

I wiped my face with my hand. I needed to refocus. I was the only one who had all the pieces.

The elevator opened, and I stepped in. I found the nickel I'd used to wedge the key cabinet shut, pinched the edge of it, and worked it out of the crack. The little door squealed open.

I felt heavier all at once. My feet pressed into the floor.

Someone had called the elevator.

Quickly, I closed the cabinet and slid the nickel back into place. It fell out again and landed on the floor. The cabinet door sprang open.

The elevator stopped, and the doors slid back. Clarista stood before me in the entry hall, flashing a look of surprise that quickly fell again. Her smooth brow lowered to darken her eyes, and her fists went to her hips.

I held my breath. "Clarista. Everything okay?"

"No, everything is not 'okay.' " She stepped back and gestured clearly that I should join her.

All I wanted to do was get downstairs, but the way her lips had gone strangely thin and the fact that she had just followed a subject with a predicate without hesitation terrified me.

I stepped out into the hall and glanced around for some clue as to what I'd done wrong.

"Did you—and I know you did, so *don't* say you didn't— remove Renee Gallagher's possessions from this hotel?" She clasped her hands and steepled her pointer fingers at me to stress each phrase.

Apparently, indignation was all the fuel she needed to propel her sentences directly to their ends.

"Yes," I said. "I thought I was only returning Clyde's things to him."

"How dare you assume that was your job? *You* didn't know if police cleared those items to be removed. *You* didn't know if they were his. And you apparently didn't know how to ask permission."

"I'm so sorry. You're absolutely right. I'll fix it."

"That's right, you will. Since you know so much about where he's staying and how to get a hold of him, you can get the things back. *Today.*"

"Absolutely, I will." Ugh. That meant yet another drive up the mountain, but if I could find an incriminating photo of Clyde before then, I could make the trip do double duty. "Thank you for giving me a chance to make things right."

"This doesn't *begin* to make things right." Her copper eyes seemed lit from behind. "You've put the hotel in jeopardy. Someone from her family could still sue us. You better hope and pray that doesn't happen."

"Yes, ma'am."

"And the only reason I haven't fired you already is because we're shorthanded with Mr. Fig gone."

"Yes, ma'am." She stood waiting for me to leave with a look on her face that said I'd better get myself moving. I didn't dare pass her to get to the elevator.

I turned toward the desk to find Doyle beaming as if he'd just been gifted a year's supply of cotton candy. "Well, well, well."

I blew past him to see if George was still in the kitchen.

He was up to his elbows at the sink, scrubbing a cutting board like his life depended on it. With a liberal dose of bleach, judging by the stinging of my nose.

I cleared my throat. "Ready to go?"

"Sorry. Yes, please." He rinsed his hands and dried them. "Take me away from this."

As we passed the stove on our way out of the kitchen, a little experiment occurred to me. "Hang on."

I turned the knob to light the nearest gas burner.

"What are you doing?" George looked like he was wondering if I was going to burn myself on purpose this time.

"Just a little test." I pulled one of the loose strands of hair that I'd gathered from the Achilles settee out of my pocket.

If it was real hair, it would catch fire and burn quickly to the end, but if it was a cheap wig filament, it would melt.

I leaned over and held the strand up to the flame. The end caught fire for half a second, and the rest of the strand softened and fell into a liquid squiggle on George's white stove top.

"Um . . ." George said.

I straightened up and looked at him. "I think Clyde is telling the truth."

When we got to the elevator, it responded immediately to the call button. I hoped that meant no one had been inside while the key cabinet was open.

"Clarista's ready to fire me," I said as we stepped inside.

"I heard. Sorry."

"Is it me, or does she make a lot more sense when she's angry?"

He laughed sardonically. "This is the first time you've seen her that way, isn't it?"

"It's jarring."

"I know. You'll get used to it." He handed me a small paper bag full of chocolate-covered bacon.

"Wow, thanks." I stuck a piece in my mouth and kept talking anyway. "I hope I won't have the chance. Coherent Clarista is terrifying."

He laughed. "Reminds me of Bea, you know?"

"Oh yeah?" I took a breath.

"The way she's usually so casual, but then when she talks about anything scientific, her language gets *so* technical and specific."

I reached in for another bite of the sweet, salty bacon. "This is amazing. Did you just have it lying around?"

"Just something I'm experimenting with. Clarista's thinking of beefing up the weekend cocktail hour."

"Beefing it up or *baconing* it up?" I asked, and got a smirk in response.

When we reached the storage room, I used the hard-won key to let us into the dim, utilitarian space again.

"So you're hoping that if you go to Clyde with definitive proof he's been here before, he'll fess up to whatever secret he's hiding?"

"Pretty much." I wiped any trace of chocolate from my fingers, located the box that Mr. Fig had told me about, and pulled several heavy, leather-bound albums from its depths.

There were three labeled *Staff*, one for the years 1911 to 1940, the second for 1941 to 1970, and the last simply reading *1971–*.

A world of loss was represented by that small dash.

There was no ending year, because my family had never finished filling the album. They had lost the house and never taken another staff photo after 1987.

I pressed my fingers to the corners of my eyes, trying to stop the hurt from coming out.

"Yeah." George put a firm hand on mine.

"It's like . . . it's a lot easier to think about two or three generations back, but when it comes to my mom's own story . . ."

"You realize it hurts too much?" he asked.

I nodded, then swallowed, gathered myself, and found an album of events including the early eighties.

We flipped through, marveling at the puffy sleeves and the puffy hair. It was hard not to get deeply distracted.

Several of the photos were accompanied by newspaper clippings describing the events.

"Here's 1983. We're getting there," George said.

"We have to scan more carefully now. We don't know exactly what Clyde looked like then." But in a few more flips, we'd found him. He wasn't hard to pick out, being one of those men whose boyish face was only covered by a thin veil of laugh lines and extra pounds.

"Wow, that's him, right?" George said.

"Definitely."

A small group of people in staff uniforms and formal wear posed on the terrace, several clearly college aged. Someone had thought it was funny to have some of the maids sitting on the young men's knees. (*Le sigh.*)

I punched George lightly in the arm. "Look at Mr. Fig!"

He reminded me of Robert Redford à la *The Natural,* handsome and still redheaded, maybe in his early thirties.

George leaned in. "He *was* young once."

My grandparents bookended the group. I could see my mother in my grandfather's high cheekbones, in the rigid bend of his nose, but nowhere else in the photo.

She would have been a teenager when this photo was taken. Maybe she was out at an event of her own.

I thought of taking time out to flip through the album and look for her, but these were events—garden parties, dinners, dedications. The family photos were in another book.

And I had to stay on track.

A copy of the dinner photo with Clyde in it was featured in the newspaper clipping on the next page. I lifted the plastic film and took the article, leaving the original photo in place. "Okay, let's go."

"Hey, by the way," George said as we stepped into hall. "The cellar door doesn't look bad to me."

I winced. "You should see the *other* side."

I'd told him in the car how I had managed to get the door off its hinges and back on again. There were definitely scratches and gouges along the trim from where I'd attacked it with the mallet in my escape.

"Eh, I can probably do a little work on it before Fig gets back." George had picked up some woodworking skills from his dad.

I knew I could trust him to fix it. "That would be amazing. Thanks."

Thinking of my escape and the hurry I'd been in triggered an idea. Until now, I'd been assuming the killer would have thrown out whatever clothing had ripped on that nail in order to destroy any incriminating evidence, but what if in their hurry to flee the scene, they'd been as distracted as I was? What if they hadn't noticed their clothing being ripped at all? What if a torn shirt was hiding in one of the guests' suitcases here in the hotel?

On our way back upstairs, I realized that, with the gravestone groupies checking out tomorrow, tonight would be my last chance to search their rooms. It wasn't my shift or my responsibility to do turndown though, so I'd have to get creative.

"Hey," I said. "Before we go, I need to take advantage of everyone being away at dinner."

* * *

A few minutes later, I waited for my cue behind the green baize door to the entry hall, cracking it open a smidge so that I could hear.

"Hey, Doyle," George said at the desk. "I've, uh, got some leftover muffins that I need to get rid of."

I grinned. He sounded like an illegal pastry dealer.

"Muffins? What kind?" I could picture Doyle's suspicious eyes.

"Blueberry."

"Really? *Just* blueberry? Nothing weird in there?"

"Nothing weird," George said convincingly.

"Pepper? Some kind of herb? Coconut flour?"

I smiled to myself. Doyle's suspicions weren't entirely off base.

"None of the above." George said as the swinging door to the kitchen creaked and Doyle's footsteps retreated.

I didn't waste any time darting to the desk to help myself to the master set of room keys. Doyle would look for them for turndown service soon, but I needed them more.

I made my way first to Leonard Chaves's room and left the door unlocked for George to follow. Each of the guest rooms was themed around a different color palette, which as far as I could tell was left over from the way it had been decorated by my family.

The Homer Room was all in green, the shade the old poet had used to describe honey. Ancient Greeks perceived color absurdly. They didn't even have a word for pure blue, and they had been surrounded by it.

A pair of Leonard's worn-looking brown loafers stood sentinel on the Persian rug at the end of the bed. I looked for his suitcase under the inlaid table by the window where guests would often stash one but didn't find it until I checked the bathroom.

George popped in just as I got to the unmentionables.

"Perfect timing," I said. "There's a pair of plaid boxers here that you can look over for tears."

He groaned. "C'mon, now. Surely you can tell on sight whether they match what you found."

"Sorry, too close to tell." I smirked.

Upon further inspection, the boxers were in excellent condition, and given that they were Leonard's only plaid item, we moved on.

As soon as we stepped out of the room, I heard someone swear. I looked around for a foul-mouthed foe.

It was Doyle on the other side of the gallery that rimmed the second-floor suites, bending over to pick up a key he'd dropped in front of the Romulus Room. Without benefit of the key ring I'd borrowed, he was wrangling all the loose ones.

I chuckled inwardly as I pulled George out of Doyle's line of sight toward the Alexander Room, where Tom and Autumn Truman were staying.

The couple was becoming more suspicious to me all the time, but they seemed at odds, keeping things from each other. If they had something to do with Renee's death, I found it unlikely that they were in it together.

"You do his, and I'll do hers," I said to George when we'd locked the door of the suite behind us.

We began our careful rifling of their clothing. Autumn had unpacked hers into the Chippendale tallboy dresser. She wore mostly timeless linens, pale silks, that sort of thing. I didn't find any plaid, and I hadn't expected to.

"Um," George said, bending over Tom's bag. "It's not what we're looking for, but it's suspicious."

He held up a few Ziploc bags of pills.

I came over to take a look. The pills didn't match the ones I had found in Selena's desk, but they were in the same kind of sandwich bags. "Oh, very suspicious."

These were blue and said *DAN 5620*. I'd run a Google search on that when I wasn't in a hurry.

"And the hoard of packaged food in here is just about immoral," George said, kneeling by the suitcase again and holding up handfuls of snack-sized Doritos, Little Debbies, and beef jerky.

I laughed.

He twisted his mouth and put everything back. "I'm starting to feel really weird about this."

"I know." I helped him zip the suitcase.

"It's unethical." He sank back on his knees.

"I know. Honestly, I'm surprised I was able to rope you into it in the first place." I frowned. "But it's a means to an end."

We checked that the couple's bags were back in place and, without having found even a square of plaid, made our way out of the room.

I wasn't surprised that George took issue with my methods of investigation, but I didn't have the same options the police did for getting warrants and doing this properly. He wasn't wrong, but I was desperate. "You don't have to keep helping me, though, if you don't feel good about it," I said, standing on the threshold.

"No, I get it. Mr. Fig is what's important here. And what seems unjust now will lead to justice for him."

"I hope you're—"

"Just what do we have here?" Mr. Wollstone interrupted from just outside his room next door. He looked as if he'd just woken up from a nap. "Two employees . . . out of uniform . . . trespassing in an occupied guest room?"

I tried to think of some quick explanation. Mr. Wollstone would love to get us in trouble. "We—"

"—just needed a moment alone." George winked at the old man and began tucking in his shirt. "If you know what I mean."

My eyes threatened to bug out of my skull, but I recovered and painted on a coy smile.

George grabbed me around the waist, and my pulse surged (from the stress of the situation).

The old man yanked out his handkerchief and coughed into it.

I leaned into George's side, the flutter behind my ribs warning me that this romantic subterfuge might not soften the leathery skeleton in front of us.

"Well," said the old man, "Lord knows I've been there." He chewed the inside of his mouth. "Although not often enough. Now that I think of it."

He glanced at us again, then disappeared into his room.

George let go of me, and I released the tension I'd been holding.

"I can't believe you said that." Warm and energized, I laughed softly. "I can't believe it worked."

He grinned. "I had a feeling about the guy."

I could hear Doyle whistling inside the Homer Room now, and I hoped that whatever we had disturbed in there, Leonard would excuse under the umbrella of turndown service.

"Anyone else's room we should check?" George asked.

"I don't think there's time. People are starting to come back from dinner, and anyway, the ones we searched already were at the top of my list."

"Should we be suspecting Wollstone?" George's phone rang. He pulled it out of his pocket and silenced the call.

"I don't think so." I shrugged. "You can answer that if you need to."

"It's okay. I'll call her back later." He put the phone away.

"How is your mom lately?"

"Oh, it wasn't Mom. It was just Bea." He started down the stairs.

Just Bea? I thought. "Just" as in "not important" or as in "we talk every day"?

I followed him downstairs and turned my thoughts to who or what else might have left that plaid fabric behind. As far as I knew, the only people who ever used the dumbwaiter were George, Mr. Fig, and Mallory Peters, the farmer who supplied us with produce and served as the current delivery person. I couldn't imagine Mr. Fig wearing plaid, and George never wore it at work. But I was sure I'd seen Mallory sporting a flannel shirt before, and if the fabric was hers, then the clue was no clue at all. She had a perfectly legitimate reason to have left it there.

Then again, if the snagged swatch *did* belong to the killer, he or she might have simply thrown the torn garment away after all.

I'd rejoiced when there'd been nothing so scientific about this case that I needed to ask for Bea's help, but if a blue-and-green plaid something had ended up in the trash, she'd be one of the only people likely to have seen it.

* * *

The last thing we had to do before leaving the hotel was return the master keys. I pushed through the swinging gate at the desk and hung them on the appropriate hook.

"Well, well, well, well," Doyle repeated, pushing back the silk curtain and leering at me from the office like a silent-movie villain.

"I think it's just three *wells*," I said, unaffected.

"Who's Clarista's favorite now?" he tried again.

"I don't think I was ever her favorite." Mr. Fig's, though. "I wonder if you suffer from some kind of inferiority complex."

He tugged at his shirt. "Stop trying to diagnose everybody!"

"Doyle," George interrupted helpfully, leaning an elbow on the desk. "Why are you working Sunday night? This isn't your shift."

"Duh. Clarista asked me to pick up an extra one. She said we all have to pitch in, or I guess that's what she was gonna say before she lost her train of thought."

He was wrong about a lot of things but not Clarista's thoughts.

"She left you a message, BTW." Doyle handed me a folded note. "Spoiler alert. It says you have to work tomorrow."

"Ugh." I read quickly, confirming what he'd said. A mandatory extra shift, bad news delivered badly. Normally I wouldn't mind so much, but I was tired and wanted to dedicate every second right now to Mr. Fig's freedom.

"At least Monday nights are slow," I growled.

He shook his head and smiled. "Not Monday night. Day shift."

"But . . . I never work day shift."

He shrugged, with that same satisfied smirk on his face.

When I got done with this investigation, I was going to have to find a way to tolerate Doyle better. He was like a beneficial mold—smelly and annoying but useful if carefully controlled.

For now, I had a lying professor to deal with who was already well practiced in manipulation.

XVII

Deep Magic

❧

The sun had set by the time we got back into George's car.

I asked him to drop me off at home so I could get the Volvo and go see Clyde.

"Nah." He swatted the air. "I'll go with you."

"Are you sure? It's all the way up on Lookout."

"Yes, but so is the Volvo, isn't it?"

I held my mouth open. "Oh no! You're right. It's at Selena's dorm. That's even farther. I'm so sorry."

"Listen, I don't want this to come as a shock, but I miss you, and I like spending time with you."

Despite his sarcasm, there was real feeling in his comment, and I held up a hand as if I could deflect it. "Okay, okay. Gosh."

"Well, you drove me to it," he said.

"You're right. Now drive me to Clyde."

In a little while, we were taking the last zig and zag of the mountain road and pulling into a parking space by the flock of little cottages resting in the twilight. I asked George to wait in the car. Clyde would be less guarded if I came in alone.

I knocked, and after a moment or two, the man appeared, leaning on the open door, like a toddler awoken from his nap. His clothes were wrinkled, his collar turned up on one side. A thin layer of grease made his nose and forehead shine. His hair stuck out at odd angles above his ears.

A whiskey-scented cloud overtook me, and I stepped back. "I've come at a bad time. I'm sorry."

"No, no. Iss fine." He opened the door wider to usher me in, revealing a half-empty bottle of Woodford Reserve and a single, empty glass on the coffee table behind him.

I hesitated. Was this a very bad idea?

What I saw in front of me was a man whose front had crumbled.

I didn't need to put a name on it. And I didn't have the expertise to.

Doyle was right. I hadn't always taken my diagnoses of others seriously, and I probably should have.

Labeling people was not only faulty but often unkind. Still, it was helpful to me to try to understand people's motivations, the perspectives that shaped their actions.

I would guess that since Renee's death and Selena's accident, grief and shame had batted Clyde around on the inside. He'd kept up a composed front, so I couldn't know that for sure, but it seemed like he was finally submitting himself to the violence of his emotions.

A man finally facing a truth long denied was a dangerous man.

But I knew as well as anyone that alcohol loosened tongues. I wouldn't get a better chance to catch him in his truth.

I followed him into the stale living area.

He had come up with another glass from somewhere before plopping his weight down on the couch. I took the armchair next to him.

Jung had written that holding on to secrets was like dosing your psyche with poison. Like the whiskey Clyde had been applying so liberally, secrets could be fine in small amounts. But kept too long or too close, they alienated a person from their community, and isolation was as dangerous as arsenic.

And that's all that could explain Clyde sitting here drinking alone. Surely someone among the grave society could sit with him in his grief. Had he consciously or unconsciously driven them away?

He picked up the bottle and filled both glasses halfway.

"Oh, I probably—I'm—" I gestured toward the car. But I wasn't driving, and I didn't have any good reason not to partake. On the contrary, the camaraderie this drink would earn me could spark better conversation (read: interrogation).

"Aw, hit'll wearov before then." He answered the statement I hadn't finished. "Unforchnately."

He shoved the glass across the table at me in a manner that was meant to be hospitable but came off as forceful and more than a little clumsy when a dribble slipped over the rim.

Yet I found his sloppiness endearing. I took the glass from him, vowing not to finish it. "You're probably right. Thanks."

" 'Course I'm right, Ivy m'dear."

Dear? Well, the fire of conviviality was off to a roaring start. I took a sip and shivered. "Mm. Nice."

He grunted in response and leaned against the couch cushion, letting his head fall back.

"So. Clyde." Even in his present frame of mind, leading with a question about his time at the hotel could make him shut down. I needed to start a little closer to home. "When will you head back to Pennsylvania?"

"Tomorrow, likely. Nobody wants me here. That's for sure."

Eesh. "Selena's still angry?"

"Women ate a dead as minagif," he said.

"I beg your pardon."

"Womenn hhate a debtt as menn a gifttt," he said.

"Gotcha." God save me from these men constantly quoting things at me. I washed his words down with a sip. "That's not Browning too, is it?"

He nodded emphatically.

Before I had time to ask what debt Selena owed him, he said, "Now this one, 'Take away luff an' our earth is a tomb.' "

"Also Browning?"

He nodded again and took a drink. "Very good student."

Still nodding, his head fell forward, and for a moment I wondered if he was asleep.

"How long had you and Renee been together?" I asked.

He breathed in and out loudly through his mouth. "Two years."

"Wow."

He laughed, sadly. "I usually say one year. That's how long my divorce has been final."

"Oh. I see." Cheater. "Well, secret's safe with me." I sipped again. "And Selena's mother—what was her name again?"

"Linda," he said, so hatefully that no name-calling was necessary.

"Where did you meet?"

"Phil-delphia."

"Nice city."

No reply.

"Why're you 'ere" —his eyes rolled up to examine my face, if drunk eyes could examine—"Ivy?"

I took another long sip of my whiskey. Smooth. It was making this whole conversation smooth. "I'm really sorry to do this to you, but—that bag of Renee's things I brought you yesterday? It turns out I shouldn't have."

"Zat witch Autumn want 'em now? As if she ever cared for her sister. She owes me, ya know? She owes me anyway, so I might as well keep 'em."

Oh gosh. "The money you invested in her firm?"

"Rright. And now she says she doesn't haffit."

"Did Renee have a lot of money?" I said.

He chuckled in a way that I assumed meant no.

"Did she have life insurance?"

"Not that I know of." His answer seemed honest.

"I'm just trying to figure out—if someone is framing you, then what do they want the police to think is your motive?" I asked.

He drained his glass, picked up the bottle, and refilled it again. "Your guess-iz-az good as mine."

He leaned toward my glass, and I waved him off, but he focused on the singular goal of topping it off, which he did with surprising finesse.

"I'd like to tell you something that not many other people know, Clyde."

When he returned the bottle to the coffee table, he looked me in the eyes expectantly but said nothing.

"It was my family who owned the house." I was surprised that the confession, though I was sprinkling it on him like tenderizer, brought me a bit of genuine relief. "I mean—the hotel before it became a hotel."

I pulled the newspaper clipping with the party photo from my bag and held it out to him.

Clyde held the clipping in one hand and his glass in another, sloshing the whiskey in it as he gestured. "The Morrows?"

I winced, worried for the delicate paper.

"They're your people?" he said.

My people. I would like to claim them, but they still felt thin to me, like the Wonder Woman paper dolls I'd played with as a kid. "Hortensius and Mary were my grandparents."

He smiled softly and nodded. "Him, I liked."

"But not her?"

"Only met her the one time, but no, not really." He shrugged. "Sorry."

I would take that with several grains of salt. Clyde was the kind of man who only liked women he could manage. I hoped he would keep the info coming, though. This was pretty good stuff, and he'd already basically admitted to being at the house.

George was more expressive when he drank too. That was a good thing in his case. Usually his inhibitions prevented him saying anything that he thought might be wrong or might paint him in a bad light. Alcohol peeled back the film, and a truer— if less refined—version of him shone through. Sometimes he'd even curse.

"What did you like about my grandfather?" I asked.

"Great question." He raised his glass in a brief toast to me. "See, Horten, he was a man's man. I mean, look at his estate, for starters . . . king of his castle, kept a couple dozen Scotches on hand 'n' a lotta fine hunting rifles."

He raised his glass again as if to the memory of my grandfather. "Wouldn't let us touch 'em, though."

"Yeah, too bad." What he liked about my grandfather told me a lot more about Clyde's own values than anything else. I had noticed the use of a shortened form of my grandfather's name, though.

For half a second, I considered asking him if he'd met my mother at the house and decided against it. His guard was good and low now, and it was time to take my shot before he was too far gone to make sense. "You're in that photo too, I noticed."

"Ha. You got me." He stared at the picture. "Been a long time since I had a woman carrying around photos of me." He winked at the younger version of himself. "Handsome devil."

"Why did you lie about being there?"

He looked up at me again, and some other version of himself, nearly as boyish as the face in the photo, possessed him. "I . . . I sstole something."

"From the house?" My mind went straight to the paintings.

Then he frowned. "No, from a . . . a clazzmate, a frien', really."

"Why?"

"I . . . I needed it." He stared at the photograph with a deep sadness. "We had just met when this was taken."

"Well, if it's bothering you, after all these years, why don't you make it right?"

He doubled over, hiding his face from me. "Nooo."

"You could just give the thing back, right? Whatever you stole? Plus interest of some kind and a hefty apology."

"No. No. It's much too late. My whole life would disappear, Ivy. You don't understand."

"Well, good grief. What could be that important?" I said.

He shook his head but kept his face hidden from the light.

Why had he changed his story? Why had he told me the truth at check-in and lied *after* Renee's death? "Clyde, when's the last time you saw the friend you stole from? Do you have some reason to believe he would take revenge on you?"

"Ssso you do believe I was fframed."

"I think so." I sipped my whiskey again. The motion had become habitual, comforting. "So who is your old friend? Anyone in the grave society? Anyone you've seen recently around the hotel?"

Clyde cleared his throat and handed the photo back to me. "No. No one like that."

And if that friend was seeking revenge, why now, after all this time?

"There must have been some kind of trigger," I said aloud, accidentally.

"Trigger. Everybody getting triggered these days. Bunch of lousy snowflakes. *M'llennials.*" He laid down on the couch now and threw one hand over his eyes.

I looked past that critique of my generation and went on. "Listen, I think I know how Renee's killer got to her, but whoever it was would've had to know the hotel—intimately."

He didn't look up.

"They would've had a plan in place long before you checked in. Clyde?"

"But"—he licked his lips—"how'd they plan when they di'n' know which room Renee and I would be staying in?"

He had a good point there, especially for a drunk guy.

"Only the club treasurer would know that," he slurred.

"Treasurer?"

"The treasurer made . . . the reservations."

Shoot. Leonard had said Clyde put forward the money for the rooms. I would've thought that meant Clyde made the reservations too. Had he handed off his credit card to the treasurer? "Clyde."

No movement. No answer.

I got up and patted his face. "Clyde, who's the treasurer? Who booked the rooms for your group?"

He mumbled something that might have been *jobs*.

Or else *Chaves*.

If Clyde were an emoji at that moment, he'd have been the one with the little *z*'s coming out its face. I couldn't revive him.

I stood up to hunt for the bag of Renee's things and found I was doing only marginally better. I realized I hadn't eaten lunch and my dinner had been that bag of chocolate-covered bacon.

Taking something from Clyde's room while he slept felt a lot like stealing. On the other hand, he was an admitted thief himself, and I had my orders.

I found Renee's bag in the bedroom and exited the dark cottage into the even darker night, removed as we were from the city lights.

Leaning against the hood of his Highlander, George looked up at the sound of the door, dropped his phone into his pocket, and said, "One more minute and I was coming in there after you."

"Pssh. It's not like he's a *murderer-er*."

I knew George was watching me make my crooked way down the crooked path, and I told myself to straighten up. I pretty much had it together by the time I reached the car.

"Uh-oh," George said.

"I'm fine." I opened the door to the back seat, threw Renee's bag in, and fell in after it. But I made a quick recovery and deposited myself in the front seat.

George got in beside me and waved a hand in front of his nose. "Whew. I'm glad I decided to drive you, Captain Morgan."

"That's Captain Woodford Reserve, for your information." I strapped on my seat belt but didn't quite complete the connection, and the buckle went flying up in front of my face.

George reached across the console with a chastising look, grabbed the shoulder strap, and pulled it across me. His hand nudged my thigh as he clicked it into place.

He paused, looking at me thoughtfully, then turned back to his side of the car and cracked the windows.

"Guess we can't get the Volvo now," I said.

"Nope."

Somewhere in the back of my head was a concern about that, but it didn't push forward into my thoughts.

I inhaled the crisp mountain air and tried to put together what Clyde had said with the rest of the clues I'd gathered.

George was taking it easy on the winding road down the mountain. He obviously thought I was in a position to be easily made sick.

It was so nice of him to drive me up here and back home again. We never got to hang out anymore, and my mind was craving the easy days when we'd been in school. We hadn't had to carve out time together when we could catch up walking home every day.

My thoughts kept wandering away from Clyde. He had flat-out refused to tell me any more about the friend he'd stolen from. Was he afraid of me tracking them down and finding out what he'd done that was so bad? A classmate, he'd said. That reminded me of something, but I couldn't remember what in my present state.

If I'd deciphered Clyde's mumble right, Leonard Chaves had booked the rooms. I wished I had been the clerk to take that call. Had Leonard specifically requested the Achilles for Clyde and Renee? He must have.

But how could he have known that was the right room to put them in, the one that could be accessed by the dumbwaiter? A simple visit to the hotel at some point in the past wouldn't have told Leonard that. He would had to have worked for the Morrow family or stayed with them at some point.

Or maybe I was thinking too much inside the box. Leonard had an obvious grudge against Clyde. Had that developed over their working history at the university, or had Leonard brought that grudge with him from having known Clyde before? Perhaps *he* was the classmate Clyde had stolen from.

If, as Clyde had told Selena, Leonard was after his job, it would explain why someone involved in Clyde's life so long ago would decide to take revenge now.

It was unlikely that Leonard would have been at the same dinner at the house, but I took out the newspaper clipping and checked the names in the caption. Each student's name was accompanied by the name of the maid who sat in his lap. Naomi and Clyde, Dana and Joey, et cetera. But no Leonard.

Headlights blinded me from the side mirror. A car had slid up close behind us. There was no place to pass on this road.

I closed my eyes to block out the brightness.

*   *   *

I woke up to find George putting the car in park.

"Oh, are we here?" I smiled sleepily. "Thanks again for driving me back to the hotel."

"We're not at the hotel, Captain."

"What? I have to take Renee's bag back. Clarista's expecting it."

"Yeah, but it's nine thirty," he said. "Clarista's long gone. And you can take it when you go in in the morning."

"In the morning?"

"To work."

"Work! I forgot." I smacked myself in the head, harder than I meant to. "Darn it."

George came around to my side of the car and opened the door. "That's why you have to get some sleep now."

"But I'm hungry." I wobbled up to standing.

George took my arm. "Okay. A quick snack, and then I'm putting you straight to bed."

"Tyrant." I looked around the parking lot and realized we weren't at my apartment either. "George. What are we doing at your building?"

"Listen. You're drunk, Ivy. And I'm not taking you to your dad in this shape."

"Whatevvv." I blew a raspberry. "He's not going to judge you."

"Well, I can't stomach the possibility of it."

I giggled as we entered the posh lobby. "Stomach."

"What?"

"*Stomach* is a funny word."

"Ohhkay." He led me into the elevator, and I leaned against the wall.

Inside his condo, I sat on the couch, and he went into the kitchen.

"You can text your dad while I heat this up."

"Oh, yeah." It took me three tries to unlock my phone, but I did as he suggested, telling Dad I was staying with George but not the reason why.

Then I got the idea to make a call.

Until his voice mail picked up, it didn't occur to me that Sunday night would be outside Dr. Larsson's office hours. But I landed on my feet and came up with a clever message, "Hi, uh,

Dr. Larsson, this is Ivy Nichols. I called you yesterday about the newspaper article on Clyde Borough. I had one final question for you. Please call me back when you can."

Totally coherent. Good job, Ivy.

I laid my phone down, saw George's white tennis shoes on the rug beside me, and followed the line of his frame upward to a steaming plate of brown meat in a shiny glaze and some kind of golden mash.

"Mmm. What's this?" I reached out to take the dish from him. We had done this so many times before. I would show up empty-handed, and George would feed me.

He drew the plate back. "Who was that?"

"A professor."

"Of yours?" he asked.

"No, no, no." I reached for the plate again. "Of Selena's."

He kept it out of my reach.

I grunted.

"Selena, Clyde's daughter?" he said. "You drunk-dialed a professor you don't even know?"

"Um . . . well." I squinted one eye and turned my hands palms up.

He shook his head and finally handed me the food. "It's leftovers. Red-wine-braised short ribs and grits."

"I'm starting not to mind so much that you brought me here." I dug in, paying little attention to anything else. (It was one of the best meals of my life, by the way, with meaty, buttery umami in spades.) When I finished, I lay back on the arm of the couch and closed my eyes.

I felt George take the empty plate from my lap. "All right, guest bedroom's all set."

"No. Too tired. Staying here," I said with my eyelids tightly shut.

Dust to Dust

"C'mon, you'll sleep better in a bed." He laughed at me and took my arm to pry me off the furniture.

I stumbled down the hall on my own, and as I sat down on the comforter in the guest bedroom, I felt his eyes on me.

He had followed me into the room and stood only inches from me, his eyebrows lifted expectantly.

Expecting what?

I realized I was holding on to him, my fingers warmed by the solid arm under his fine-textured shirt sleeve.

My eyes stuck there a second, and the same little tremor I'd discovered when Mr. Wollstone confronted us this afternoon rattled my middle again.

I had just enough inhibition left to drop my hand before it got awkward.

George jerked up to standing.

Or maybe it *was* awkward. I couldn't tell in my current state. I didn't know if my feelings meant anything right now. "Thanks for letting me sleep over."

"Sure," he said, backing up a step and straightening his shirt without looking toward the bed.

I kicked off one shoe, then the other, and let my head fall against the fluffed pillow.

George stared at the floor, pursing his lips crookedly. He flicked his eyes at me and then kept them on the door.

That was his thoughtful face. What was he considering?

My hands tingled. For a moment I thought he would stay, hoped he would stay.

He went back to the door and put a finger on the light switch. "Okay, sleep well."

"Good night," I said.

He waited for me to pull the covers up before turning off the light.

219

XVIII

Our Earth Is a Tomb

◞

Monday morning should have been one of the worst of my life. I hadn't slept well, despite the comfortable bed. I'd gone to sleep earlier than I was used to and had woken up *much* too early so I could work day shift. (George had set an alarm for me.) Now my body clock was all turned around.

The gravestone stans were going home today, leaving me with nothing except theories, ponderings about my own mortality, and a wicked rope burn on the business side of one foot.

And above all that, pressing down on me like a guilty secret, was the knowledge that while I had slept at George's, Mr. Fig had spent his third night in jail.

It should've been a terrible morning.

But George was there.

He whistled in the kitchen while he made me some kind of fancy French egg dish (oeufs coquette?) and sent me off with his car key and a travel mug full of hot Earl Grey.

He wasn't due at the hotel for several hours and said he'd get a ride in with tonight's *sous-chef*, which I knew was a sacrifice 'cause making conversation with that guy was like rafting without a current.

The seriousness of the day didn't stay buried for long, though.

Details of the night before began flashing into my mind as I drove George's car through the early-morning streets to the hotel. Crossing the bridge over the oil-black river, I blushed thinking of how I'd clung to George in the bedroom the night before.

Surely we both knew I hadn't meant anything by it. I was simply worn out and drunk. I climbed the hill of Third Street past the Art District and had another flash of memory.

Had I made a phone call?

Son of a witch. I jerked the steering wheel and nearly hit a speed limit sign.

I'd called Dr. Larsson back. I'd left him *my real name.* He'd been so suspicious at the end of our last call. And now he had my *number.*

My stomach somersaulted as I reached the hotel. I parked, grabbed Renee's bag from the Highlander's back hatch, and ran inside to change into my uniform.

Well, *run* would be an overstatement. I was limping from the burn on my foot, and I only had one good arm. I felt like sticking a patch over one eye and greeting everyone I passed with a hearty, "Argh!"

But at six in the morning, I didn't pass anyone. The servants' hall was as quiet as if the house stood empty.

After dressing, I crept upstairs while the guests were still in bed, somehow more wary and lonely than during my usual shift. I'd grown used to one AM.

I changed the newspaper on the desk, switched around the signage, and checked for any office business to attend to. I had at least an hour to myself before anyone would be up and about, an hour in which to dwell on the fact that the gravestone group was checking out soon, and along with them my chances of naming a killer.

Sure, there was that bit of cloth I'd found in the dumbwaiter, but there was only a chance labs would reveal DNA, and even then, I'd have to make Detective Bennett believe the killer had used the dumbwaiter to access the room.

And those strange drawings. No one had stepped forward to threaten me or claim them. Had Mr. Fig been wrong about Bob the thief having returned?

Acting as opening clerk, I preheated the oven and put in the croissants George had proofed overnight. A server would get here later to ready the rest of the breakfast and put it all out in the morning room.

The fragrances of those pastries plus coffee, eggs, and bacon drifted toward me at the desk over the next hour, and guests crisscrossed the entry hall on their way in and out of breakfast, including Autumn and Tom at about eight fifteen.

In all the hubbub yesterday, I'd forgotten to Google those pills in Tom's suitcase. I took a second to do that now. They were diazepam, generic Valium. I searched for side effects, too, and it looked like his fatigue and increased appetite could be some of them.

Autumn had said he'd been tired since giving up drinking, and Valium, as it turned out, could be prescribed for alcohol withdrawal. It looked like Tom and Selena were both taking prescription pills without prescriptions, and that was too coincidental to not mean something.

I heard Clarista's high heels approaching.

My stomach braced for confrontation.

But she slipped through the door from the servant hall and directly into the morning room.

I needed to tell her I'd brought back Renee's things, but I'd let her get a cup of coffee first.

After a few minutes, I popped my head into the morning room. Clarista was in the middle of a conversation with Furnell and Parker at one of the tables, her face bright and smiling as if someone had just told a joke.

"Well, so the rest of the evening . . ." She watched their faces expectantly.

"Oh," said Furnell. "Nothing special, really."

"We were supposed to see the graves again," Parker said.

Furnell smiled. "Bud, I think we saw all the graves here. Twice."

"But remember? We were walking that gravel path by the Aeneas statue. It was five o'clock on Saturday. I said, 'Dad can we come back to the graves again?' You said, 'Sure, bud. How about on our last night?' I said, 'Yes, please.' "

Furnell rocked his shapely head back and trumpeted a hearty laugh that filled the room. "This kid, aw, this kid is gonna do me in."

Parker didn't laugh with him.

"Okay, buddy, we'll do that before we leave this morning."

"His memory is practically photographic," Clarista said.

"Echoic," said Parker.

His father bobbed his head. "A lot of people think all kids on the spectrum have some kind of savant capabilities. They don't usually. Parker's memory isn't perfect, but it's really very good, better when it's something that he's really into."

Furnell chuckled again, and Clarista laughed with him.

I wondered how much Parker knew that I didn't. He had witnessed all the gravestone club's meetings, where all the arrangements for this trip had probably been made.

Leonard had called to make the bookings, but I didn't know who had *decided* that Clyde and Renee should stay in the Achilles Room. Had Parker witnessed that discussion at a meeting?

Clarista wouldn't want me interrupting their conversation or their breakfast. I'd catch them on their way out of the morning room.

Bea was dusting the hall furniture when I got back to the desk.

"Any word on Mr. Fig?" she asked.

"Not yet."

"I hope bond will be set at some kind of reasonable level." She picked up a vase on the front desk and swished her feather duster under it.

"I do too."

She stopped cleaning for a second and leaned toward me, her eyes on my face. "Getting up early really took its toll on you."

"Um, yeah, it's just that I'm not wearing any makeup 'cause I got ready at George's, so . . ."

"Oh." She drew her eyebrows together, then relaxed them with effort. "Okay."

I probably should have corrected the assumption she was making, but I didn't want to.

Her lips buttoned together as if she needed to stop them from betraying any emotion.

"I better get to work." She held her head up as she started toward the stairs.

"Yeah, see you later—oh, hey," I said. "This is going to come across as weird, but have you seen anything plaid in the trash around here?"

She shrugged. "Nope."

"And that wig you found thrown away. Was it blond?"

She narrowed her eyes. "How did you—"

My cell phone rang.

I looked at the screen. *Dr. Larsson.*

"Sorry, I've gotta take this," I said to Bea. "Hello?" I answered.

"Is this Ivy Nichols?"

"Yes."

"Hello, Ivy. Dr. Larsson here. You called me last night."

I watched Bea climb the stairs and felt a little guilty. "Oh, yep, yeah, I was—"

"You had another question for me?"

Furnell and Parker left the morning room and headed up the stairs. I was missing my chance to question them about the Achilles Room booking.

"I—I have to be honest with you, Professor." It was time to let it all out. "I'm not writing for a student paper. I've been trying to figure out who killed Dr. Borough's girlfriend. An innocent man has been arrested. I wondered if you would tell me about the classmate that you said called about him."

He paused, and all was silent on his end of the line. "Oh, well, all right. She was a good friend of Clyde's back in grad school."

"She? What was her name?"

"Uh, Naomi . . . I can't remember the last name. Started with an *R*, I believe."

Naomi. Naomi was one of the maids in the newspaper photograph. The maid sitting with Clyde, actually.

"And what did she want when she called?"

"Uh, well, I don't know that she wanted anything in particular, really," he said. "She just seemed to want to know about him, about what he had been up to. I told her to send him a request on Facebook. That was six months ago."

"Oh, I thought you had just talked the other day."

"Yeah, she called the other day too. Can't say what she wanted, really. We just talked about Clyde's daughter some."

"What about her?"

"Oh, just how she was doing, the kinds of things she was struggling with."

Her struggles? This Naomi was looking for another weak spot to get to Clyde. That had to be it. "Thank you. Thank you so much," I said. "You've helped a lot."

I hung up the phone and ran downstairs to get the newspaper clipping out of my bag in the changing room.

There she was, Naomi Hagel, sitting on Clyde's lap.

That was the connection. She'd worked at the hotel during Mr. Fig's time here, and she knew Clyde.

When I got back upstairs, I examined her little face but couldn't connect her to anyone I'd seen at the hotel or anywhere else. Of course, it had been decades since this photo was taken.

I wondered if one of the hotel guests had changed their name to disguise their identity. But none of the women were even the right age. Naomi would be, like Clyde, in her early sixties now. Autumn was closest but still probably ten years too young.

I pulled out my phone and Googled Naomi Hagel. Unsurprisingly, nothing relevant came up. She'd likely been married and changed her name, maybe more than once in the last few decades.

I stared at my screen, but there was nothing else to look up, nothing I could think to do to help, nothing that could remove the fear of not being able to save Mr. Fig.

* * *

The next two hours were uneventful, which made them excruciating. All I could do was stand behind the front desk and fret over Mr. Fig. Somewhere in the courthouse, he was awaiting arraignment.

I was so angry with myself, with the legal system, and especially with whoever had really murdered Renee.

Between ten fifteen and ten thirty, all the remaining gravestone guests came down for checkout.

Autumn and Tom were the first.

I smirked as Doyle followed them down the stairs, lugging Tom's heavy suitcase. He had been roped into helping with the busy checkout day in Mr. Fig's stead.

The Trumans turned in their keys, paid for incidentals, and sat down to wait for an Uber to the airport.

Next were Furnell and Parker, who were supposed to ride back to Pittsburgh in Deena's Porsche. They absconded into the library to kill time until the ladies came down.

Meanwhile, Mr. Wollstone flew out of the morning room like a hornet released from a jar. "I've been waiting for a coffee refill for fifteen minutes!"

I managed to answer him without gritting my teeth. "I'll bring it to you myself as soon as I finish this checkout."

As I was speaking, the elevator dinged and the doors opened, revealing Velvet and Deena, both wearing sunglasses on the tops of their heads. Behind them, Doyle looked like a pack mule—albeit a well-dressed one.

The two women shuffled to the desk, and Doyle continued to the garage with their luggage.

Velvet looked the room over. "Well, I guess we beat them down."

"That's awfully violent. Who did we beat?" Deena said.

Mr. Wollstone tapped his fingers on one side of the desk, completely ignoring their conversation.

"I mean, we beat Furnell and Packer getting downstairs," Velvet said.

"You'll find them in the library," I said.

Velvet followed my direction while Deena stepped up to the desk, her head just clearing the raised ledge. "What do I owe ya, sweetheart? I know there were a couple lunches and dinners."

"I'll just go see." It occurred to me as I slid into the office to pull up her charges on the computer that this was a near-perfect setup for the kind of big reveal that always marked the end of classic murder mysteries. Everyone present on the night of Renee's death was here together, with the exception of Clyde and my dear Mr. Fig.

As I wrote up the itemized receipt, I heard Deena say, "Shoot. My credit card's expired."

"Here, use mine," said a voice far enough away that I couldn't identify it.

I returned to the desk and exchanged the written receipt for the credit card in Deena's hand.

The first name embossed on its shiny plastic stopped me midbreath. I was certain now who had killed Renee.

Naomi—the maid who'd worked here so many years ago, the old classmate of Clyde's—stood in front of the fireplace with her back to me.

No wonder I hadn't recognized her. She was nothing like the young woman in the photo, and she was nothing like what she appeared to be.

The vague bitterness I'd been carrying around for days condensed now that I really saw her, and I stared as if I could bore a hole into the back of her skull.

I hated her for sending Mr. Fig to that stinking jail. I hated her for letting an old man, and a good one, take her place.

But how could I prove she was Renee's killer? If Bennett couldn't find her DNA on that swatch from the dumbwaiter, I had nothing.

Either way, I couldn't let her walk out of this hotel thinking she'd gotten away with it.

I thought of Clarista's gun under the desk. I'd taken a safety course with my dad years ago and been to the shooting range a few times, but that didn't mean I was ready to fire at a real person, even a murderer. Not to mention that I'd only been *told* about this particular gun. I didn't know if it would be easy to handle, if the safety was on, or if it was already loaded.

There was thunder in my chest, but I tried to hold my hand—and my voice—steady. "Here's your card back, *Naomi*."

Several guests swung their heads around—at the tone in my voice, I imagined.

Naomi turned around too, and I searched her face. Obviously, hair color was going to change over nearly forty years, but this woman looked twenty years older than she should.

Clearly, she had aged herself on purpose so that Clyde wouldn't recognize her. But how?

Naomi Velvet Reed stepped up to the desk and snatched the credit card from me. "I *go* by my *middle* name."

"You do *now*," I said.

Velvet. Velvet had arrived early enough on Wednesday to cause the leak. Velvet had been able to slip away from the tour unnoticed while Deena went to the restroom. Velvet knew enough about literature to stage the murder and frame Clyde.

Her artificially wizened face widened with the realization that I was onto her, eyes darting from side to side as if checking to see if anyone else had caught on.

Deena looked back and forth between us, confused.

"Parker," I said.

The boy shifted his head a little. He was listening.

"Who was it that suggested Clyde and Renee stay in the Achilles suite?" I asked.

Without speaking, Parker raised his pointer finger from his side until his arm was parallel with the floor, then aimed it straight at Velvet.

"That's not true." Velvet took a step back.

"Deena brought pierogies," Parker said. "It was the January meeting. I wore my gray-striped shirt."

Furnell backed up his son both literally and metaphorically. "I remember the pierogies. Potato, right?"

"Cheese." Parker angled his head toward Velvet. "Her ankles are too young."

I sucked in a breath. I remembered her young ankles peeking out from her caftan at the pool.

"You remarked yourself how observant the boy is," I said to Velvet.

"Well, even if I did make the room suggestion, that has nothing to do with anything. I was just being thoughtful, I'm sure. Anyone would agree the president of the club should have the master suite."

"When you were able to name the mountains so easily, I should have wondered if you'd been to the area before." My mind was running a thousand watts an hour now. "Whoever killed Renee understood the hotel's blueprint and planned the murder well in advance. *You* used to work for the family here. You understood that the dumbwaiter would give you access to Renee."

"What's going on, Velvet?" Deena said, then rounded on me, employing her spiked hair and fierce eyes to go from sweet to intimidating in two seconds. "You've always been a nebby little Debbie! You've been sticking your nose into our business since the day we got here."

I was genuinely sad for her. "Your friend isn't who you think she is, Ms. Nixon."

"What in the world could you mean by that?" She gripped her eyeglasses emphatically. "I just got my prescription updated. I can see clear as day who she is."

"The two of you act like sisters, so I assumed you'd been friends forever, but you haven't, have you?"

Deena's frown turned to interest. "Six months."

"I should've known," I said. "There's no trace of Pittsburgh in your accent, Velvet. You moved to the city for Clyde, didn't you?"

"Now, wait a minute," Velvet said.

"Tom, open her suitcase," I said. "You won't find any pills, but you should find some stage makeup and, with any luck, a torn piece of plaid clothing."

With a vaguely concerned expression, Tom set the open bag of pork rinds he'd been eating on the desk and turned toward Velvet.

Instinctively, she grabbed the handle of her rolling bag, but Tom wrenched it away from her, laid it on the floor, and unzipped it.

"This is ridiculous. This is a violation of privacy," Velvet yelled as if to the whole room, then said to me, "You tell him to stop, or I'll have you fired for this."

Tom, who'd been digging around in her makeup case, made a sickened face, said, "Ugh," and held up a piece of wrinkled skin.

"What the . . . ?" Furnell peered at the thing and then leaned back as if he didn't want it to touch him.

"Prosthetic wrinkles," I said. "For her face." I could see into the suitcase now. There was a piece of plaid that matched the swatch I'd found, line for line.

"There's a few more in here. And this." Tom held up a bottle of liquid latex.

Velvet's anger had overwhelmed her now. She held her head so tightly it seemed to vibrate.

"Velvet?" Deena was starting to put things together. She shook her head and stared at Velvet's skin. "You always wear your makeup. Always ready before me in the morning n'at. Is this why you wouldn't skinny-dip with me?"

Under the counter, I entered the code Clarista had given me on the safe keypad.

It beeped, and I flinched.

But no one seemed to notice.

"I don't understand," Autumn said, as if coming alive to the scene for the first time. "What did *you* have against my sister?"

"Nothing," I said. "It was Clyde she wanted to destroy. He stole something from her a long time ago, and for some reason she decided now was the moment to get her revenge."

That did it. Velvet had to step up and defend herself.

"You don't understand." Her lips almost snarled. "He committed a crime, and he was rewarded for it!"

"The great thesis idea he had?" I said.

"The great thesis idea he stole!" She chopped the air with her hand. "He was a little ahead of me in grad school. He pretended to be my friend and stole my entire concept before I could present it to my committee. He simply took it from me. And then he was handed a career!"

"But why now?"

"I lost everything a few months ago—well, every piece of the measly life I'd managed to create for myself. I was fired. My husband left me."

"And you thought everything would be different if you had written the thesis that Clyde wrote?"

"Yes. You see, don't you? That was the beginning of everything that went wrong for me." She waved her arms wildly.

I opened the safe and laid my hand on the gun. The safe beeped again.

Velvet's eyes narrowed. She threw her weight forward, leveraging against the desk to reach me.

I leaned out of reach, but she shoved my sore arm.

I fell back a few steps. In the moment it took to regain my balance, Velvet felt under the counter and snatched the pistol from the safe.

She swung it in an arc across the room. "Everybody back."

XIX

Southbound and Down

~

A chorus of screams rang out in the hall. My own voice felt disembodied.

Deena, God bless her, reached up for the gun.

But Velvet, no longer pretending, was obviously younger and stronger. She threw a hard elbow into Deena.

The old woman flew backward.

I darted forward as if I could catch her, but I was stuck behind the desk.

Deena's small body smashed onto the thin rug.

The group let loose another round of screams.

Leonard stepped toward Deena.

"Stop!" Velvet showed him the end of the pistol. "Nobody move."

Did this kind of thing really happen? I wished I hadn't brought the gun into this at all. I'd only given Velvet the leg up she needed to overpower us.

Her hands shook slightly.

Maybe there was room here to stop her before she did something terrible. Something *else* terrible.

Tom stepped in front of his wife.

But Autumn wasn't afraid. Her gray eyes glowed with hatred. If she had her hammer and chisel now, this whole scene would look different.

Maybe Tom wasn't protecting her—maybe he was preventing her going for the gun.

Propped on one elbow, Deena sneered. "How could you, Velvet?"

Velvet's attention was drawn to her erstwhile friend.

"Now, Tom," said Deena, monotone.

Tom shifted two steps to the right and lunged at Velvet from the side.

He grabbed the gun with one hand, breaking it from her grasp in two easy seconds.

Velvet screamed in frustration and swiveled toward the elevator.

"You're going nowhere." Tom pointed the gun at her as if he did it every day.

"Neither are *you*."

All heads turned to the front entrance. The voice was Clyde's.

With our attention fixed on Velvet, none of us had noticed him come in.

"What?" Tom said.

"How dare you give *my* daughter drugs!" Clyde marched to Tom and socked the big man in the jaw.

Several people gasped again.

Tom's head snapped back and forward, but he held on to his footing and the gun, as if one eye were on Clyde and the other on Velvet.

"Drugs?" Realization washed over Autumn's face. "That's it. *That's* why you've been so strange." She narrowed her eyes and widened her mouth. "How were you *paying* for them? Tom . . . tell me you weren't the one stealing from me."

"No. It wasn't me . . . not really," Tom said.

I took the chance to pick up the phone and dial 911.

Autumn had been simmering, and now she boiled over. She lifted a hand and struck Tom across the face.

"Hello," said the 911 operator.

Clyde's assault hadn't fazed the big man, but Autumn's left him raw. Tom stared and reached for her.

He had taken his eyes off Velvet.

I opened my mouth to answer the operator. "Hi. I'm at Hotel 1911—*Tom!*"

I was too late.

Velvet wrenched the pistol from Tom's hand.

And aimed it right at me.

"Hang it up!" she yelled.

"What the . . . ?" Clyde said.

I obeyed. At least I'd given the operator a location.

Clyde held up his hands innocently like a hostage negotiator. "Velvet, what are you doing, dear?"

Thankfully, there was no hostage.

She smirked at him, and I half expected her to rip off her prosthetics like a thriller movie villain. Instead, she pushed the elevator button.

"Where are you going, Velvet? You don't have a car," Furnell said.

"Good point," she said. "Tom. Keys."

"You'll have to shoot me." Tom stuck out his chin.

Velvet steered the gun in Autumn's direction.

Tom grunted and tossed the key fob with its little rental tag toward her.

It landed short.

"Ivy, bring me that," Velvet said.

She sure knew how to give orders. Her hand wasn't shaking anymore.

I bent down, snatched up the fob, and approached her from the side, arm extended as far as possible. I didn't want to be anywhere near the end of that pistol.

The elevator slid open behind her. She stepped aside, holding the door with one hand. "Get in."

"No, Velvet," said Deena.

I continued to stare at the gun, uncomprehending.

"You. Ivy. Get *in*," Velvet repeated.

"Me?" So this *was* a hostage situation.

Silently, I did as she said. Better me than Deena.

Several guests muttered.

"For God's sake, you don't need a hostage, Velvet," Clyde said.

"I'll decide what I need. Thanks very much," Velvet fired back, and jabbed the basement button on the control panel.

The elevator doors slid toward each other.

Deena shouted to the room, "Yinz, get down to the garage!"

I tossed Tom's key fob out through the narrowing crack.

Velvet groaned and slapped me across the face with the barrel of the gun.

Pain seared up the side of my head, and I fell against the elevator wall. But I stood up again. She hit like the frail person she'd pretended to be.

"I guess we'll take your car," she said.

* * *

We got out on the lower level, and Velvet prodded me into the staff dressing room.

I'd never been at the wrong end of a gun before. The tension was unbearable. I knew she didn't want to kill me yet, but what if she accidentally fired?

I could taste blood in my mouth as I grabbed my bag and felt for George's car keys. Why hadn't I just told her I didn't have a car? "Where do you think you can hide? Everyone knows who you are now."

"Shut up or I'll shoot you in your good arm." She was finding her groove, working that gun as if she'd memorized her part from some hard-boiled detective film. She directed me back into the narrow hall. "Out."

I was looking for a moment to somehow take the pistol from her. Maybe after we got in the car. At least I still had my phone.

Outside, the air felt heavy and still, but it couldn't be more than seventy degrees out here.

"Toss me the keys," she said when we reached the staff lot. "And your cell phone."

Damn.

I did as she said, all the while thinking someone from upstairs would catch up to us, but they'd gone to the garage and didn't know where George's car would be parked or even that we would be in George's car.

She opened the door to the back seat, then took an extra moment to be sure I wouldn't be a hazard. "Facedown on the floorboard."

I hadn't thought I could feel more vulnerable than when she was aiming the gun at me, but after I laid myself down like she'd said to, I couldn't even see what she was doing. Would she hit me again?

"Reach forward." Her voice came from the side of the car near my head now.

I stretched my arms blindly overhead. "You drew the pictures and hung them on the walls."

She put a length of seat belt into my hands. "Tie yourself up."

I didn't do a very good job. I couldn't see what I was doing, and anyway, why would I do it well?

But she used her own hands to tie another knot in the belt and jerked it hard.

My arms yelped at the joints.

She couldn't have done that with one hand, I realized. She must have had to lay down the gun.

Now was my moment.

I reached out for her hands, found them, and pulled up so I could see the seat beside me.

The gun was right there.

But she cinched both my hands in the strap, snatched up the gun, and slammed it into the back of my head.

My scalp stung, and tears pooled in my eyes.

Velvet got into the driver's side, started the car, and peeled out onto the road. "So which way to the interstate, Miss Marple?"

The torque of the seat belt wrenched my arms over my head. My head still stung. My skin puckered and burned where the seat belt cut into me. I couldn't answer her.

"Never mind—I don't trust you. Hey, Siri," she yelled. "Route me to Atlanta."

"Okay, routing to Atlanta," said the disembodied voice of her iPhone.

I wondered where the gun was now. I turned onto my side so I could breathe better. If I had to be here on the floor of a car,

I was thankful that it was George's so the mats weren't full of dried grass or mud or gravel. "Where are you headed?"

"I'll let you go as soon as I can," she said. "I'm not a monster."

"I find that hard to believe, coming from a murderer. And from someone trying"—a hard bump in the road took my words—"to torture Mr. Fig." Was it too coincidental to think she hadn't been just a maid at the house but *the* maid who had been fired for the painting theft?

"Torture? I simply want him to pay for his crimes, just like Clyde."

"And Renee. *Renee* paid for them."

"That had to be done."

"But why? Wouldn't killing Clyde's daughter hurt him more?" I asked.

"Clyde wouldn't be as obvious a suspect in his daughter's death. And the point wasn't just to *hurt* him but to disgrace him. I couldn't prove he'd stolen my work, but I could change the way posterity would remember him and make him serve out a sentence that would punish him."

"No matter that it was for the wrong crime?" I struggled with the strap, but between Velvet's knot and the seat belt's own pull, I couldn't loosen it at all. I tried not to think about what was going to happen to me at the end of this ride.

"Anyway, Renee was an easy target," she went on, as if I hadn't spoken. "I knew she'd have one of her passive-aggressive headaches at some point during the weekend. And I was determined to be ready for it."

I remembered the headache and the magic pill Clyde had gotten from Velvet for Renee. "You drugged her, didn't you?"

"I had to make sure she wouldn't hear me coming into the room, or if she did that she wouldn't put up much of a fight," she said. "You know, you're really a lot smarter than I gave you credit for before I found you hiding like a mouse in that armoire."

"It was you who came back. To seal up the hole?"

"You got it, babe," she said.

"And then you left that book of poetry for me at the desk?"

"Yes sirree."

"But how'd you get away from the tour group to commit the murder?"

"That's the thing about being an old woman. You become nearly invisible. It's like a superpower." A dark laugh seeped out of her. "Deena was the only one who would've noticed, and she slipped off to the bathroom."

Speaking of old women, I wondered where Deena's crew had ended up. I'd bet they had taken that fast Porsche of hers.

They'd had time to leave the hotel before us. They could be anywhere now. My best shot was to distract Velvet from the road. If Deena caught up with us, it would be better if Velvet didn't notice right away.

"You really thought this out," I said. "Especially the bit with the paintings."

She was silent.

"I guess you won't get any money out of Mr. Fig now, though."

"I didn't want his *money*," she said. "I wanted him to admit to what he'd done."

"He didn't steal the paintings."

"I saw him being all friendly with the thief. He was in on it!" she shouted.

"No. I know him. He wouldn't have done that."

"Whatever." She sighed. "Either way, my friend suffered because he didn't admit the truth. I should've outed Ralph Fig when the Morrows fired her, but I'd just found out that Clyde had gotten approval for his thesis idea—*my* thesis idea. I was too devastated to put up a fight."

So she was a friend of the maid they'd let go. "Did you know Clyde well before all that?"

"Oh yes, that was the thing. We were good friends for a year or two before. I think he justified it to himself that way. Like deep down he thinks every woman on whom he bestows his very valuable time and attention owes him something."

That was grim, but I could see how she could be right. I didn't know Clyde like she did. "Did you meet at the mansion?"

"He came to one of their fancy dinners, and I was working, of course. He flirted with me, and we got to talking, realized we were both going after the same degree. But it was always a little unbalanced between us, like he thought he was mentoring me or something because he was going to a nicer school than I was and was a year ahead of me."

"I'm still grappling with how you tricked all those people into believing that you were, what, twenty years older than you really are?"

She laughed again. "Well, even without the stage makeup, I'm not sure I look as young as I am."

"Why not?"

A song began playing softly over George's car speaker—a song from the playlist on my phone. I was sure of it. My phone was paired with the car, which meant she hadn't turned it off.

"For starters, let's say I've a had a heck of a lot harder life than Mr. Golden Opportunity."

"Haven't we all?" I still couldn't see a lot, but Siri directed us to Fourth Street. We weren't that far from the interstate on-ramp. If Deena's crew didn't catch us before that, they might never.

"And you betcha I've made a few alterations, stopped dyeing my hair, for example, but it didn't take that much. Don't get me started on how society's made us believe women under seventy don't have gray hair."

Then again, on the open road, the Porsche could outrun this Toyota. If they knew which way we were headed.

I wished I could text someone in the group.

"Befriending Deena made your whole charade more believable." I couldn't take this position anymore. It hurt, and I couldn't see a thing. "You used her."

"It wasn't entirely an act, dear. I enjoyed getting to know her. She's a snazzy lady."

We stopped at a light. I used the seat belt tension to pull up to sitting.

"I'm sorry, but I've—no—no, I'm *not* sorry. Excuse me. I'm not sorry." Velvet waved her hands around while she spoke as if casting curses through time at all the people who had hurt her. "I've suffered too much for far too long to let anybody ruin this, even some pretty young thing like you."

Even sitting up, I couldn't take a full breath.

Then another sensation became clear to me. Although the bumps of the road had disguised it for a while, my heart was now thumping too hard to be ignored.

Fear swallowed me. *No. No. No.* I clenched my eyes shut.

"I've had a hard life." She was really going now. "Born in poverty, raised myself up to go to college, and then some arrogant misogynist comes along and takes it all from me."

"You're blaming him for *all* of it?" I said with the little breath I could muster.

She went on like I hadn't spoken. "Anyway, I guess I never recovered from all that. Can you blame me?"

I tried to focus on the pressure of my body against the car seat behind me, the texture of the rubber floor mat below me.

But her voice was so straining, so overpowering.

" 'Cause that son of a gun went on to win awards! And fellowships! And published work in illustrious journals, and you know what I did? You know what? I taught high school in a rinky-dink, hole-in-the-wall—"

"No matter where or who you teach, teaching is a noble, undervalued . . ." My voice died as I ran out of air. My head felt disconnected from my body.

"*Whom* you teach."

"Okay." I tried to make my brain work. Maybe this wasn't the panic. Maybe this was really a heart attack. Was I dying this time?

I pushed down through the feelings, not past them. I let myself fall toward the fear, lean into the lack of control.

"You didn't have to take my phone, by the way," I said on the first good breath I caught.

"Oh, you Millennials and your precious phones. Like babies with pacifiers."

I had been both praised and criticized over the last few days for being my particular age. Now I would employ it for my own ends. "But what was I gonna do with it? *Hey Siri*-ously, send George a text that I'm being held hostage and taken in his car toward Atlanta?"

I held my breath. If Siri had heard me, she'd respond over the car speaker. It was turned down low, but would Velvet hear too?

But the woman started talking again, too loud for me to hear the speaker at all. "I'm sure teaching at that level is fine for some people, but I was supposed to be somebody special." She revved the engine. "And he robbed me of all that."

She took a sharp turn, and my shoulder slammed into the car door. From my floorboard viewpoint, I saw the top of a familiar steeple of a church at the end of Fourth Street. Were we climbing the on-ramp to Highway 27?

"But why take your revenge now?" I said. "After almost *forty* years?"

"You know what, Ivy, that is an appropriate question. It really is." She bobbed her head up and down.

She reminded me of Clyde's classic "great question."

"See after Clyde betrayed me, after his dissertation was published, I showed my professors my notes—I was a year behind him and just getting started writing, but I had my notes in order. Those blowholes refused to believe me, of course. Clyde had his good name and his good connections . . ."

While she talked, I focused simply on breathing. Just inhaling for as long as I could and exhaling for as long as I could.

Velvet went on. "I pushed it down, tried to forgive and go on like he hadn't destroyed all my prospects. I finally went back and got my master's and got married, and then—" She screamed with frustration. "Then six months ago my husband left me, left me for some no-good, trailer-trash home wrecker."

"I don't follow." It was odd how she felt a need to prove herself to me. Then again, it wasn't *for* me, really. She was justifying herself to herself. Some part of her felt guilty. Because she wasn't a sociopath. Bipolar, maybe, but not sociopathic.

She was still talking. "And that's when I thought—you know what? I never woulda married that cad if it weren't for going back to school when I did, and whose fault was it that I went back to school when I did?"

"Clyde's, I guess?"

"Ding-ding-ding. So, star pupil, if you've grasped history, we can move on to economics. After my husband left, the powers that be decided they'd had enough of teacher raises for a while and voted down a budget increase that would've raised my salary just enough probably to cover all the supplies I buy out of pocket every year. To heck with that, I said, and I took my toys and went home."

We were gaining speed, coming up to the place where we'd merge onto the interstate, I thought.

Was that a squeal in the distance? Maybe a police siren, or was that wishful thinking?

My heart wasn't slowing down, but the pain in my chest no longer sucked up most of my attention.

"And suddenly I had a whole lot of time to surf the internet," Velvet went on. "And whose face popped up on the Facebook? Good ole Clyde Borough's! And the little devil on my shoulder said, 'Now's your chance.' But I didn't rush in. I stopped to consider—*would punishing Clyde, taking everything he loves away from him, really make you feel better?* And there was no way to answer that hypothesis without running the whole experiment."

"And you began by vandalizing his house."

"Exactly. But that wasn't nearly satisfying enough, although it did cost him quite a bit in insurance deductibles—shoot!" She screamed the last word.

I started. What had she seen that made her say that?

"I can't believe it!" she shouted.

I had to see. I struggled against the seat belt and pulled myself up into the seat.

It was Deena's bright-orange Porsche coming up on our left. The windows were down and Deena was yelling something from the driver's side. Tom stuck his head out the passenger side, waving an arm like an air-traffic controller. It looked like Clyde, Autumn, and—Doyle?—were in the back.

Velvet released a stream of expletives.

There was a split coming up. If she couldn't get over, she'd have to take the exit.

Deena nudged into our lane. *Go, Deena. Go, Deena.*

But Velvet didn't let up.

The split was coming for us. We were aimed straight at the guardrail.

At the last second, Velvet braked and swerved behind Deena. My shoulder knocked into the car door again.

"Ha-ha!" Velvet screamed.

Darn it.

Deena changed tactics. She'd started to brake. Traffic had picked up here, and Velvet had to slow down to keep from hitting the Porsche.

The police siren I'd heard earlier was louder now. I turned around.

Blue lights flashed on the roadway behind us. At least three patrol cars were heading this way, but Velvet was flying now.

"Suffering savages!" She saw the lights too.

The I-75 split was coming up ahead. Velvet would go right at the fork for Atlanta. If Deena chose the wrong direction, there was no way she could catch us.

She craned her neck around. "What are you doing? Get back in the floorboard."

She held the gun in one hand and steered with the other, but she couldn't shoot me while I was behind her.

The police were gaining on us. Would they see which way Velvet went in all the traffic?

I couldn't take the chance. All I had to do was knock Velvet off the road. There was a concrete barrier on one side, a guardrail on the other.

It was dangerous for us both, but I couldn't let her get away. "I told you. Get down!" she screamed.

I was still breathless and weak coming out of the panic, but I finagled the middle seat belt across my body and into its buckle. I shoved my foot between the front seats and kicked the gearshift into neutral.

The engine groaned.

"What did you do?" Velvet shouted.

Before she could recover, I thrust my foot up past the seat.

And jammed it into the side of her head.

Velvet's skull bounced off the driver's side window. Her hands jerked the steering wheel.

The car swerved.

We slammed into the guard rail, and the world started spinning.

All I could think of was George.

XX

The Road Back Home

I was tired, on the whole, of ending up in ambulances.

Cords and pumps and such surrounded me, but thankfully, none of them were hooked up to me. The first responder's assessment was that I was fine except for some bruising. Funny the amount of pain that could be included in the word *minor*.

As if she hadn't just taken a bad fall herself, Deena had waited at the open end of the ambulance while I was evaluated.

I was going to miss her.

Autumn, Tom, and Clyde stood in a tense exchange a few feet behind the white-haired woman.

Doyle, who I guessed had come along on the promise of something interesting to do, chatted up one of the first responders, his hair burning orange as a Tic Tac in the afternoon light and his thumbs in his suit pockets. Somehow he reminded me of the mayor of Emerald City.

Traffic was down to one lane on this side of the interstate. Emergency vehicles were scattered all over the place.

I had given a short statement to the police, and now Velvet was being questioned.

Deena followed my gaze, frowned, and then decided, evidently, to think happy thoughts. "We didn't know what we were gonna do, but it was gonna be something."

"You did do something." I reached out and squeezed her hand. "Thank you for coming after me."

"Furnell and Parker wanted to come too." She adjusted her peacock bag on her shoulder. "But Furnell thought a high-speed chase would be too stimulating for the boy."

"Yeah. I'm sorry I didn't get to tell them good-bye."

My attention was caught by Autumn's voice raised at Tom. "But why would Renee steal from me?"

"Because *he* was threatening her!" Clyde pointed a finger at Tom.

Tom sighed heavily, which was all the admission I needed.

I thought back to our conversation at the convention center. "It wasn't that *Selena* was threatening to turn Autumn's company in for hiring those workers. It was you, wasn't it, Tom? You found out what Renee was doing, and you threatened to tell Autumn if she didn't give you the money you needed for the drugs."

Tom glanced at me, then Autumn, and nodded once.

Clyde looked like he was going to hit Tom again. "And then you used the money to buy pills for Selena!"

"No, she *made* me give her those," Tom said. "I swear."

Tom had been alone in the conservatory the night of the murder, and then Selena had pocketed the stash two nights later. That was where the exchange had happened, but why had it happened?

"How could *she* force *you* to do anything?" I asked Tom.

He turned to Clyde. "It's your wife's fault—"

"Ex-wife," Clyde said. "And how?"

"I said Selena was blackmailing the company. Really, she was blackmailing me. When Linda got mad about being fired and about Renee stealing her husband, she told her daughter that Renee was hiring illegals." Tom was angry, as if he had a right to be. "And that's how the little brat figured out I was getting the money from Renee, from the company."

He looked at Autumn now. "Selena was going to tell you the whole thing if I didn't give her the pills she wanted. But, I swear, I didn't know Renee was getting the money to pay me out of your books . . . not until last week."

"So you decided to take your revenge on Selena by nearly killing her?" Clyde said.

"No." Tom said. "I gave her perfectly good stuff . . . if she took too many—"

"They were blood pressure pills!" Clyde pulled a small bag out of his pocket and thrust it at Tom. "*She* thought you were giving her something for *anxiety*."

Tom glanced at the bag. "No, I didn't give her those. Those aren't from me."

Deena looked horrified.

Blood pressure pills . . . like the ones Deena had lost.

Velvet was still talking to an officer a few yards away.

"Hey! Did you have something to do with this?" I yelled. "Did you *steal* Deena's pills?"

Velvet glanced at Deena and back at me but didn't deny it. She couldn't justify hurting Deena, even to herself.

If she hadn't been, or at least seemed like, an unassuming old white lady, she would already have been handcuffed and put in the back of a patrol car.

Maybe the officers were waiting on someone familiar with the case.

Speaking of the devil, Bennett pulled up behind the ambulance in an unmarked black car with flashing lights. George exploded out of the passenger side, and I sprinted to meet him.

We talked at the same time.

"Are you al—"

"I'm al—"

"Thank God."

"Yeah, everything's okay . . . except your car," I said.

He looked over my shoulder at his poor Highlander, which had broken through the guardrail and lay on its side in the median. He shook his head. "I really wasn't that attached to it yet."

Bennett left the driver's side of the car with less urgency. He began a conversation with one of the officers, and I enjoyed the look of embarrassment hidden in his face as he pieced things together.

Before I knew it, a uniformed officer had handcuffed Tom.

Bennett must have had time to look into Tom's little habit.

Tom called out to Autumn as they walked him to a patrol car, but she stood silently, watching him.

In a matter of days she had lost her sister and now, at least for a little while, her husband. I wondered if she'd be able to hold on to her company. I thought of my grandmother Mary trying to keep the Morrow holdings intact after my grandfather's breakdown.

Autumn approached George and me where we leaned against the guardrail. Her face was controlled as usual, but her arms trembled at her sides. She looked at me intently. "How sure are you that that woman—Velvet, Naomi, whatever the heck her name really is—killed my sister?"

I screwed up my mouth. "Um, like a hundred percent. She confessed to me in the car."

Autumn bobbed her head seriously.

Bennett interrupted. "Miss Nichols."

"Detective." I nodded with a victor's smug politeness.

"I understand you stated there was a gun in the vehicle with you."

"Yes, I was taken hostage," I said. "Any of these people can tell you."

"And where is the weapon now?"

"They didn't find it in the car?" I said.

He shook his head.

The truth struck me all at once. I turned to where Autumn was standing, now six feet away.

One hand in her purse, she watched Velvet with the focus of a cat stalking her prey.

Several things happened in quick succession.

I yelled, "She's going to shoot!"

Bennett dove for Autumn.

The gun went off. Together Autumn and Bennett crashed to the ground.

My eyes snapped to Velvet.

It seemed an impossible chance, but Velvet was lying on the asphalt, holding her stomach. Two paramedics rushed to kneel beside her.

Autumn had gotten off her shot before Bennett crashed into her.

He rolled her onto her stomach now, and a uniformed officer put her in cuffs. Somehow she was still so calm.

"Why would you do that?" I said to Autumn. "We caught her."

Standing up again and adjusting his suit, Bennett gestured that he would allow it.

Autumn looked up. "But who knows what they could prove in court." She struggled for enough breath to speak. "I loved my sister. If I had just gotten her away from Clyde . . ."

"She made her own choices," I said.

The officer near Autumn let her roll onto her side but kept a hand on the cuffs. "I explained everything to Clyde in the car, but he was just going to let the police take care of her. As if that would work."

"Yeah, but . . . now you'll go to prison," I said.

She closed her eyes and opened them. "What's left for me here anyway? A bankrupt company and a husband who used my sister to steal from me?"

"Tom loves you," I said.

Resentment and hurt flitted across her features. "Then he should have done better."

The officer made her stand and led her to the same patrol car as Tom.

I wasn't the only one around here who had trouble trusting other people. Autumn couldn't trust Renee to take the reins of her own life, and she couldn't believe the justice system would convict Velvet.

I heard the squeak of wheels behind me.

A few yards away, handcuffed to a stretcher, Velvet was being loaded gingerly into the ambulance.

"She's not as old as she looks," I said to the paramedic.

* * *

The ambulance had driven away, and so had the patrol car and Deena's Porsche with everyone who had come in it.

I had explained to George how I'd figured out Velvet was the killer.

He stood there rubbing the back of his neck and staring at the ground. "So many lies. I wonder what might have happened if Clyde hadn't had a chance to take the wig before the police got to see Renee."

"It's a good question. He might have been arrested instead of Mr. Fig."

"And Velvet never would have been found out. But it's no use asking questions like that, I guess," he said. "Especially when you've brought the truth out, like you do."

I shrugged.

"But Clyde was right to be paranoid," George said.

"Yeah. It's no wonder he suspected his ex-wife of vandalizing his house. He wouldn't have thought of Naomi returning after all these years, but I think the guilt of what he'd done had its effect on him. He was afraid of karma."

"And he was hassling Autumn about the money she owed him because he'd lost a lot in alimony?"

Exhaustion and injury were catching up with me, and I had to sit down, there on the gravelly side of the road. George did the same.

"Seems that way," I said. "Tom was blackmailing Renee about her hiring of undocumented workers so he could fund his drug problem. And Renee was keeping him at bay with money from Autumn's company."

"Ah, which is why Autumn couldn't pay Clyde."

I reached up, prodded the back of my head gingerly, and winced. There was a huge knot from the gun. "Yes, somehow—and my money's on her mother—Selena found out about Tom strong-arming Renee, and he paid Selena off in pills. Velvet simply capitalized on all that was rotten between them, knowing Clyde's desperation and paranoia, not to mention a bit of a fascination with death and Victorian poetry, made him a believable suspect in Renee's death."

"Wild." George ran one thumbnail against the cuticle of the other, then looked up as a tow truck passed us at a crawl and stopped in front of the overturned Highlander across the road. "You know, I used to think it was a bad habit of yours that you kept . . . putting yourself in places where you don't belong."

That sounded like a nice spin on *nosy*. I leaned away enough to turn and frown at him, but I kept silent, knowing there was a compliment on the tail end of his statement.

"Remember that petition you started in eighth grade?" He threw his head back a little as he laughed once. "To turn one of the boys' bathrooms into an extra one for the girls?"

My eyes widened. "Not *extra*. We needed it more than you did."

"Anyway." He shoved me with his elbow. "I figure Mr. Fig and I are really lucky that you are the way you are."

Was he encouraging me the way he always did—or was this something more? I looked down at his lean denim-covered legs stretching out into the road past mine, his white tennis shoes glowing in the angled rays of the sun. And I held my breath, trying to keep the lid on that feeling about him, whatever it was, that I'd had right before the crash.

Seconds ago, with Velvet taken away and the expectation of Mr. Fig's freedom, my world had been a still summer lake, warm and calm.

But now my breathing had gone all shallow and quick. George was the best and oldest friend I had. If I could just bury that instant when I'd seen his face during the crash, I could keep everything the same.

Couldn't I?

His little gestures toward me had either become more ardent over the last week, which meant his feelings about me were changing, or I had simply noticed them more, meaning my feelings . . .

"You okay?" he said, watching my face.

"Um." *No.* Why was I so tense?

There was only one explanation. But I couldn't stand to think it.

I felt nauseous and petrified. I always got bored of the people I dated. If this thing George and I had, this easy thing, shifted into . . . it couldn't last.

I turned back to his face, his raven hair framed by a clear blue sky.

The problem was that if I had woken up in the hereafter instead of that ambulance, I knew my biggest regret would be not having told him that I . . .

And here he was beside me, and not a thing in the world, save my own fear, could stop me.

His eyes scanned my face, and I could tell from the set of his wide mouth that he was going to say something important.

Should I launch into my thing or let him go ahead?

While I deliberated, his mouth opened. "Do you . . ."

"Yes?"

"Do you still have that newspaper?" he asked.

"What?" That wasn't what I'd expected.

"The picture of Clyde at your grandparents' party?"

"Um, yeah, it's in my bag." The police had retrieved it from the Highlander after the crash. "Why?'

"It's just that . . . Clyde said something that made me wonder. Can I take a look?"

I fished it from my purse and passed it over.

He held the paper between two hands and peered into the faces in the photo. His eyes widened, and he unfolded the page from where it was creased under the caption. He looked at me and then away again, an expression of horror on his face.

"For God's sake, what is it?" I said, grabbing his hand to see the photo.

"Before Clyde left a few minutes ago—you were talking to Deena, and he didn't want to interrupt you—he said to thank you . . ." He brought a fist to his mouth.

My eyes were torn between searching for clues in the photograph and seeking them in George's face. "Okay. And?"

"And he said you were the spitting image of your dad . . . when your dad was a teenager."

He held the newspaper where I could see and pointed to a name below the fold. I hadn't noticed before, but the caption continued there. My grandparents were listed, but then, above George's thumbnail, was another name. A name that didn't make sense at all.

Paul Morrow.

I could feel some part of my subconscious already putting things together, even as I struggled to understand. "Who—who's that?"

George's thumb moved under a face now, a boyish, teenage face, bright blue eyes and full, ruddy cheeks. I knew that face.

My dad.

"But . . ." I couldn't form words. It was as if this new information shot into my brain, obscuring everything I knew about my life with misunderstanding. "My dad's name is—isn't Paul Morrow, George. My dad isn't a Morrow. My . . ."

"I know. I know." George held on to my arm. "But that's him, isn't it?"

I felt my stomach clench unwillingly. Whatever was in it rose up through my throat. I pulled away from George and wretched onto the road.

"Damn, Ivy." George sighed. "I'm so sorry."

He walked away and returned with napkins and a bottled water. "Here."

I coughed, then took them and wiped my mouth with the rough paper. "I'm okay."

"It's a lot," he said. "Of course it would make you sick."

I swished and spit with the water a couple of times, trying to clear the acid from my mouth.

"I guess you two need a ride somewhere?" It was Bennett, who had walked up and nearly stepped in my vomit.

I wished I'd been able to save it for the inside of his car.

"Yeah," George said, and gave Bennett the address to my apartment.

We climbed into the back seat of his unmarked black sedan. I was moving slowly with the weight of the news and the soreness from the crash.

I sat with the wad of damp napkins in my hand and shook my head. "Why did he lie? All this time, George?"

"There must be some explanation."

* * *

The drive felt like an hour, during which I lost myself in anger. Everything I saw was filtered through the narrow tunnel of it. It had been just the two of us for so long. My dad was my roommate, my friend, my whole family. Nothing he could say could excuse his hiding this from me. But I had to confront him anyway.

Are you home? I texted him.

Yep. Need something?

Headed that way, I replied. *Liar*, I thought.

I looked down into the pit of my fears and realized some part of me was always waiting for the people I loved to leave me or let me down. I guessed that was the attachment disorder talking, but putting a name on it didn't undo the damage.

It was why I had taken it so hard when friends stopped calling after I dropped out of college. Maybe it was the reason I had never dated anyone longer than a month. And it made sense of my extreme reaction to a small thing like my dad getting a girlfriend.

Even with George—I hadn't been able to admit to myself that anything was going on there because I was afraid I would be disappointed. Or that he would—what? Leave?

Seeing my dad in that photo had interrupted my confession. Our moment, mine and George's, had expired in the heat of my anger, and I didn't know if I could revive my courage.

I held the photo in my sweaty fingers and stared at the faces in black-and-white print. I had only imagined that I could find my mother's features in my grandparents' faces. I'd seen what I wanted to.

Bennett stopped the car under the bare-limbed flame tree.

"I need to go in alone," I told George. "It's not that I mind you hearing anything I'm going to say."

A thought broke in unasked for: *because I love you*. I set my mouth and continued. "Just that he needs to feel free to say whatever he needs to. The truth, I hope. Even if it hurts."

"You're right. It's time for that. No more sidestepping." He turned toward me. "By either of you."

"Okay, I hear you."

"Remember how he forgave you for lying about working at the hotel."

"That was different! This is my whole life, George."

"I get that, but sometimes loving someone means assuming they have the best intentions."

I nodded and got out of the car. He was right.

"Call me and let me know you're okay," he said.

I dragged myself up to our door as if the weight of my dad's lies was shackled to my feet.

Where was his family now? Surely there had to be someone left alive, nearby? Why had he lost touch with them?

I'd spent all these years denying my own curiosity in order to spare his feelings.

But he hadn't spared mine.

I unlocked the apartment and took one last look down at Bennett's car pulling away.

I threw the apartment door open, banging it into the wall of the tiny entryway as I stepped through, and then slammed it home again.

Dad appeared at the mouth of the hall. "What in the world is the matter?"

I threw my bag across the room.

It slid on the linoleum and came to a stop under the kitchen table. "Twenty-eight years of you lying to me. That's what the matter."

This was where it had to happen. In this apartment.

Here where we'd eaten hundreds of frozen dinners and drunk thousands of cups of tea. Where I'd grown plants in the pots he'd made—the *pots*, I realized, that Morrow artistic talent handed down! For the last five years, this place had been the closest thing we'd had to a family home, and it represented everything we meant to each other.

I could never be at home here again.

He stopped a few feet from me. "Ivy, I don't know what you're talking about. I have never lied to you."

"Where is the rest of our family? Why are we so alone here?"

He stood frowning at me.

"Why didn't I get to know my grandparents? Why do you never talk about them? What's wrong with a man who never talks about his family? None of this is normal. *None of this is okay!*" I picked up a mug from the counter and threw it against the floor.

Linoleum isn't very hard, but the handle popped right off.

He glowered at the mug and back at me. "If you want answers to your questions, you'll have to stop yelling and throwing things."

Stop yelling? I gave him better than that. I stopped speaking altogether and stood there stabbing my eyes like pitchforks into his.

"What brought this on, Ivy?" he said. "Nothing has changed. It's always been you and me. I know you miss your mother, but the two of us, we've always been enough, haven't we?"

I pulled the newspaper clipping out of my back pocket and tossed it toward him. It fluttered to the floor, and I took some petty satisfaction in him having to bend over to retrieve it.

"Wow." He jerked his head back and raked a hand through his silver hair. "I don't remember this."

"You tried to hide it from me. But I found out."

"Hide what?"

"That *you* are the Morrow. Not Mom!"

"Yeah." His eyes narrowed, uncomprehending.

"Is that all you have to say?"

He held his mouth open a second. "Ivy. If you're saying you believed your mother was a Morrow instead of me, I had no idea that you thought that."

The expression fell off of my face, and I froze in front of him. "What?"

So how had I come up with that narrative? I took a minute while he thought about what to say next to examine my own memories. There weren't many that applied. Dad hadn't brought up the family, and I hadn't asked. Most of the times I remembered them being discussed were before my mom had left. Maybe that was why I'd thought they were her family. She was the only one who'd ever talked about them, and it was always *Your grandparents this* or *Your great-aunt that.*

She'd never said *my parents, my aunt.*

So I had assumed. Poorly. "Oh."

"Yeah. I don't know at what point that became the story that stuck with you, and I do take some of the responsibility here." He shook his head gently several times. "I think I must have buried this topic under so many layers of . . . shame, Brené Brown would say, and pain. You probably never felt safe bringing it up."

"*You've* read Brené Brown?"

He held up both hands as if at gunpoint. "I listened to the audiobook on the way to some house calls, okay, but that's not the point—"

"Sorry—"

"That's all right, just . . . the point is, I didn't know you wanted to know all of this, and I should have." His chest seemed to cave in, and he tucked his chin. "I should have talked about it."

"Okay. So, what happened to you?"

"Are you aware at all of how the family lost their fortune?" he asked.

I nodded and frowned. "Mr. Fig told me about the stock market crash. And the instability after that."

"That's a kind way to put it." He sat down. "Ralph always was kind."

"Ralph?"

"Mr. Fig, as you call him."

"You know him? You remember him?"

"Of course. Everyone loved him. They would have made him butler if he'd been just a little older." His eyes sparkled. "He took me by storm. He was so cool. He used to drive this Jaguar—"

"Cool? Mr. Fig?"

"I mean, sure, he could be a little exacting."

"A *little* exacting? Dad, the man once had Bea rewash a whole load of linens just because she found a Dum Dum wrapper in the dryer."

He laughed. "Yeah, that sounds about right."

"Listen, I wanna talk more about the young Mr. Fig, but what are you telling me? What happened to you and your family?"

"I was angry, disappointed, when we lost everything. All my life, they had fed me these ideals of what it meant to be 'a Morrow.' And then it felt like they just gave up. The economy tanked, and I didn't see, Ivy, how hard my mother was working to hold it all together," he said. "The bank took the house, and from my perspective, my parents let it happen. They lost the home my ancestors had kept together for generations.

"I had to leave private school and wear clothes from Goodwill, which—I know—is not that bad, but when your name is Morrow and kids know who you are, they delight in your misfortune."

"Kids are the worst," I agreed.

"Even while my dad was still around, he was just so pitiful after his breakdown, the heart attack—I don't know how much you know—but he was also just so stubborn. He refused to explain anything to me about what was happening." Dad leaned forward and looked at me intensely. "I feel terrible about the way I treated them, Vee. I was immature, and I handled it all badly. By the time you came along, I just never wanted to speak of it again."

I had the instinct to lay a supportive hand on his, but I didn't get up. "It must have been hard, losing your parents so early. And I know there must be a lot more you haven't said yet."

He cocked his head. "Didn't you ever wonder why your mother's maiden name wasn't Morrow?"

"I just figured she'd been married before, I guess. I didn't think that would be a favorite topic of yours either. Anyway, that was easier to explain than your name not being Morrow."

He shook his head. "Wow."

"So why *isn't* your name, my name, Morrow?"

"I changed it. I was that angry, and I was eighteen. I thought I had to reinvent myself. I'm sorry, Ivy."

"Wow." I closed my eyes a second, as if that would stop the flood of new realizations.

"I . . . abandoned my family, really. Just when they were hurting the most. I couldn't go back to them after that."

My dad had been so stable for so long. It was impossible for me to picture him as the leaver. He was the one left behind. At least when it came to our little triad.

"I'm sorry, Dad." I meant it on so many levels. I was sorry for yelling at him and sorry for all the pain he'd carried. I had questions that would fill the weeks ahead, but right now, I just wanted us to be whole again.

He pulled me close to him, then pushed me away just as quickly with a face like he was disgusted. "What have you been doing tonight? You smell like the exit line of the Tilt-A-Whirl."

I smiled. "Oh that? That's only because I puked a little while ago."

XXI

The Thing With Feathers

~

Disappointment was inevitable, conflict unavoidable. But maybe—maybe neither of those things had to mean quitting on a person. Maybe neither had to mean someone leaving.

I'd taken some painkillers and a nice long nap after the talk with Dad and woken up around dinnertime, still only beginning to process all the pieces of my life that looked new to me in light of what he'd shared.

But it wasn't long before I was thinking of George again. I was used to having a hundred casual thoughts of him in a day, but now, having admitted to myself how I really felt about him, my body kept reminding me of the discovery. Every time he came to mind, my cheeks went hot.

And then there were the deliberate reflections on everything we'd done and said for the last few weeks. I was trying to nail down when things had shifted for me.

I had a text from him asking how I was feeling and another from Dad saying he'd gone to pick up tacos for us.

I could see us, George and me together—me bringing a little healthy flexibility into his life, him grounding me.

Of course I could see it. We'd been doing that already for years.

I was getting ahead of myself. I knew he loved me but not if there was anything more than friendship coming from his end.

But the possibility there made the risk worthwhile.

Before I could change my mind, I showered, slapped a big Band-Aid on my cheek to cover the nasty black welt from Velvet's pistol-whipping, popped two more ibuprofen, and got on my old Schwinn.

In a little while I was knocking on George's condo door, my sweaty palm hidden safe inside a brave fist. Something about this hallway—the crisp paint lines, the velvet carpet runner, the art deco sconce lights—made me feel exposed and inferior. George's building wasn't nicer than the hotel, but I was *used to* the old Mustard Mansion and felt at home there.

I knocked again.

When he finally opened the door, the gap was only wide enough for him to stand in. He'd obviously spotted me through the peephole, because he wasn't surprised to see me. "Ivy. Hi."

Weird to use my name like that. What was going on? I tried to read his face. It was like there was something he had to say and didn't want to.

"Hi." I took a breath.

"You feeling better? After everything that happened today?" Behind him, the hard angles of his white leather sofa were all I could see in the dimly lit interior.

Why didn't he just let me in?

"Yeah, a little sore. Are you hiding something in there?" I said. "Don't tell me you got so lonely you adopted a cat. I promise I'll make more time for you after midterms."

He squinted his eyes and barely smiled at my joke.

My nerve faltered. This wasn't starting out at all the way I'd hoped.

Maybe going in loaded, with this laser focus, wasn't the best way to approach this conversation. Maybe it'd be better to wait until we were just hanging out sometime and the moment felt right again.

"Actually." He smiled at me . . . politely . . . as if there was something wrong, as if I'd just received bad news and he was trying to be kind about it. "Bea is here."

Those three words normally wouldn't alarm me, but his tone of voice and the sympathetic look he sent me signaled something more. Signaled danger.

He stepped aside a few inches, revealing behind him his little bistro table set with candles and some kind of dinner and Bea in one of his two chairs. She looked gorgeous in a tiny blue dress that would've matched her eyes if I had been close enough to see their color.

He had cooked for her.

They were having dinner.

This was *a date*.

Damn. Damn. Damn.

George watched my face.

"Oh." I nodded rapidly to affect nonchalance and understanding.

I totally pulled it off, of course. There was no way my best friend of a decade and a half could see right through my little charade.

"Hi, Bea." I swiped a hand in a halfhearted wave, and the air felt cooler than it should've on my damp palm.

She waved back heartily and grinned behind George's back as if this were a victorious moment for us, as if we were on the same team. And we should have been. We were friends.

As were George and I. We were all friends. All friends, except that they were also on a date.

I looked at George with what I hoped was an encouraging smile and thanked God that I was able to keep my head. "Good for you. Cool. I only had five minutes anyway."

I took a step backward.

"Bea was under the impression," George said, "for some reason, that you and I were . . . something more than friends."

He said it like the idea was only mildly off base.

"*Really?*" My voice spiked an octave. "Glad you got that straightened out. This is your first date, then?"

"Yeah, I guess so," he said. "You okay?"

"Sure, yeah, just tired from today, you know."

He hadn't told me what he'd cooked for her. That was unexpected.

He nodded thoughtfully. "Okay. Well, rest up. I'll call you."

"Yeah, great. Let me know how it went," I said, already turned toward the elevator, already turned away from him.

Hope was still the cruelest thing I knew.

* * *

I downed several quiet cups of tea that night and the next day thinking of George.

He filled my consciousness now as much as he had last fall when I was working to clear his name, but every thought I had of him was now accompanied by the ache of loss and longing.

The truth wasn't my friend.

George didn't commit himself lightly, but once he was into something, he was all the way in.

If he had begun this thing with Bea, I had to let him see it through.

Or not, another part of me said. *Maybe he loves you but he's afraid. Maybe you haven't given him any evidence that he could act on. Maybe the kindest thing to do is intervene before his relationship with Bea gets too serious.*

And round and round they went, these parts of me.

Clarista called me Tuesday afternoon to say Mr. Fig had been released, and even though it was the outcome I'd expected, I was so relieved for him that I cried.

I couldn't wait to get back to the hotel to see him. But maybe he would take some time off to recover.

I pictured him being handed back his shoes, his wallet, his watch, walking out of the jail without so much as an apology from anyone, but with his head held high again in the fresh air.

I felt a little like I'd just gotten out of jail too, a cage of denial about my feelings that I'd built myself. The honest light on the other side wasn't much easier to bear, but the pure joy I felt about Mr. Fig being cleared made it easier to set aside my own regret and jealousy for a while.

On Tuesday evening, I turned my thoughts to my dad and the people that I now understood to be his family. A wealth of knowledge about them was within reach now, but the first question I wanted answered was the one that had bugged me all week.

If anyone knew where my grandparents were buried, surely it was Dad. I worked up the nerve to ask him, no small thing after my own long-running moratorium on the subject.

"We'll need to go back to the hotel for that," he answered mysteriously.

* * *

We parked the Volvo in the staff lot. Seeing the car here was normal. Having my dad on the property was not.

"This used to be the kitchen garden." He glanced around. "These birch trees were always here, screening the garden from view. Shorter then, though."

"I guess you ate well."

"That we did."

"It occurs to me now why you have such good table manners," I said.

"Ah, well, yeah." He wrinkled his nose. "Hard to shake those after so many important dinners where I had to impress so many people."

"At least you're not bitter."

He laughed. "I'm sorry. It wasn't all bad."

"So if you spent most of your life avoiding this place, why did you take the call to come and fix the leak last week?" I asked.

"It's hard to explain, but . . ." He put his arm around me as we walked, as if for warmth. "Maybe it's because I'd seen you doing all these hard things, going back to school again, working here even after your accident last year, just staring your demons right in the face. I just thought, I should try to face mine too."

He stopped at the edge of the tree line and looked up at the house in the growing dark. The row of wavy-glassed French doors sparkled with golden light, and I wondered if he was picturing those candlelit dinners he had so hated, or perhaps his own father.

As we watched, a human silhouette stepped from the dining room out to the terrace. I recognized the backlit outline of Mr. Fig's neat hair and square shoulders at once.

I ran up the steps, every ounce of me aching to hug him, but I saw the serious smile on his face and thought better of it. I stopped in front of him and stuck out a hand. "Welcome back, sir."

"Thank you so much, Miss Nichols." He took my hand in both of his and gave it a wholehearted shake. "I owe you my life."

"Well . . . I don't know about that."

Mr. Fig's gaze went behind my shoulder.

Dad had joined us. "Ralph." They shook hands. "It's great to see you."

"You're looking well, Mr.—Nichols, isn't it?"

That funny intonation Mr. Fig always put on my name—this was why.

Dad smiled softly. "I appreciate the way you've been looking after my girl."

"I've been repaid tenfold," Mr. Fig said.

Dad must have sensed that we had things to say only to each other because he drifted away toward the back corner of the house.

"I figured out who taped up the drawings," I said.

"Oh?"

"It wasn't the painting thief. It was Naomi, a friend of the maid who was fired after the theft all those years ago. She was trying to drive a confession out of you."

"Gracious me." Mr. Fig grasped and tugged one jacket cuff and then the other.

"She was Velvet Reed . . . or pretending to be Velvet, at least, and she was also Renee's killer, but maybe Bennett already told you something about that."

He frowned. "It's rather hypocritical to commit murder and still judge another person for theft, don't you agree?"

I chuckled. "Yes, I do."

"Speaking of which, Miss Nichols, you know that I abhor speaking of money, but I'm afraid it is necessary to ask you to talk with me about the same when you come to work tomorrow."

"You're giving me a raise?" I asked.

"Well, yes, that is a very good idea, and furthermore, there is the matter of my debt to your family. Now that everything is out of the bag, as they say, I'd like to set you up better for the future." There was no guilt in his expression, only resolve and affection. "Of course, the amount won't be anywhere near the combined value of the paintings that were stolen, but it will be a step toward reparation."

My eyes were hot and damp. I wanted Mr. Fig to keep his money, and yet, this was what he wanted. And let's face it, I could really use a car. "Thank you."

"Good, then." He ducked his head in a short, energetic nod, smiled, and slipped his hands in his pockets. "I'll see you tomorrow."

"On the *morrow* then," I said with a wink, and turned to see Dad peeking into the conservatory. A thought occurred to me. I looked back at Mr. Fig. "You called him here for the leak? On purpose?"

"It seemed long past time for him to come home. And for you both to come clean."

This was the answer he had predicted would come to me when we were in the basement passage. All this time, he'd known that my dad was a Morrow, and he hadn't told me.

I set my teeth crookedly. I could choose to hold it against him, but only if I was going blind to my own choices. I had a lot of experience in justifying the keeping of secrets, and Mr. Fig had his reasons too.

As if reading my mind, he said, "It wasn't my secret to tell."

I took a breath and nodded that I understood.

When I caught up to Dad, we started toward the back lawn.

"Hey, is there still a big, old date palm in the conservatory?" he asked as we passed it.

"Oh yeah, and lots of other great trees."

The copper gas lights blazed up as we reached the top of the garden.

"I used to climb that one," he said. "There was a big tangle of branches like a platform, and I could hang up there and spy on people for hours."

We walked down the terrace's grand staircase. Below us, the nearly full moon lit the marble statues as if from the inside and painted the grass an electric blue.

"So, why Nichols?" I said. "Why that name? Did it belong to someone else in the family?"

He cinched up one corner of his mouth and shook his head.

"What? Tell me."

"It's stupid," he said.

An owl hooted from the direction of the old stable.

"If anyone has a right to know, Dad . . ."

"It was all I had left—nickels, a little more than pennies."

"A pun? My last name is a pun?"

"I was eighteen." He took a turn before we reached the fountain so that we stepped off the gravel path and onto the lawn.

My feet squished in the thick grass, the ground still saturated after the snow.

"So why wasn't I able to find their graves on my own?"

"Mm, yeah. It's because the estate used to be bigger than this, Vee."

"Really?"

"Oh, yeah, acres of forest and meadow."

We gave the old stable a wide berth. I was happy to see he also avoided it, confirming the spookiness I always felt about the place. Later, I'd ask him if there was a reason.

"But after the house was donated to the city, they sold off this part, everything past the fence here." The high iron fence was lined with a yew hedge as tall as a house. He gestured at the rooftop that peaked above its horizon. "The property was divided into three plots, actually. That's when they built these houses. Broke my heart all over again."

We had reached a small break in the yew hedge that I hadn't paid any attention to before. He pulled a latch, and a gate squeaked open. In the late-winter quiet, the fountain's burble still carried across the grounds toward us.

"If this fence was put in after you left . . ." I said.

"Yeah, I came here a few times after. After Mom died. But not since the place was turned into a hotel. Didn't feel right."

"Are we trespassing now?" I asked.

"No. This kind of thing is covered by law. That's why the gate's here. They have to provide access as long as there are living relatives."

On the bluff edge of the neighbor's backyard, a knee-high fence made a neat square around two lone gravestones. They were simple and small, nothing like the grand statues on the other side of the fence.

A feeling stepped into focus that had been foggy since the moment Mr. Fig had confirmed my family's graves were here on the property.

For the past few days, as I'd looked for my grandparents' headstones, I'd been propelled by a strange mix of dread and denial, but now, with them here in front of me, a new sense of attachment washed through me. I hadn't expected to ever feel this way in a cemetery.

"Dad passed away"—my dad cleared his throat—"before we actually lost the house. I had already moved out and gone to live with a friend.

"They chose this out-of-the-way place because it was in this peaceful meadow, at the time, and that suited these modest stones better."

"Yeah, I agree." I noticed the dates on my grandmother's stone. "Nineteen ninety-three? The year after I was born. How old was she?"

"Only sixty-three. Liver disease. They let her be buried here with him, even though we were gone from the place."

"That was kind. Why liver disease? Did she drink too much?"

He nodded sadly.

My top lip got all tight and wobbly. Maybe this was the kind of thing Mr. Fig had been apprehensive about me finding out. "Tell me something good about her."

"Oh. Well, how could I narrow it down to just one thing? For starters, she had the most beautiful singing voice in the world."

"You get it from her, then."

My whole life my dad had sung little tunes around the house. He had a voice like a clarinet.

"And she was the most competent person," he said. "She had a great head for business, which she never needed until Dad was gone."

Tears leaked in at the corners of my smile. "What about him?"

He inhaled and tightened one cheek. "Mm, now Dad was a charmer, but one of those people who it was authentic for—do you know what I mean? It was never for show. He just liked making people feel special."

My tears flowed freely now. I'd never known them, so how could I have such a powerful feeling of missing them?

All of the good qualities he told me about them were talents I saw in him too—his natural charisma, his ability to pick up the pieces after a crisis. I had missed so much not getting to have them in my life.

Knowing him was a bit like knowing them. Still, more of a good thing was always more.

"I keep having these realizations," I said. "Like that I always thought Mom got her mental health issues from the Morrows, and now, that doesn't add up."

He looked at me like he had a stomachache. "No. I think her challenges were more about what she experienced growing up. She never said so. She wasn't able to look at it, but her family gave her those challenges, just not genetically, like ours."

"I don't understand how a lie could make more sense to me than the truth."

"But that's why we lie to ourselves, to make sense of things we can't understand." He reached down and picked some moss off his father's gravestone. "We tell ourselves we could've stopped things from happening, stopped people from leaving us, stopped them from hurting."

"So, my anxiety, it really doesn't come from her?"

"It came from me." He shrugged.

I put a hand over my mouth, then folded my arms. "But, but you seem so . . ."

"Normal?" He grinned.

"I wouldn't go that far."

"It was you, babe." He looked into my eyes. "You gave me the reason I needed to fight it."

A house or two down the block, someone called a dog. A car blaring hip-hop passed in the distance. And I, Ivy Nichols, began to understand my father.

It wasn't for me only that he didn't drink coffee. He took long walks and found creative outlets. He told me to take my meds because he knew the consequences, firsthand, of letting the anxiety get out of control. I wondered if he'd taken pills at some point too, but this wasn't the moment for asking.

A string of memories flashed through my mind, and I sucked in a breath. I remembered him after my mom left, and now that I knew about it, his anxiety was obvious. The way he hadn't dressed himself some mornings, the way he used to pace the floor, the days I found him curled in a ball on his bed.

And just like that, the last trace of hostility about his secrets left in me was drowned in appreciation for him.

"Dad, did the things in the secret passage help you?"

"What?"

"The machines, the books, the special room," I said.

"Ivy, what are you talking about?"

My throat seized up. Could it be that he didn't know? And if I showed him, would it be okay? Would it hurt him that there was a secret so big in his boyhood home—that his parents hadn't told him, if they knew at all themselves?

"Dad, I have something to show you. I don't know if you'll like it."

"Well," he said. "Do *you* like it?"

"Oh yes, very much." He would be my road to the past, and I would be his way back home.

XXII
Deeper Magic

～

I led Dad through the conservatory toward the camouflaged opening to the basement passage. In the uneven darkness between lampposts, we ducked under a rough tree branch that overhung the path like an old man's arm.

I felt him watching my face and looked back at him. "What is it?"

He smiled. "The day I took the call to come here for the leak, I went home later and thought about you being in this house."

"Yeah?"

"Of course I'd imagined you here before that, but it was different . . . having seen you here . . . in your uniform and everything."

I slipped my arm through the crook of his. "And?"

"And I knew you would love this place, and you do."

"I do. There's a lot of competition for my favorite room here, with the gardens and the library, but this is definitely in the running."

We had crossed to the western side of the conservatory now, and I paused in front of the orange tree.

"Have you ever read the Aeneid?" I asked him.

"Doesn't everyone in school?"

"Ha. Maybe at the fancy schools you went to. I barely knew what it was when Mr. Fig brought it up."

"This was when?"

"Remember the fall I had last year? 'At work'?" I made the air quotes with my fingers.

He frowned slightly and nodded.

"That was how I discovered this passage under the first floor. The second time Mr. Fig was with me, and we found the things I'm about to show you. And he explained what he meant by *sic itur ad astra*."

"So we go to the stars?"

"*So we go, thus we go*, depending on the translation. Mr. Fig said it to me last year. It's from the Aeneid."

"Yeah." He paused, concentrating on something, although probably not the thick aspidistra where his eyes landed. "*Sic itur ad astra*."

Mr. Fig had sat down with me in the garden after we'd come up from the passage that day and told me how Apollo "bestrode a golden cloud" and visited Aeneas's son during battle. "Mr. Fig got a bit sidetracked telling me how important the book was, how the writer—"

"Virgil?" Dad asked.

"Right. How Virgil started with these random legends about Aeneas wandering around after the Battle of Troy and from that wrote the Aeneid, which became a national epic."

"Yes, because it gave reason and importance to the story of Rome's foundation and a whole bunch of other things."

"Yeah, anyway, so Aeneas and his son Ascanius, they were trying to build a new life for their people after the fall of Troy, and Virgil must have understood how their failing to save Troy weighed on them.

"But while Ascanius is fighting in the place that will one day become Rome, Apollo tells him 'Troy is too narrow for you.' That's the one quote I remember."

"That his past failures do not define him," said Dad. "He is an heir of gods and an ancestor of gods to come."

"Yes. I thought you hadn't been down here?"

He shook his head. "I haven't. But this part of the story is very familiar to me."

I cocked my head. He was being mysterious, and it wasn't like him.

I made sure we were both clear of the opening and, with a pointed look at Dad, found the heron in the ironwork along the wall and pushed its wing down an inch. The creak of the lowering panel was familiar to me.

His mouth popped open along with the panel.

I wagged my eyebrows at him and handed him my phone with the built-in flashlight turned on. "After you, sir."

He took the handrail and stepped down without hesitation. "Well, it doesn't smell amazing."

"Yeah, I wish we could just leave it open all the time and let it air out."

We reached the bottom of the steps, and I put a hand on his shoulder to stop him. I flicked on the light and pointed up at the thick stone lintel at the top of the open archway in front of us.

Dad looked up and read the words engraved in the stone. "*Sic itur ad astra*. Wow, my family was weird."

"And wonderful," I said. "So this is what Apollo tells Ascanius—that it's his 'fresh courage' that is his family's path to the stars—to glory, in other words."

Dad grabbed my hand and squeezed it, and we passed under the arch together.

"When he built the house, Murdoch had this secret basement put in for his wife Lillian."

"*A secret basement?* A secret passage. All this time?" He shook his head. "What—was it closed up for a hundred years, then?"

"No, we're pretty sure they kept using it even after Lillian."

"We?"

"Mr. Fig and I."

He nodded, as if getting used to the idea of my friendship with the old man.

"I'm interested in what you make of it, though." I paused in front of the door to our left and sighed.

"What is it?" he said.

"It's just—I never thought of you and me doing this. All this time, I imagined Mom was the connecting piece and that that piece was gone forever."

He looked at me, and the light caught on the moisture in the corners of his eyes.

"So the first room has a couple of machines in it," I said. "They were cutting-edge technology at the time, must have cost them a fortune."

We stepped into the room on the left, and I flipped on the light. The long, silver tube of the fever machine glimmered in the brightness.

Dad dropped his jaw again and scanned the machine and the space around us. "Good golly Miss Molly."

I opened the lid of the fever machine and explained it to him.

"It's incredible," he said, turning the knobs and tapping the dials. "Did it work at all? Or was it a bunch of hocus-pocus?"

"I've looked into it. There's actually a modern doctor inducing fever to treat depression. It's a bit theoretical at this point, I think, but it has something to do with body heat generating electrical impulses in the spinal cord and the brain and generating serotonin."

Dad smirked.

I must sound like Bea about now.

Dad turned toward his right and examined a stack of shelves holding brown glass jars and blue bottles with faded labels, handling each piece with the same reverence I would, like we had dug our way to the burial chamber of a lost pharaoh. "And all of this?"

"I'm not sure about everything, but this"—I laid my hand on something that looked like a complicated beverage dispenser with dusty thick glass and an oxidized spout—"is a radium water jar."

"Radium? They drank the stuff?"

I nodded and smiled grimly. "Thought to cure all sorts of madness."

"Jeez. I think I may need to sit down." He put his hands on his waist, taking it all in. "All this time. How'd you figure all this out?"

"That's a great segue to the next room."

I led him across the hall, all the time with him giving me this funny look, like he saw me differently now.

I turned on the light in a room with a giant bookcase on each wall and a small armchair with a simple side table in the middle of the room.

"Another library?" His eyes gaped, and he spun from one stack to another, raking his eyes over the old volumes, our sacred family texts. "But why? Why keep books down here when there's a library upstairs?"

"The best I can figure is that these titles were either scandalous just to own or would've caused people to talk."

"But why not keep them in a locked cabinet upstairs?" he asked.

"That's where the chair in the middle of the room comes in. If Murdoch, I imagine, or any other member of the family was seen reading these, it would have fed the rumors that the family was already trying to silence."

"You're right." He sighed. "There's not much privacy when you live with a household staff."

He tilted his head to read the titles on the old editions. "William James. *The Principles of Psychology*. Sigmund Freud, *The Interpretation of Dreams*. That one I've heard of."

"The other bookcase has a bunch of old copies of the *American Journal of Psychology* and the *Journal of Educational Psychology*," I said.

"This place is so psychoanalyzed, even the bookshelves have issues."

I laughed and handed him a tiny volume more pamphlet than book. "This one explains the fever machine. And this one"—I flashed another cover at him—"talks about treatment with radon."

"You've spent a lot of time down here, huh?"

"Well, I'm lucky to share the interest with my ancestors." I wanted to keep it light. I wanted to wink at him, but a wave of emotion rose in me, and my next words shook. "Actually, it's more than some kind of academic hobby . . . I think these rooms might have been sort of sacred to our family. This was their secret, and now I'm one of the few people in on it."

He put one arm around me and squeezed me, then kissed my head.

"And what's down the hall?" He stuck his head out the open door.

"A bedroom." I waggled my eyebrows. "And a hydroelectric bath chamber."

He jerked his head back. "Something about that—I mean, *bath* and *electric* shouldn't be in the same sentence."

I laughed. "Yeah, it looks kind of like a claw-foot tub covered with a canvas sheet that has a hole cut out for your head."

"I think I'll have to see that another day. These two rooms may be all I can take in at the moment." He stared through the doorway as if it could open the past to him. There was awe, but also frustration in his face as he tried to take in a hundred-odd years of history at once. He leaned against the doorframe for support. "I don't understand. How did Mr. Fig know about this place when I didn't?"

So Dad shared my sense of disconnection from the Morrows.

"Apparently your dad avoided the place and forbade anyone from coming down here, but his sister, your aunt, was still living in the house, and she brought Mr. Fig down here and told him about some things."

"That must have been Tulia. She was a force to be reckoned with, always disagreeing and undermining my dad, but often with good reason. She had a little dog that followed her around, and she used to have him bite Dad's ankles when she thought he was being unfair."

I laughed.

He leaned against the doorjamb. "My mom must have respected my dad's wishes and not shown me this place. But she told me the story of Ascanius anyway."

"Sometimes it's enough to bury the seed of an idea in a kid. I feel like you must have done that with me too, but less intentionally? Otherwise, why would I be so interested in psychology?"

"There's more passed down in our DNA than I can understand," he said. "Why are we so much like the people we've never met?"

"Your dad, though, wanted to ignore the particular 'gift' that had been passed down through our family tree, didn't he?"

"And you see what a lot of good that did," he said.

"If there's anything I've learned over the last year," I said, "it's that thinking positively about a problem and ignoring the way it affects you doesn't make it go away."

"Murdoch, though, he did his best for Lillian, to keep her out of those horrific asylums."

"Yeah." I took a long, deep breath. "He did what it took to keep her here, to take care of her . . . like you did for me."

Maybe I was getting to the heart of what it meant to be a Morrow.

He sat down in the armchair, running his hands along the dusty, leather arms. "I'm trying to figure out what the right thing to do now is. I suppose we should let the owner know all of this is here."

"But Clarista would open it up to guests, let them tour it and gawk at it. I can't bear to think about that." I felt more connected to my family right here than anywhere else in the hotel. I understood what this place meant, but other people wouldn't.

"It's her property."

"Can't we just . . . keep it between us for a while?"

His head wobbled. "No one else knows besides Mr. Fig?"

"Well, George."

He exhaled slowly. "I don't want you to get in trouble if someone else finds out. *When* someone else finds out."

I bit my lip and let my eyes drift to the little table beside the chair Dad was sitting in.

I'd never looked at it from quite this angle before, and I saw for the first time that the wooden apron of the table was decorated with a small molding shaped like an eight-pointed star.

Dad followed my gaze and turned in the chair, bending down so his head was nearly level with the table. With an upturned hand and a thoughtful look, he felt the underside of the tabletop. "Huh. This is awfully thick."

Was he thinking what I was thinking?

He knocked on it once, and sure enough, it thudded like a ripe watermelon. *Hollow.*

I reached out and pushed the star with a finger.

It shrank soundlessly into the wood behind it, and the table apron popped forward a centimeter or so.

A hidden drawer? Curiosity jolted me upright.

Dad looked at me, a question obvious in his eyes—*did you know?*

I shook my head.

"Do you want to . . ." He indicated the drawer.

"You go ahead."

He wedged a finger in the top edge of the crack and inched the drawer out to half again the length of the table. Inside, on a felt lining the color of a dusky sky, lay a leather-bound book with a monogram embossed on the cover.

Dad's and my eyes widened as we looked at each other. I reached in, lifted the book out gently, and ran my fingers over the grooves of the letters—*MLM*.

Multi-level marketing? I thought. Was my whole family the origin of some early pyramid scheme?

I cracked the cover and read from the inside flap. "Marigold Lillian Morrow."

"My grandmother," Dad said.

I handed the book to him.

He smiled, focusing on the elegant script. The pages fluttered in his hand.

"What is it? Her journal?" I asked.

He turned the next page over.

I held my breath.

Coming around behind him to read over his shoulder, I heard the staccato step of a high heel in the hallway outside the room and glanced up.

In the doorway, a pair of copper eyes blazed in an angry round face that was about to give voice to several complete sentences.

"Hi." I swallowed hard. "Clarista."

Acknowledgments

Writing this book in 2020, a year in which we all suffered collective and personal losses, wasn't easy. I couldn't have finished without dipping into a source I (nerdily) call my "second well," which was fed all year by my family, good friendships, and the Author of life.

I'm convinced that, through no fault of my own, I have the best literary agent in the world. Annie Bomke, thank you for your Mr. Fig–like commitment to doing your job with excellence. You go above and beyond, and because of that, this book is twice what it could have been.

To my editor with the well-fitting given name, Faith Black Ross: thank you for seeing the heart of this story, for asking the right questions, and for your careful and patient work. I'll forever be grateful that this series landed in your proficient hands.

Shout-out to my Hotel 1911 Bellhops, the incredible street team who helped get the word out about *Murder at Hotel 1911* and *Dust to Dust* and shared in the excitement of my launch.

To my Chattarosa critique partners, who so often carry the burden of seeing the worst first version of everything, how could I do without you? (*Add more detail here showing the author's blushing and gushing, etc.*)

There are so many people who were a gift on a global level last year—essential workers on the front lines of the COVID-19 pandemic; truth-tellers in an era polluted with disinformation; justice-oriented pastors; and intrepid teachers who kept right on teaching kids—even mine!—to explore, persevere, and most of all, to read.

Finally, I'm grateful to mental healthcare workers and those who keep talking about mental health in the public sphere. There was never a year we needed you more.